The
House
at Magpie
Cove

BOOKS BY KENNEDY KERR

A Spell of Murder

The
House
at Magpie
Cove

Kennedy Kerr

bookouture

Published by Bookouture in 2020

An imprint of Storyfire Ltd.
Carmelite House
50 Victoria Embankment
London EC4Y 0DZ

www.bookouture.com

ISBN: 978-1-83888-885-5
eBook ISBN: 978-1-83888-884-8

For Kathryn, who gave me the idea.

Prologue

The beach house swayed and shook in the wind. There was a storm coming in. The grey clouds off the Cornish horizon sat heavy like judges in a court, pendulous and dark over the silver sea. Suddenly, a clap of thunder echoed across the beach and startled a flock of magpies nesting in the ruined roof of the house. They flew out, chattering like a scolding mother in the silence.

Abby watched the rain come, wondering why the house looked so different to how she remembered it. She knew it so well: the slightly off-kilter balance of the wooden floor in the lounge; the wide front door, its paint badly flaked so it was hardly blue anymore, revealing a cracked cream undercoat peeling off in the salt air.

Upstairs, Abby knew where the landing would creak, and where to walk around the edges to avoid waking up her parents; she knew how far it was from the back door to the hidden slip of rock that appeared at low tide. If you clambered over the rocks, exposed sand led you to a private hollow, unlooked-over by anyone walking by. She knew the smell of the salt air and the sea purslane that grew around the beach. She knew this place well: Magpie Cove, where she had lived all her life until she was seventeen.

Abby knew that she was dreaming. And as the storm rolled in, she knew what it brought with it. In the dream, she turned to run from the shadow that always came; the shadow that chased her along the beach, away from the house. She ran and ran, her breath ragged in her throat, but it was no good; now, like she always did in this dream, she fell, catching her ankle on a rock hidden in the sand. And she begged the dream to let her wake up, because she knew what was coming for her. Abby knew what was in the storm, and she woke up screaming.

Chapter One

'No one's lived here for a time, by the looks of things. Fair amount of work to be done.' The solicitor handed Mara the house keys and gave her a sympathetic smile. 'Not quite the luxury beach retreat, I'm afraid,' she added.

'This is it?' Mara looked around the deserted beach; it was the only house on this cove, though there was a small wooden shack at the other side, and she could see the roof of another house beyond a promontory that reached into the Cornish sea. She knelt and zipped up her son John's coat against the wind, and beckoned her daughter Franny back to pull a purple knitted hat down over her black curls.

Her nine year-olds were the kind of twins that were so close they sometimes spoke in an incomprehensible secret language; they were growing out of it, but they were still an island, the two of them, a unit which didn't include her. Mara was sometimes allowed into their secrets, but often not. She wondered what it would have been like to have just one child, or for John and Franny – Frances, not that she ever answered to it – to have been born a few years apart. Would they have shared their secrets with her then? It seemed that Mara's family was full of secrets; perhaps it was in their DNA.

This house, it turned out, had sheltered generations of her family. As close to DNA as a wooden house aged by salt and wind could get, it had creaked under the feet of Hughes women since 1900. And yet, today was the first day Mara had ever seen it.

The solicitor, a woman perhaps her own age, was dressed practically in a sky-blue rainproof parka with the hood up and some tough-looking lace-up shoes. She had introduced herself as Clare in a no-nonsense but kind voice. Mara appreciated the kindness and Clare's straightforwardness; both were in short supply in her life right now.

'This is it,' Clare agreed. 'Shame it's been so neglected. Might have been a boarding house once, I s'pose, given the size, but it's hard to say. Must have been rebuilt a fair few times to still be standing all these years.'

'Hmm.' Mara peered up at the wooden roof: it didn't look strong enough to hold up to the wind. 'How many bedrooms has it got?'

Clare looked at the paperwork and shook her head.

'Doesn't say here, but I'd say maybe four or five? Big place, just needs some love.'

'Mummy, can we explore?' John pulled against her, impatient to get away. Mara pointed to the house.

'Stay where I can see you. Don't go behind it,' she instructed, pulling her own long, loose coat around her. It was August – thank goodness it was still the summer holidays, because she didn't know whether she'd have to find another school for the twins or not – but it was windier than she expected next to the sea.

Mara pressed the keys into her palm. 'I didn't know it existed until last week.'

'Oh?' Clare raised her eyebrows enquiringly, but Mara didn't elaborate any further. 'Well. It's yours now! The deeds are here.' She handed Mara a thick envelope, bound with a blue rubber band. 'I'll be in touch about the rest of your mother's estate. There's not much, as you know.' She turned her gaze to the house, frowning. 'You're planning to sell it, then?'

'Uh-huh.' Mara watched the children as they raced in circles on the sandy beach: Franny's hat had blown off towards the sea and was caught on the wet rocks that led to the water. Her daughter was explaining something in detail to her brother. Mara wondered absently what it was this time – the life cycle of a clam, common seaside birds and their nesting habits, or an old favourite, perhaps the story of the first woman to go over Niagara Falls in a barrel?

She didn't have a choice about selling it, not now. Gideon's words reverberated in her mind: *She's moving in. It's over between you and me. You need to leave.* Her husband of twelve years had thrown her out; he'd offered to keep the children, though he hadn't objected too strongly when she'd insisted they come with her. Straight-backed, she'd walked out of the house she'd thought was her forever home, one hand in John's and one in Franny's. It wasn't even her crime: Gideon had been unfaithful. He'd been sleeping with his executive assistant for the past two years.

Every time Mara thought about it, she felt sick. She'd felt even sicker when she'd had to explain it to the twins. She had to keep explaining, too. Today, John had wanted to know why Dad wasn't coming to see the beach house with them, and yesterday, Franny wanted to know if they'd see Gideon at the weekend. She felt awful trying to justify the fact that Gideon was spending all his free time with his new girlfriend – she wanted to say *mistress*, it had more of the sense of betrayal in it – and hadn't made time to sit down with Mara to talk about access.

'Right. Well, good luck!' Clare shook Mara's hand. 'Can I give you a lift back to town?'

Mara shook her head.

'I've got a car.' She smiled, tiredly. 'My husband let me keep that, at least.'

Clare nodded, following Mara's gaze to the black SUV parked on the dirt road behind the house. She reached for Mara's shoulder and squeezed it.

'Chin up. It'll be all right,' she said, her voice loud over the wind. 'Things will improve. I promise.'

What a cliché, Mara thought. *His assistant.* He couldn't even be bothered to go farther than his own office to find love – although, knowing Gideon, she doubted that love was really the motivation. In twelve years of marriage, he'd told her he loved her twice. Once on their wedding day, and once when the twins were born. Dutiful *I love you*s. Contractual, obligatory *I love you*s. No excess.

She should have known. She should have seen it coming. But she hadn't.

Sometimes life takes the tiller and steers the boat over the falls, her mother Abby would have said; she had been the one who told Franny the story of Annie Edson Taylor, the first woman to survive going over Niagara Falls in her woman-sized barrel. *No point trying to steer upstream.* Abby had been fond of boating, rivers and waterfalls as life metaphors. Mara had tried to *steer the boat of her marriage upstream*, as Abby would have said, against the cold tide of Gideon's disinterest in her for so long that, now, as the boat hurtled them towards oblivion, she felt a kind of strange calm. It was good not to have to work so hard anymore.

Sometimes, life takes the tiller, rips it off and stuffs it down your throat, Mara ruminated, mocking her mother's soft Cornish accent in her own head, then feeling instantly guilty. None of this was Abby's fault.

Life wasn't a boat ride. Or, perhaps, you thought you were sailing peacefully down a river on a yacht, but in fact, you were plunging over a deadly waterfall at a hundred miles an hour with your rat bastard of a husband standing at the top, waving you goodbye. Annie Edson Taylor had at least made her own barrel and stuffed it with pillows.

Still, she had the car. Gideon had taken pains to point out its impeccable service history and recent MOT as he handed her the keys, like he was doing her a favour. Like he wasn't kicking her out of her own home and moving his – she searched for the right phrase in her mind, but all she could come up with was *fancy woman* – well, he *was* moving his fancy woman in. *She is fancy, ergo, I am not fancy*, Mara thought.

She stifled the impulse to laugh, because she knew it was the kind of wild laughing that would lead to tears, and she couldn't break down in front of the children.

'Come on, let's look inside!' she shouted.

The weather was turning and it was going to rain any minute; at least if they looked inside, they'd be able to shelter for a while and then she'd drive them back to the little hotel they were staying in in St Ives, along the North Cornish coast from Magpie Cove. She had enough money to stay there perhaps a couple of months while she put the house up for sale, and then, as long as it sold fast enough, she could buy somewhere small for her and the twins. She missed St Ives: her house, like many, sat on steep hills overlooking the pretty harbour which twinkled at night with the lights from the yachts and fishing boats; you could enjoy plump oysters and a glass of champagne in the evening at one of the modern harbour restaurants, watching the stars come out and the moon rise. Or, from the raised deck of her old house, which sat above an ample garden, she could watch the boats coming in and out with a cup of coffee between the school run and whatever else she had on that day.

Any new place she bought wouldn't be fancy, not like their house on Cedars Avenue, one of the most desirable streets in St Ives, with its double garage and top-of-the-range kitchen, but at least it would be hers. Like Annie Taylor, she could at least make her own barrel.

Chapter Two

Part of the roof was missing.

When Mara opened the door, the creaking noise startled seagulls that were nesting somewhere upstairs, and they flew out, shrieking. The warped wooden floor creaked as she walked on it, and a damp stain had flowered on the wall facing the sea. Mara wrinkled her nose in distaste.

'Oh dear,' she murmured, as she took it all in.

The beach house was a two-storey wooden construction with a porch that ran the length of the front of the house, and wooden steps (now broken and half-rotted away) that led up to it from the beach. The house itself was oriented sideways, so that its front faced the beach, with the back of the house facing an outcropping of rock. The west side faced the sea.

Immediately inside the front door was a square sitting room that might once have been cosy. The floorboards spread across a wide room with light blue walls; there were darker patches here and there where pictures had once hung, not counting the damp. A white-painted kitchen dresser stood on one side; a couple of blue-and-white plates sat on the shelf, covered in dust. A door led to another large sitting room that looked out over the sea; it was damper in there, and the old blue wallpaper was peeling off. A pair of rattan easy chairs faced out to sea: the seat was missing from both of them. Otherwise, the only furniture left was a ratty cream sofa, a warped, empty bookshelf and an oil lamp which stood on top of it. Abby had not left much.

At the rear of the main sitting room, a large kitchen spread across the back of the downstairs. Mara walked over and inspected it for signs of functionality, but the stove appeared to have once used gas canisters, and there was nothing connected. A few utensils sat in a pottery jar sticky with dust and ancient cooking residue.

'Look, Mummy! A box!' Franny raced past, her wet shoes leaving sandy prints on the wood. Mara opened her mouth to tell her daughter to take her shoes off, then closed it again. There was no point; people would be coming to view the house soon, no doubt tramping sand all over the place. Franny lifted the lid of a deep wooden chest and looked inside. Mara thought it had probably been a blanket box once; she walked over, curious to see what was inside, if anything.

John had already disappeared into the kitchen and was opening cupboard doors and closing them again.

'John, don't slam those doors,' she called out. Anywhere there was a door, John would swing on it, lean on it or play with the handle: she was always terrified he'd catch his fingers in the jamb. Whereas his sister talked incessantly, John always had to be moving. A door handle turned and released. Fingertips drummed on tables. Standing on one leg, and then the other.

Looking down, Mara reached into the box and pulled out a mildewed cushion, showing it to Franny.

'Yuck. Put it down.' Her daughter made a face and peered back into the box. Mara leaned the cushion against the side of the box; she'd have to clear out all this old stuff before putting the house on the market.

Franny reached in again and pulled out a rag doll with red hair in a thick plait. She hugged it delightedly.

'Look, Mummy! A doll!' she cried happily.

'That's lovely, darling.' Mara sat back on her heels and watched as Franny inspected the old toy. It had certainly seen a lot of love, but it seemed to have escaped the mildew, at least.

'Can I keep it?' Franny hugged the doll to her chest. 'I'm going to call her Marianne. That's her name.'

'It's her name?'

'Yes. She told me. Also, it's like your name, a little bit. Marianne seems like a good name for a doll that lives in a house by the sea – it's quite romantic, isn't it?'

'Ah, I see.' Mara stood up. 'Yes, very romantic.'

'Dad would like this house,' Franny added, pointedly.

'Mmmm.' Mara made a noncommittal noise and walked into the kitchen to avoid any further discussion on the subject. She thought how odd it was that this was all hers now, when she hadn't known anything about it last week. It had been enough of a shock that Abby had died so quickly; within a few weeks, cancer had developed, and taken her mother faster than anyone expected. Some weeks later, the solicitors had got in touch about her mother's estate. *What estate?* Mara had asked, still shell shocked, whole days going past with her having no real memory of what she'd done. She must have made the twins meals, but she didn't remember it.

John had found three saucepans in one of the cupboards, had upended them on the floor and was playing them like drums with a blunt pencil. Mara tried to open the back door, but it was locked and she couldn't see a key anywhere.

Abby hadn't even owned the house she lived in; it had been rented. She'd never owned anything much as far as Mara knew, but then there was this place, an address in an official letter. Abigail Hughes leaves this property to you. A house that her mother had never, in forty years, mentioned to her only daughter.

As she turned the back-door handle again, there was a knock on the front door. Surprised at the sound – why would anyone knock unless they'd seen her go in? The house obviously wasn't lived in – she went to open it. Clare stood on the doorstep holding a large box.

'Me again.' She held the box out to Mara, who took it and put it down immediately; it wasn't light. 'Sorry, I got halfway down the road and remembered it. The box was left with us for safe keeping with your mother's will.' She was slightly out of breath.

'Oh. What's in it?' Mara asked, curiously, but the woman shrugged.

'No idea. It's been in storage for the past few years. Sometimes people want to store valuables with us, meaningful documents, that kind of thing. Could be anything.'

'Hmmm. Oh, I'm sorry. Come in.' Mara waved vaguely at the lounge, but the solicitor shook her head.

'Thanks, but I've got to be off. Forms to process, paper to stamp. As I said, any questions or issues, let me know.' She raised her hand as a goodbye and made her way back over the rocks to the sandy beach and to the road at the top where her car was parked.

Mara squatted on the floor and regarded the box. It was medium sized and taped up neatly: Abby was – had been, she corrected herself – neat to the point of obsession. Growing up with a neat freak as a mother was a challenge when your idea of neat involved piling all the books you were reading into a shaky tower next to the sofa. Mara slid her finger carefully under the tape at the edge of the box and snapped one end open. It had been years since she'd sat down and read a book – although of course she'd read stories to the twins. Why had she ever stopped reading for her own pleasure?

Peeling the tape carefully from the top of the box, she listened to the twins who seemed to be playing some kind of game on the landing; she hadn't even seen upstairs yet. She knew why she hadn't read a book in years: Gideon hadn't ever specifically said it, but he disapproved. In fact, he had a way of never specifically saying anything, yet making her feel inferior for anything from her driving (too slow, but in the event she drove faster, he barked at her to be careful, the children were in the car), hair colour (she was a dark brunette; he openly admired women with blonde hair he saw at parties or when they were out shopping or picking the twins up from a club or class) to her political views (he rolled his eyes when she raised the subject).

Well, at least now the book police aren't around. Gideon never read, outside whatever legal briefs he had to read for work. He gave the air of considering himself too important for something as fanciful as reading a novel or a play or a poem. Privately, Mara had always thought that anyone who didn't like books was either boring or an idiot. *Turns out, I was right.*

The thing was, that although Gideon was pretty unpleasant to her, he was a great dad. He made up plays with Franny – which always turned out to have some kind of legal theme, though Franny didn't seem to mind – and patiently painted the backdrops for her productions of *The Princess and the Pea* or *Rumpelstiltskin*. He played endless hours of football in the garden with John and talked to him when he had a nightmare, often up into the small hours himself, preparing for a case. Sometimes she'd wake up in the middle of the night and find one of the twins – usually John – asleep on Gideon's office sofa, with Gideon working at his desk. She'd pick John up and return him to his bed. Gideon, when he was working late, would usually sleep in his office and take John's place.

That's why Mara had stayed for as long as she did: Gideon was a devoted father. It was just that – as far as their own relationship went – things weren't great. She supposed that she had also believed that she could never do any better. Her confidence had never been high as far as men were concerned.

She opened the flap of the box. Inside, there was a clear plastic bag. She took it out, noting a few notebooks that lay underneath. Inside the bag was a bundle of letters.

She listened to Franny's voice upstairs for a moment which had taken on a familiar, monotonous tone; it sounded as though she was telling John one of her stories, which could take a while. Mara thought it was likely that the new doll was expected to listen, too.

She hadn't worked since the children were born, because Gideon had said, *I earn enough to support us; you should concentrate on the kids.* And that had been fine; she'd wanted to, she'd been happy to support the family, being a stay-at-home mum. Yet, despite the fact that he had wanted her to, Gideon never seemed to respect her for it. He would make remarks about her lack of experience at work, that she wasn't savvy about things, that she was naïve.

Well, I'm not naïve now, she thought. *Not about cheating husbands, anyway. That cherry has been well and truly popped.*

Mara undid the rubber band that held the letters together and looked at them curiously. They all had the same name and address: Paul Sullivan, at an address in Helston, perhaps a forty-five-minute drive away from St Ives, as long as the traffic was okay. Every one of the letters was unopened, and each one had been stamped RETURN TO SENDER. She turned the bundle over in her hands thoughtfully.

Now, she had to find a job. She had studied literature at university, but a literature degree, some long-ago office experience and eleven years of being a stay-at-home wife and then a mother qualified her for precisely nothing, as far as she could see. She'd applied for a couple of jobs, but she didn't feel confident. All the more reason to sell this place – at least it might buy her some time to find a job if she had some cash to carry them through.

'Mummy! Come upstairs!' Franny's voice called down the stairs.

'I'll be right there, sweetie,' Mara called back. Should she open the letters? It felt wrong – they weren't addressed to her. Yet Abby had wanted to make sure she had them after she died. There must be some kind of important information she was supposed to have.

Mara had slid her fingernail under the flap of the first letter in the bundle when there was another knock at the door: Clare had forgotten to tell her something, she supposed. She frowned and went to open it, absent-mindedly carrying the letter with her.

Chapter Three

The man looked surprised when Mara opened the door.

'Oh, hi. I saw someone moving around and wanted to make sure everything was okay,' he said, taking a step back from the door. *Kind eyes*, Mara thought.

'Everything's okay.' Mara realised she was standing with her hands on her hips; she wanted to read the letters, whatever they were. 'Can I help you?'

The man had an easy smile; wry amusement flashed in his deep blue eyes.

'Well, now, I'd kind of decided that I was going to be the helpful one.' His dark blond hair was slicked back with water and he wore a black wetsuit with the top rolled down and a faded blue rugby shirt on top. He looked like he had just thrown the top on and seemed to be in the process of pulling it down, but not before Mara saw a flash of a toned, muscular stomach underneath. She blinked and looked away.

'Everything's fine, thanks,' she replied curtly. 'This is my house.'

It was strange to say it, but, oddly, the beach house did feel like hers already. Even the fact that it was decrepit felt familiar and homely, not that her house for the past twelve years could ever be described as either decrepit or homely.

Nothing in her house was ever more than three years old: the freezer, the sofa, the light fittings. Gideon liked everything to be new; in retrospect, Mara realised his obsession for novelty should have made her suspicious a long time ago. Yet all it had done was keep her busy. She seemed to spend her life researching the best shade of paint, the best floor lamps and the best drawer organisers.

The beach house was the opposite of her house with Gideon and the twins, but there was something about it… Perhaps it was simply the fact that it was hers. Something that only she owned. Still, it wouldn't be hers for long.

'Your house?' The man cocked his head on one side, quizzically. 'It's been empty a good while. There was an older woman that used to come down sometimes and stay for a while, walk on the beach. I thought it was hers?'

'That must have been my mother. She… passed recently.' Mara wondered why she was having to explain herself to this passer-by.

'Oh. I'm sorry.' He looked genuinely sympathetic, and Mara felt herself thaw a little. Behind the man, a girl, perhaps in her twenties, emerged from the sea, also wearing a wetsuit and carrying a surfboard. She approached the man and nudged him on the arm.

'Hi, Brian. Want to go back in?' she asked, smiling politely at Mara.

'Sure, sweetie. I'll be right there.' He gave the girl a warm smile which had more than a hint of what Mara would describe as 'come to bed eyes'.

'One of my students,' he explained. 'That's my base over there.' He pointed to the wooden shack at the other side of the beach.

Mara thought the girl looked like she wanted to say something more – like, *hey, stop chatting some woman up in my lesson time.* Mara thought she would probably be thinking that herself if she was halfway through a surf lesson with this guy – but she just pulled her long blonde hair into a wet topknot with an elastic band and gave Brian a thumbs up, then turned away, walking back to the shoreline.

'You were friends with Abby?' Mara asked him, curious.

'Oh, not really. Just used to say hi now and again, sometimes we talked about the weather, the beach. She used to have a lot of hanging baskets and plants around the outside of the house.' He pointed to a couple of large terracotta pots on the porch which held some withered stems and leaves. 'Gave me cuttings a couple of times.'

'Mum loved plants.' Mara felt a lump in her throat and looked away, controlling herself.

'I'm Brian, by the way. Brian Oakley. I teach surfing on this beach, so we'll probably run into each other quite a lot.' He held out his hand and she shook it; his skin was rough in places, but his touch was warm and reassuring.

'Mara. But I'm selling up, so I doubt we'll see much of you.'

'We?' Brian's eyes flickered to Mara's left hand where she still wore her wedding ring; she hadn't even thought of taking it off yet. She probably couldn't, now, anyway; since having the kids her fingers were fatter than they had been when she and Gideon had got married. It had been at a registry office, she had worn a plain skirt and a nice white blouse, in the afternoon Gideon had had to go back to work. If she wanted the ring off, it would have to be cut off.

'Me and the kids,' she answered shortly.

'Well, I'll be sorry that the old place doesn't get to stay in the family. Hope whoever buys it gives it some love.' Brian rested his wide palm on the peeling paintwork of the doorframe, as if he was comforting the old timbers with his touch. 'I'm a carpenter as well as a surf teacher; mind if next time I'm here I drop a business card through the door? For the next owner. They'll be wanting to make some repairs.'

'Sure. It needs a lot of TLC,' she admitted.

He held her gaze for a moment; unexpectedly, she felt herself blush. *Oh dear lord,* she thought. *Who is this guy?*

'It's still beautiful, though,' he replied seriously.

Mara looked down; she was still holding the letter, and she suddenly remembered that she had been waiting to read it.

'Okay, well, nice to meet you.' She looked up again, nodding politely. There was no point getting friendly with the locals. He turned to go.

'The pleasure was all mine, Mara!' he called out, giving her a friendly wave.

She closed the door, and realised she was smiling. She rolled her eyes. *Don't be such a sucker for a nice smile and some toned abs, Mara,* she thought. *That's not who you are.*

She reflected for a moment that maybe it *could* be who she was, now that she was single, and would that be so bad? But she shook her head and walked back to the ratty sofa to read the letters instead. Abs could be on her agenda some other time in the distant future.

Chapter Four

The letters were all addressed to one person, Paul Sullivan.

Mara had never heard of a Paul Sullivan; Abby had never mentioned him. She was sure of that. But Abby, aside from her fondness for her grandchildren and for nautical metaphors – oh, Abby was secretive. Mara knew there were huge holes in the story of her mother's life. Mara had never known her grandparents, or any other family member. Abby had refused to tell her who her father was, and why she avoided all contact with him. Mara grew up loved, but in the dark.

Mara sat cross-legged on the wooden floor in the lounge and regarded the cardboard box that held the letters. Maybe this was it, finally; in death, was Abby willing to tell her secrets?

She opened one of the envelopes carefully and took out a folded piece of blue writing paper and a photo. Turning it over, she was surprised to see her own face looking out, next to her mother's. Mara was seven or eight in the photo, she thought, judging from her two thick brown-black plaits and her dress with the orange and brown fabric; Abby was still so young, somewhere in her mid-twenties, and smiling sadly at the camera. Mara fought to hold back the tears that returned to her eyes, her throat clenching hard again, and opened the letter itself.

May 5, 1989

Dear Paul, my darling boy,

Today is your third birthday. I hope you have a happy day with a cake and candles, jelly and ice cream and lots of presents. I have sent a present for you to your mummy and daddy; I hope you like it! I don't know what toys you like, but I asked at the toyshop and the lady there said that these trucks are what all little boys want this year. Happy birthday.

I hope you are happy and healthy. I enclose a picture of me and your sister Mara. She is eight years old now and she goes to primary school. She likes peanut butter sandwiches, reading and she plays with her dolls a lot.

I love you so much, with my heart and soul, and please know that I will always love you.

I will always regret giving you away, but please know that I did my best. I did what I thought was right. I'm sorry, Paul. Please forgive me.

Your loving mother,
Abby

Mara stared at the letter in shock.

I will always regret giving you away.

I love you so much, with my heart and soul, and please know that I will always love you.

My darling boy.

She checked the name at the end of the letter again, and the home address. Abby had definitely written these letters.

It seemed that she, Mara, had a brother.

She dropped the letter in shock; her hands felt oddly unable to hold it. She scrabbled at the floor to pick it up again, dust and sand getting under her fingernails. She rubbed her hands against each other to bring the life back to them. She felt cold all over.

A brother. A *brother!* All her life she had wished for siblings. For family. But there was none. Always a wall of silence when she asked, or an unhelpful proverb, *Gone water doesn't mill anymore,* one of Abby's favourites. Mara wondered if it was a Cornish phrase; it seemed to mean 'don't live in the past'. *Water under the bridge* was another favourite.

But there was a past to be lived in. There was a brother, another past she hadn't been allowed.

She had a brother – or a half-brother? She had no idea – and she'd never known anything about him until now.

Mara hid her face in her hands as the shock washed over her once again, raking up her recent grief and the stress of the separation into one awful, tearing sadness. She began to sob uncontrollably until the children, hearing her, ran down the rickety stairs and approached her warily.

'Mummy? Why are you crying?' John hugged her, and Franny stroked her hair.

'Mummy's sad. Mummy, would you like a biscuit?' Franny asked. Mara snorted a bittersweet laugh, taking in a deep breath: she often offered the children a biscuit or a sweet when they'd hurt themselves. 'Something sweet raises your blood sugar levels if you've had a shock. Have you had a shock, Mummy? Because you should put your head between your legs if so.'

'Oh darling, I don't think we have any biscuits. But thank you for the thought.' She held out her hands for both of them and enveloped them in a hug.

'Come and see upstairs. We found four bedrooms and a toilet with a wooden lid. In my room there's a hole in the roof and I can see straight through it!' Franny pulled away, out of the hug, but John stayed with her. Mara dried her eyes with some effort; she knew that John got anxious when she cried.

'There's a hole in the roof?' Mara asked. Franny bobbed on the spot excitedly.

'It's perfect! I could lie in bed and watch the stars! And there's a fireplace with a dead pigeon!'

'Oh, that's… lovely.' Mara's heart sank a little at the realisation she was going to have to get rid of the dead bird; it wasn't exactly what potential buyers wanted to find.

'Come and see!' Franny danced in a circle.

'All right, sweetie. In a minute. Let me just finish looking at these old letters, and then you can show me.'

'I'm going back up! I'm going to look for cave paintings!' Franny shouted excitedly and ran back up the stairs.

John stayed next to her, sitting solemnly cross-legged in imitation of Mara, as she opened the other letters, looking for more information. Yet each letter was more or less the same. Abby had written to Paul every year on 5 May, his birthday, and every Christmas. Each time, she enclosed a photo of herself and Mara.

Mara remembered that Abby had been very protective of her expensive Polaroid camera. It had always seemed odd to Mara that her thrifty mother, who would walk from one end of town to the other to save 10p on a bag of potatoes, would have splurged on such a luxury. Mara remembered the photos being taken; it was a routine. At the time, she hadn't thought much about it, but now a wave of understanding washed over her. It had all been for him. She didn't know how she felt about that.

She opened more of the letters, showing John the photos. Every year between 1987 and 2005: photos of Mara and Abby, photos of Mara at ten, twelve, fifteen. In the pictures, Mara grew older, her shyness continuing to shape her smile. Abby grew older, though not old; in the last picture, she would have been in her early forties at the most.

'See, that's me, and that's Grandma.' She pointed herself out to her son, who looked curiously at the pictures. Franny could never be persuaded to be interested in photos or family stories.

'Grandma looks so young.' John stared at the pictures. 'You look like Franny.'

It made Mara wonder what Paul had been like as a child. Had he been like John, a frequent victim of nightmares, who, though he was quieter and more introspective, also ran straight to the boundary of any space he was in, who had to be rescued from running into roads and restrained from the edges of cliffs, kerbs and ponds? Or had he been like Franny, a chatterbox, a frequent know-it-all, a reader and imaginer of worlds, whose stories were long and elaborate? What kind of man had he become?

Abby had been seventeen when she'd got pregnant with her daughter, though Mara never knew more than that. When she had been old enough to understand, she had assumed that it was a mistake. Few people planned to be a parent at that age, never mind a single mother at seventeen. Why hadn't Paul ever read these letters? Why had they been returned? Who had looked after him as a child if it wasn't Abby?

There were thirty-six letters in all. She bound them up carefully in the elastic band and put them back in the box, but kept the photos. Somehow, that felt right; they were hers and Abby's, after all.

'Who was Grandma sending all these letters to?' John asked, watching as Mara shuffled the photos into a neat pile. Mara paused for a second as she considered how much to tell him.

'I guess they were to your uncle,' Mara answered. 'Isn't it nice, looking at all these old photos of Grandma and me?'

'Uncle Bruce?' Bruce was Gideon's brother.

'No, sweetie. An uncle you don't know.'

'You're not crying anymore, Mummy. I think you should put all of these pictures on the wall so you can see them every day and be happy.' John pointed to the peeling painted wall above the wide stone fireplace. For a moment, Mara visualised a fire lit in the grate, a cheery glow in the room and the house filled with plants and books; she saw the old photos arranged in a frame above the mantelpiece, and she saw herself curled up on a comfy old leather sofa, reading to John and Franny as they listened to the sea.

Her phone vibrated; she looked at it and saw she had a number of new messages. She clicked on one. It was from Gideon, telling her she had a month to get the rest of her stuff out of the house. Her heart sank. There was no way she could afford to live here – it was uninhabitable as it was, and she had no money to do the repairs that were needed. The children couldn't sleep in a house with broken windows and bedrooms with no roof. She sighed and slipped the box into a cupboard.

'I don't think we can stay, sweetheart. Come on, let's get your sister and go back to the hotel.'

John looked disappointed.

'Can't we live here?' he pleaded, but Mara shook her head.

'I'm sorry, baby. We've got to sell it.'

'But I like this house! Franny likes it too. You can see the sky from her room.'

'Well, that's not exactly ideal.' Mara sighed again, going up the stairs carefully.

John trudged up the stairs behind her. On the landing, Franny rushed over excitedly and took Mara's hand, guiding her into a beautiful large, light bedroom with a stunning view over the bay. An antique four-poster bed, still made up with a slightly grubby but lovely embroidered Shaker-style quilt, stood in the centre of the room, with a tall brass standard lamp next to it and a French-style antique wardrobe on the other wall. There was a fireplace with a white stone mantelpiece and an art deco tile surround; moving closer, she saw that the tiles featured a design of golden yellow irises and blue cornflowers on a white background.

'Look!' Franny presented it proudly to her. Mara took in a deep breath. It was so beautiful that she didn't know what to say.

'This is your room!' John beamed delightedly. 'You can put your clothes here. And here's a vase for some pretty flowers.' He opened the wardrobe door, and held out a pottery vase he'd found inside.

'It's lovely, darling,' she agreed, her heart aching. This house *was* hers. She imagined waking up every day to the glittering blue sea outside, and the idea made her shiver with delight. The joy in John and Franny's voices, and the love in their eyes for this old place – that was the most magical thing of all. Could they stay? Could they ever possibly make it work?

Her phone buzzed again and she looked at it fearfully.

She didn't want to give up this view, and she certainly didn't want to give up the happiness that being in this house had given the children – this was the brightest they'd been in months. But she couldn't see a way to make it work.

Yet, her heart tugged at her. There was something about this house; it felt like home, and if there had ever been a time when Mara needed a home, it was now.

Chapter Five

Serafina's was one of two cafés in Magpie Cove.

Mara's beach house was one of a few houses actually on the beach. Further back, there sat a line of faded Victorian terraces that overlooked the sea from a promenade with steps down to the beach. The Cove was prone to occasional storms, and so most people lived further into town.

Behind the terraces, a winding high street followed an original cobbled lane that predated cars; in fact, if you drove into Magpie Cove, you could only get so far and then had to leave your vehicle in a car park and walk into the village. There was, however, a slim road that led to a dead end next to the beach, which is where Mara had parked when she visited the beach house.

Unlike St Ives with its bustling streets of fudge makers, ice cream parlours, tea shops and Cornish pasty takeaways, Magpie Cove's high street featured an antique shop, an art gallery and a small shipwreck and smuggling museum alongside a small bakery and a local butcher. Of the two cafés, there was a nice-looking one with plenty of people in, Serafina's, and another at the end of the street. Its drab décor looked like it hadn't been refreshed for many years, and, anyway, the sign in the window was flipped to 'closed'. Despite not living that far away, she couldn't remember ever having come to Magpie Cove herself before now; she hadn't needed to. Clearly, Abby had mysterious reasons for keeping Mara away.

Serafina's it is, then, Mara thought. She desperately needed a coffee – preferably triple strength.

It was two weeks after she and the kids had first visited the house, and Mara had just been at the estate agency in St Ives – Magpie Cove was too small to have one. The news wasn't great. In its current state, the beach house would only be likely to raise half of what she needed to get a new place. In St Ives, where they'd always lived, a small house with a garden – what she'd need for her and the kids – wasn't cheap. She'd barely afford a one-bedroom flat there.

The kids had gone back to school now that it was the beginning of September, and she was glad they weren't with her today, because she felt like bursting into tears. What on earth was she going to do? She couldn't afford to make the repairs to the beach house. The roof alone would cost thousands, and the survey had thrown up some pretty serious damp and subsidence: oh, and the whole place needed rewiring. *Great.* Aside from that, she could also see that the school situation was going to get difficult pretty quickly. The twins had gone back to their old school in St Ives, which was nice on one hand because it provided them with some much needed normality, but Mara wondered how long it would take for word to get around that she and the kids were currently bunking down in a cramped hotel.

Living in a scruffy hotel and the proud owner of a decrepit beach house, she thought sarcastically. *Could life get any better than this?*

When she'd dropped them off at school that first morning, there had already been some looks. Some sympathetic, but some not as kind. Mara had no doubt that she'd be getting fewer dinner invitations from now on, and that was fine with her, quite honestly. She worried for the twins, though. She didn't want them to be excluded or seen as different; in their school community, poverty was synonymous with disease. She didn't think she imagined that some of the 4x4-driving, carefully blow-dried mummies had shied away from her at the school gates today, either. As if her misfortune was catching.

There was the added worry that Gideon might not continue to pay the school fees, or perhaps he'd expect her to chip in. It wasn't a conversation they'd had yet. That said, Mara knew that the twins attending private school was important to him, for their benefit, but also for his social status. Refusing to pay would make him look bad – to John and Franny, but also to his friends and work colleagues at the legal firm. All the other lawyers' kids went to private schools.

On the other hand, since Gideon was currently balls deep in his executive assistant – Mara shuddered at her own phrase – maybe the kids' schooling was becoming less important to him.

She hoped it wouldn't: when it came to the twins, he had always been a good father. He loved them. He played cricket in the garden with John on the weekend, took Franny to the science museum in London and set up a telescope in her room so that they could watch out for the international space station and meteor showers. But this whole situation had thrown Mara a curve ball and she didn't know what to expect anymore.

She pushed the glass door of Serafina's open, which produced a cacophony of bells ringing; she looked up, surprised, to see several colourful ribbons hanging from the inside doorknob, each with a number of acorn-sized copper bells tied onto them. Some people glanced up and smiled as she walked in, but most were either deep in conversation, laughing, or working at laptops with a half-drunk coffee next to them. At one table, a woman about her age was listening to her friend with a serious expression.

The café was long and thin: wide enough for a table on each side of the door and a long counter that stretched back into a square at the rear, thronged with people talking and laughing.

Paintings and drawings dominated the rough whitewashed walls. Mara noticed that there were discreet price tags next to most of them. Cheery reggae music played in the background.

As she made her way to the counter, Mara's phone buzzed: it was Gideon again, the fifth text this morning. He wanted to know how it had gone at the estate agency. He was anxious for her to get the house on the market so that he could 'feel secure' about the children's future.

Maybe if you wanted them to feel secure, you shouldn't have slept with your assistant, she thought angrily, turning the phone to silent as she scanned the hand-lettered blackboard coffee menu behind the counter. Gideon loved his children, but he'd been blind in terms of what his infidelity would do to their family.

'What can I get you?'

The woman who asked her was perhaps in her fifties, very petite, with light brown skin and a glamorous mane of white hair. She wore a long bright pink peasant dress and several fine gold necklaces that bore a variety of pendants: a golden shell, half a heart and a rose-and-cream-coloured cameo. Over the top of the dress she'd slung a citrine-coloured fluffy cardigan which Mara knew would have looked awful on her, but this woman had a kind of effortless chic which made the combination look great. Mara noticed a handwritten 'HELP WANTED' sign taped to the chalkboard behind her.

'Ah… a large cappuccino, please. With an extra shot?' Mara set her bag on the counter to rummage for her purse. 'For here?'

'You got it.' The woman turned away and manipulated the large silver coffee machine, expertly pouring milk into a mug to froth, twisting levers and pressing buttons. She placed a squat blue pottery mug on the counter and finished the coffee by making a foamed milk heart on the top.

'There you go, my darling. Three pounds.'

Mara's gaze lingered on several cake stands on the counter, each of which held either a delicious-looking gateau, or a stack of brownies or fruity flapjacks.

'Homemade. The brownies are vegan, but you'd never know it. As for the cakes… I recommend the walnut and pecan.' The woman winked at Mara, who couldn't help smiling.

'Well, if you recommend it, then yes. I'd love to try a piece,' she agreed. Why not? Her life was going to hell – she might as well enjoy a piece of cake. 'Can I sit at the counter?'

'No problem. Let me get you a plate.' The woman cut a generous slice of the tall, moist, nutty sponge, lined with three generous layers of caramel-coloured buttercream and put it on a blue pottery plate that matched Mara's mug. Both were a kind of modern willowware, Mara thought –though she wasn't an expert when it came to pottery – with a countryside scene depicted in a vibrant blue on a white background. Mara tapped her card on the reader and looked around for somewhere to hang her coat. The woman held out her hand for it.

'I'll hang it up for you on the door. There's a coat stand over there, but it's so full. Just let me know when you want it.'

Mara passed her coat over. Being in the café was improving her mood; just something as simple as someone making her a cup of coffee and hanging up her coat made her realise how little anyone usually cared. She felt her earlier tears welling up again and wiped at her eyes furiously. The woman behind the counter gave her a curious look.

'You all right, darling? Can I help?' She leaned over the counter in concern; Mara felt a nervous cry-laugh escape her.

'I'm so sorry. I'm fine, really. It's just been quite a morning.' She sipped at her cappuccino which was thick, strong and chocolatey.

'Want to talk about it?' the woman asked, cocking her head to one side; it was a sympathetic gesture which warmed Mara's heart.

'Between my own life and everyone in Magpie Cove that comes here to spill their guts, I've heard or done it all. Unshockable, me.' She grinned, resting her elbows on the counter.

'You've got other customers. I wouldn't want to take up your time.' Mara sniffed, picking up a paper napkin from the counter and blowing her nose. *Get a grip, Mara*, she berated herself.

'My café, my rules. Anyway, Zeke's on duty. If he ever stops chatting up girls, that is!' the woman called out. A good-looking teenage boy with dark skin and wavy hair looked up from where he stood, leaning casually against the other end of the counter and waved. 'Zeke! Take over behind the counter for a bit, okay?' she yelled, and the boy made his way back behind the long aluminium bar.

'I'm here, chill.' He rolled his eyes affectionately at the woman.

'I have zero chill, Zeke. You know that,' she replied, and tossed him a tea towel. 'Here. Clean up a little? I'm taking a break.' The woman stuck her hand out and Mara shook it. 'I'm Serafina Lucido, by the way.'

'Mara Thorne.' Her married name had been hers for so long that it was automatic to use it, but for the first time, she realised it wouldn't be hers much longer. 'Well… Mara Hughes, I suppose,' she added. Hughes was her maiden name. *Maiden. An unmarried virgin.*

Soon to be unmarried, anyway, she thought. *And I don't care if I never have sex again, frankly. Definitely overrated.*

'Nice to meet you, Mara Hughes.' Serafina grinned. 'So. Divorce, is it?'

'Yup.' Mara conceded. Her phone lit up: another text from Gideon. Serafina followed Mara's eyes and saw her look of despair.

'Your ex?' She indicated the phone.

'He wants me to call him. I'll do it after my coffee and cake.'

'You take your time,' Serafina coaxed. 'I can relate.'

'Have you… I mean…?' Mara realised it was rude to ask if this stranger was divorced, but Serafina's manner made her feel like they were already old friends.

'Heavens, yes. Been there, got the T-shirt.' Serafina pulled her lips tight. 'Not pretty. Still, at least it was a long time ago. You have children?'

'Twins. They're nine.' Every time she thought about what divorce would do to the twins, Mara felt a fresh wave of *you're-a-bad-mother* wash over her, despite the fact that it wasn't her fault. Even though it was Gideon who'd cheated, it was still there in the back of her mind: if she'd been better, he wouldn't have strayed. If she'd been sexier, cleverer, a better mother. If she'd fascinated him in the same way that his assistant, Charlotte, seemed to, then maybe he'd never have left them. Maybe she should have worn sexier knickers. Dyed her hair blonde. Something.

She took a deep breath.

'Anyway. I just inherited a house down on the beach. Gideon's all over me to sell it quickly so I can get a new house for me and the kids and he can have our old house with… her. But I've just had the survey done and the beach house is a total wreck. I doubt anyone would want to buy it, the state it's in.' Mara cut a corner of pure buttercream icing from her cake and ate it. It was delicious: sweet caramel with a hint of salt; buttery on her tongue. At least the cake was good. No, the cake was *amazing*.

'Darling. You have got a solicitor. Right? Your ex owes you half of everything. You should either get the family home or half its value. Here…' Serafina fumbled under the counter for a minute and handed Mara a business card. 'Aimee's great. She didn't do my divorce, but she's done them for quite a few people in Magpie Cove. Give her a call.'

'Oh. Thanks.' Mara took the card, wondering how she'd even afford a solicitor, or divorce lawyer, or whatever you needed to get divorced. The idea was still so new.

'Hughes… not related to Abby Hughes, are you?' Serafina frowned; she jutted her chin forwards, peering at Mara closely. 'My goodness, I don't know why I didn't see it before now! You're the spit of her.'

'She was my mother,' Mara replied.

'She left you the family house!' Serafina exclaimed, a look of discovery on her fine features, eyes twinkling. 'The old Hughes house on the beach. Not been lived in a long time, though she used to visit the town now and again, just over the past year. I'd see her walking on the beach, end of the day sometimes, if I needed some air. She never came in here, though.'

'Why not?' Sipping her coffee, Mara looked up as she heard the bells by the door jangle again, and was momentarily distracted; the man that had just entered was the same one from the beach; he was a handyman, or something. A carpenter. That was it.

Mara felt a warm yet unfamiliar sensation in her diaphragm. As she looked down at her plate, she realised she was feeling butterflies in her stomach. Before she had a chance to wonder why she suddenly felt like a schoolgirl whose gorgeous Head Boy had just walked into the common room, he was standing next to her, unzipping his dark blue waxed jacket. It brought out his eyes, she realised, then couldn't believe she'd noticed that at all and stared at her cake again, mortified.

'Oh, hello again.'

Mara looked up and found the man – what was his name? She racked her brain, but it had gone – smiling down at her. She'd forgotten how tall he was. Under the waxed jacket he wore a plain light grey T-shirt that hinted at a broad chest and flat stomach.

His eyes twinkled with the same friendly amusement as before. She looked away. This never happened. She'd never even thought about any man other than Gideon since they were married, even after she had stopped loving him – which, in retrospect, had happened a few years ago, not that she had admitted it to herself at the time. Still, she'd never noticed other men that way. Perhaps it was more out of habit than anything else.

'Hi.'

'You two know each other?' Serafina looked from Mara to the man and back again.

'Not really. We met briefly at the beach house the other week, that's all.' Mara ate some more cake to have an excuse not to say anything for a minute.

'Brian,' he reminded her. 'You're Mara, right?'

'Right.'

'Did you decide what you're going to do about the repairs?' he asked, pulling up a stool to sit next to her. Mara hoped he wasn't staying; she'd been enjoying talking to Serafina, and Brian made her feel uneasy.

'Um... not really. There's so much to be done. I don't have that kind of money, and I need to sell. You'd be better off waiting for the new owners and asking them.' It was sad; she liked the old house, and she could see its potential. But she had no choice.

'Ah. Sorry to hear that. I hoped you might have reconsidered. Serafina, can I get a double espresso to go?' he asked the café owner, and Mara felt relieved though some small part of her, inexplicably, suddenly wished he'd stay and talk to her a little bit longer. *Stop it,* she rebuked herself. *A carpenter with washboard abs sits next to you in a café for five minutes and you can't control yourself. Is this what being divorced is going to be like? I hope not. Niagara Falls in a barrel. You should set yourself a goal like that. That woman knew what she was doing,* she thought manically. *She was all about the barrel. Not so much the carpenters with great bodies.*

'Five minutes,' Serafina called out. 'Just got to get something from the back.' She shot Mara a meaningful look and disappeared into a back room. Mara suddenly suspected that this espresso was going to take longer than usual.

They sat in uncomfortable silence for a moment.

'Nice day out,' Brian observed. Mara looked out of the plate-glass windows at the front of the café and saw that the September sunshine had turned into driving rain.

'Good for the flowers,' she agreed.

'You know where you are with rain.' Brian grinned at her; she met his eyes, shyly, and looked away.

'In Cornwall?'

'Well, yes, true. But I was also referring to… I don't know. There's a soulfulness about the rain,' he continued, shrugging.

'I think I'd find it more soulful if I didn't know that it's raining through the massive hole in my roof.' Mara raised an eyebrow.

'Hmmm. That bad, then?'

'Pretty bad. Subsidence, damp, needs a new roof, needs to be totally rewired. Goodness knows what else. Redecorated, I guess,' she added, glumly.

Brian looked at her thoughtfully.

'You know, I've been looking for a development project.'

'Have you?' she asked politely, taking a big mouthful of cake. *Ohhh, it was good.*

'Yes. The beach house would be perfect, I have to admit. Listen. I could do most of the repairs and then when you sold it, I could take a percentage. You'd still make money if you can sell it for what it's really worth. Not just what someone will give you for a wreck.'

Mara looked up in surprise.

'What?'

'What I said.' Brian shrugged. 'More money in property development than carpentry. This could be the perfect project, if you were interested?'

'I… I don't know. I don't even know you.' Mara stammered as her phone lit up again. CALL ME. Gideon's text messages had now reached the ALL CAPITALS stage.

'Well, maybe we should have dinner or something, and we can talk it over in more detail?' Brian's expression was hopeful. 'I think it could be great.'

Is he talking about the house or something else? she wondered, as Brian kept her gaze. *Dinner?*

Before Mara could reply, a woman came up behind Brian and put her arms around his waist.

'Brian! Didn't you see me? I was waving at you!' she exclaimed. Mara caught Brian wince, but it was swiftly replaced with a big smile.

'Petra! No, I didn't know you were here, sorry. I just came in for an espresso to go. How are you?' He kissed the young woman on the cheek. 'Mara, this is Petra Blake.'

'Pleased to meet you,' Mara replied politely. Petra was perhaps twenty-five, pretty, with an upturned nose and a mass of long, curly red hair. Mara thought of those pre-Raphaelite paintings that always featured women with flaming hair and noble faces; Petra resembled the Lady of Shalott, Circe, or one of those other mythical women. *No barrels for Petra,* she thought. *No stretch-marked thighs to ram inside a custom-made wooden casket and pad out with pillows. Definitely no saggy stomach reverberating against the Niagara undertow.*

'Oh, hi!' Petra beamed at Mara, and placed a proprietary hand on Brian's muscular thigh: it was obvious that she wanted him to herself. 'How do you two know each other?'

'Oh. Well, we don't, really.' Mara wondered what to say. 'We just met a couple of weeks ago, on the beach. Brian was talking to me about repairing my beach house.'

Petra frowned, and then her face lit up.

'The Hughes house? That's yours?'

'It was my mother's,' Mara said, hoping she wouldn't be forced to say the words *she passed away*, but Petra seemed to understand.

'Oh. I see. I'm so sorry.' Unexpectedly, the young woman took Mara's hand and squeezed it. 'I'll pray for her.'

'Er… thanks.' Mara gently drew her hand away. Brian gave Petra a sharp look.

'I don't think Mara's quite used to Magpie Cove yet, Pets. Maybe don't freak her out on day one by holding her hand.' Mara thought he sounded as if he was her dad, not her boyfriend. *Not my place to judge*, she thought.

'Oh, she doesn't mind, I can tell. Don't be so grumpy, Brian. Jeez.' Petra made a face at Brian. 'Listen, Mara. I'm usually around here mid-morning. I tend to come in for a coffee break unless I'm deep into a painting. If you want to chat, or anything, just come over and nudge me. I love that old beach house. I always think about who must have lived there when I'm down on the beach, surfing.'

'Oh. Is that how you know each other?' Mara looked between them.

'It's how we got together.' Petra looked apologetic. 'Little did I know that my wholesome desire to get in shape would result in me dating the local girl magnet.' She rolled her eyes. Mara stifled a laugh.

'The course of true love never did run smooth…' Mara remarked, watching Brian's reaction.

'Ha! True love.' Petra gave Brian a cynical look. 'I don't think that's in your plan, is it, babe?'

Brian raised an eyebrow and shrugged.

'You seem to know more about it than me, Petra,' he replied in a snarky tone that wasn't anything like his usual charm.

'See what I mean? Grumpy old man.' Petra rolled her eyes.

'Well, it's time I was going.' Mara got up and picked up her phone. She'd been stupid to think that a man like Brian wouldn't have a girlfriend, or more than one – not that it mattered, anyway.

Just for a minute or two she'd started to think about Brian's idea to partner on doing up the beach house, but it was just some pipe dream: it was unthinkable that she'd go into business with some local handyman when they'd only just met in a café – not when she had the kids and a divorce to think about.

'Oh, do you have to go?' Brian reached out a hand and caught her lightly on the arm; it was only a brief touch, but it shot a sudden bolt of electricity through her. *What the heck was that?* Her eyes met his in surprise and saw that he'd felt it too. He released her arm almost immediately; a second passed when neither of them knew what to say.

'Sorry. I… I have to go,' she stammered. 'I have to make a phone call.'

'How can I reach you? To talk about the development?' he asked, but Mara was making for the door, her heart pounding.

'I've got your card,' she replied, over her shoulder.

'It was nice to meet you!' Petra called out. 'Remember, I'm here most days!'

Mara waved at Petra. She liked her, actually. Maybe it wouldn't be so bad to have a chat now and again.

'Hey! Mara!' Serafina called after her, having reappeared at the counter: she held up Mara's coat. 'Don't forget this!'

Mara felt herself blush. She scurried back and took her coat from Serafina.

'Thanks so much.' She smiled shyly at the café owner, who was watching her with amusement.

'Come back soon!' Serafina called out. 'We should talk!'

Mara realised they'd been distracted from whatever Serafina was going to tell her about Abby. Oh well. Probably just some local gossip.

Outside the café, Mara looked at her phone. Eight texts and four missed calls from Gideon. She felt the good mood from the café evaporate into the air; the rain threatened to soak her immediately.

She took a deep breath, pressed Gideon's number and waited.

'What took you so long?' Gideon demanded; he didn't even say hello.

'I got caught up.' She couldn't think of a better excuse.

'So?'

'So what?' She stalled for time. She didn't want Gideon to know about the state of the house. For some reason she felt protective about it, as if it was an ill relative of hers that needed her. And, she realised, she didn't want to tell Gideon the price the estate agent had quoted her, because she knew that, despite his making out that he wanted it to give her some financial stability, he would love the fact that it was worth far less than Mara had expected.

She really wondered why he'd ever married her in the first place.

'The valuation, Mara. Tick, tock.'

She gave him a number, but not the one that the estate agent had given her.

'Shame it wasn't more.' Gideon's tone was thoughtful.

'I thought that was a reasonable amount.' Mara hoped he didn't know she was lying. She hardly ever lied, but when she did, she went bright red. Thank goodness he couldn't see her right now, blushing like a sunset in the middle of the street.

'You would,' Gideon dismissed her. 'Fine. Well, I've got to go. I'll check back in a few days and see how the sale's going. If it doesn't go quickly I might need to take over the process. Time is of the essence, after all.'

Yeah – for you, Mara thought, pressing her lips together to stop it blurting out. *You can't wait to have me off your hands so you can walk off into the sunset with Miss Botox.* She had to be civil with Gideon, or he might take the kids. He'd threatened to, if 'settled accommodation of a reasonable standard' was not provided by Mara in the time specified in the letter she'd received from his lawyer. She doubted he wanted the kids around, full time at least – it would mess up his new love life – but he could make things difficult.

'Okay, bye then.' She rang off with a falsely bright tone and pressed the end call button fiercely.

As far as Gideon was concerned, she had her inheritance and that was that: whatever the value, the deal was, she got it all to herself and he got the house. Otherwise, he'd threatened that he'd take half of it like he was entitled to as her husband, and he'd fight her for custody of the kids too. She *thought* he was probably full of crap and Serafina could be right. As his wife, it was likely that she was entitled to half of everything he had too, if she wanted it, and that wasn't nothing… but the idea of fighting Gideon in court wasn't attractive – he was a lawyer by profession, after all. Serafina's advice was good, though: she clearly needed to talk to a solicitor, otherwise Gideon could do whatever he wanted.

She looked down the street, taking it in more detail than she had before. The antiques shop had a dusty façade, but the sign on the door said 'Open'. Mara took a moment to look in the window and realised there were quite a few things she liked: a jewel-coloured Tiffany lamp, tall silver candlesticks and a charming rose-patterned porcelain tea set, which would have looked beautiful in her old kitchen. If she'd visited before the divorce, she would have gone in and probably bought a few things.

Further down the street there was the other café with its 'Closed' sign and, on the other side of the street, a traditional butcher next to a small bakery. She hadn't stopped at either when she'd first walked down. It made Mara wonder what other little treasures there were, tucked away in Magpie Cove.

A few doors down, Petra and Brian emerged from Serafina's with their takeaway coffees and turned away from her, heading into the village. They were talking and laughing. *Must be nice to be in love,* Mara thought. She pulled the solicitor's card Serafina had given her from her pocket and sighed.

If love leads to needing to make a call like this, then you can have it. I don't want it, she thought, tapping in Aimee's number into her phone and pressing 'call'. She spoke with Aimee's assistant for a few minutes, and arranged an appointment with the solicitor, watching Brian and Petra stroll down the street and out of sight. When she put the phone back in her pocket, she felt unexpectedly relieved. It was a start, at least.

Time to start standing up for yourself, Mara, she thought. *Time to start a new life.*

Chapter Six

The more she pulled out the old, sea-air-warped wooden furniture to clean behind it, the more Mara realised the scale of the damp in the house. It was everywhere – shadows reaching up walls, wallpaper peeling off in the hallway, rotting floorboards. She had had to send the kids out to play on the beach for fear that John's foot was going to plunge through the damp wood into the recess beneath, or Franny would catch a cold on her chest from the moist chill in the late September air: Franny was particularly susceptible to chest infections.

The twins hadn't needed much encouragement to disappear onto the wet sand, even though it was as cold out there as it was inside. They loved the beach, and every day that week they'd begged Mara to take them back to the beach house to explore some more. Their lives were usually so structured and scheduled: school, homework, carefully chosen play dates. Yet they adored discovering new corners of the ratty old house and playing on the sand, not doing anything in particular, just making their own fun. Mara watched Franny chase John over the top of a dune, her coat unbuttoned and streaming out behind her like a cape. At least if they were running, they'd keep warm.

Even though it was cold inside the house – a house with a hole in the roof was hard to keep warm, after all – Mara was working up a sweat from the labour. She'd tied her dark hair up in a light blue scarf, and taken off the bulky cardigan she'd put on that morning at the hotel, leaving her in a white vest and some paint-splattered denim dungarees. She had put on thick-soled trainers to protect her feet, because of the splinters that stuck up everywhere.

'It's just as well I'm selling you,' she muttered. 'Though, who would buy you, I don't know. A sucker for punishment, for sure.'

She tried to imagine her mother living here, but couldn't. Abby had never talked about this place. Not once. Was it because of the letters? The lost child? Some kind of bad memory – about why Abby had had to give the little boy up – linked to this house? But Brian had seen her mother here, a short time before she died. Had Abby always come here without Mara knowing? Or had it just been before she died that she had – what, made peace with the place? Serafina had mentioned that she'd seen Abby at the house in the past year but not before, but she hadn't had time to explain if she'd known Mara's mother.

Mara stopped sweeping and stared out of the window at her children again. Abby had had so many secrets. What if there were more? Had she ever really known her mother? She had always thought she had. She resolved to go back and ask Serafina what she knew.

Having swept the worst of the detritus from the floor – dry leaves, paper, faded beach plastic – she piled the recycling in one bag and rubbish in another, thinking about the letters again. Who was Paul Sullivan? Where was he now? He would be a few years younger than Mara. The letters Abby had written had all been returned unopened, so he obviously didn't live at that address in Helston. She wondered why Abby had continued to write them after the first couple had been sent back. Wasn't that proof that whoever lived there had moved on?

Mara opened out one of the flat-pack boxes she'd brought with her, taped it together and started stacking the variety of non-matching plates, bowls and cups from inside the painted Welsh dresser in the box, wrapping each piece in brown paper.

Some of this could go into storage. Wherever Mara and the kids eventually ended up, they'd need stuff.

It was strange, though, looking at the crockery. Who else had eaten their dinner from it? Mara had grown up with no family other than Abby. They were a unit, the two of them: Abby refused to talk about her own parents or even if she had any siblings. When other children talked about staying at their grandparents' house or going to their auntie's birthday party, Mara had no comparison.

It was a close, sometimes suffocating relationship. Mara had grown up fast as Abby's only friend, a maturity she had never asked for. Listening to Abby sometimes cry and beat her fists against the walls at night; living in a miasma of regret and sadness that had always encircled her mother like fog, but which her mother never explained. A fog that had threatened to suck Mara in too, even though Abby had tried so hard to appear positive and bright for her daughter. Wasn't that why Mara had married Gideon? Because he was the first person who came along and asked? He had given her a way out of that house with its sadness rotting the walls, just like the damp in the beach house.

Cheery, Mara thought. She always tried to jolly herself out of being sad, but it was pretty hard lately. The barrel woman, Annie Edson Taylor, the one Franny always talked about, had become a minor obsession in her mind. It had started off as a joke she was having with herself, but now she thought of Annie when she was starting to feel really crappy and worried about everything. In a strange way, thinking about a middle-aged Edwardian woman who had voluntarily risked her life to prove a point made her feel like this new life might be possible, somehow. No one was asking Mara to thrust her middle-aged body into a screaming white-water waterfall. All she had to do was make three meals a day, get a divorce, sell a beach house and move on with her life. By comparison it was easy, although some days, she would have preferred the barrel.

The front door blew open in the wind. Mara sat back on her heels and watched two seagulls hover in mid-air above the sand, navigating the current of the air as if they were ships at sea. Beyond them, a black-and-white bird with a red beak flew across the beach to join its mate on the rocks leading to the water. Mara frowned for a moment, trying to remember what she knew about birds. Was it an oystercatcher? She thought so. Beyond the birds, she spotted Franny and John crouched in the sand.

Looking back, she knew that Gideon had seen in her what he needed, too – someone young and weak and all too grateful for a nice house and two children. Someone who didn't ask for anything, who didn't demand, because she had never even dreamed that anything would come of demanding. Someone who was already shrunk by the weight of responsibility. She was small and malleable enough not to complain when she was squashed into a smaller box by a determined hand.

If she was truthful with herself, Mara knew that she had never really been a child. Most children demanded and sulked and tried to get their way, which was normal, which was okay – John and Franny did and she was happy for them that they did, because it meant that they weren't so fearful of her being sad, deeply, awfully sad – that they were unafraid to be anything less than perfect. They didn't mind annoying the crap out of her sometimes. It was okay.

Or perhaps they were just less sensitive than Mara had been. Either way, she reflected, she had been so frightened to misbe-have, to do anything other than what she was told and to fit in, because – what?

She watched the birds, tears running freely down her cheeks now.

Because everyone had left her, and she only had Abby left. If she was bad, Abby might leave her too. So she was as good as she could be. She fitted in. She did as she was told.

And then Abby had died, and she *was* completely alone in the world, apart from the kids, thank goodness for them. And by then she had realised that she didn't love Gideon, and had never really loved him, apart from a kind of gratefulness at first. And being good and fitting in and bending and folding according to everyone else's expectations hadn't worked, because now Gideon, who had presumably chosen her exactly because she was so eager to please, had left her for someone who apparently demanded an awful lot, and he appeared to love it.

There was a mildewed pillow nearby and Mara grabbed it and punched it, over and over again. She was suddenly furious. Furious at Abby for dying. Furious that Abby had never brought her here as a child in the summer. Furious at all the fun she had missed out on.

'There was no FUN!' Mara shouted, hugging the pillow. 'Other children had fun! Why did everything have to be so sad?!'

Why was she even here, clearing out this house like a good little girl? If she was going to sell it, it didn't matter that it was a mess. There was already a bloody hole in the roof, how much worse could it really be? She sat down on the floor, where a damp rug immediately leached heat from her. *Stop. Just stop,* she told herself. *You don't have to be perfect anymore.*

But I do need to sell it, she told herself, even though she was starting to love it here. Despite the hole in the roof and the peeling-off paper and the bloody damp.

I wish I didn't, though.

She sighed, and stood up, putting the damp cushion into the rubbish bag. She doubted it could be salvaged.

There was the sound of running feet coming up the beach – the children. Probably hungry. She wiped her eyes and tried to rearrange her face into something normal.

'What is it?' she raised her voice, looking around, ready to frown at them both for muddy feet or something similar.

But instead, she looked up to see Brian Oakley standing in the doorway, with a soaking wet Franny lifeless in his arms.

Chapter Seven

'Oh my—' Mara ran to Brian and held her arms out instinctively for her daughter. 'What happened? Franny! Is she… is she awake? Franny?' Mara's heart was pounding. Franny's face was white as the foam on top of a wave. She touched her daughter's cheek; miraculously, Franny opened her eyes.

'I'm okay, Mum. I just tripped on the rocks.' Franny's voice was weak and wavery.

'Twisted her ankle, I'd say. I had a look and it doesn't seem broken, but you might want to take her to hospital to be sure.' Brian laid Franny down gently on the ratty old sofa and looked around. 'You'll need to get her out of those wet clothes. Got any blankets, change of clothes, that kind of thing? I'd say put her somewhere warm, but—'

'You were out there… surfing?' Mara hugged her arms around herself; she was suddenly freezing cold.

'Great weather for it. It's fine if you've got one of these on,' he explained. He was wearing a wetsuit again, and shoes made of the same material.

'I want Daddy,' Franny shivered; her face screwed up and Mara could see that tears weren't far behind.

'I know, sweetie,' she crooned, hugging her daughter. 'But he's not here right now. We'll give him a call on the phone later, okay? Let's get you warmed up first. You'll feel a lot better.'

Mara had found blankets in a hall cupboard that weren't too mouldy when she was cleaning up earlier, and she remembered them now. Brian turned away and spoke quietly to John as Mara stripped Franny of her soaked clothes and wrapped her up in her own discarded cardigan and a couple of the blankets, taking care to avoid moving Franny's ankle which was already swelling up quite badly. Mara rifled through her bag for the snacks she'd brought for the kids, and hugged Franny to her as she dutifully drank a carton of orange juice and ate a cereal bar. Mara fretted. They couldn't stay here: the electricity was cut off, there was no way to get a warm drink inside Franny. Didn't sweet tea help shock? What she wouldn't give for a cup of tea. *Bloody tea, bloody beach house, bloody rocks,* she thought.

'Do you want me to take you? To the hospital, I mean?' Brian sat down next to Mara on the sofa. John was standing by the door, looking uncertain.

'Maybe. Yes, I think so. I mean, no. I have a car, so I can take them. It's fine.' She smiled as warmly as she could, even though her heart was still racing.

Mara shivered. 'John, what happened? How did she fall?'

'It wasn't my fault!' John had tears ready in his eyes: Mara knew that look. He would blame himself, even if it he hadn't done anything.

'I know, sweetheart. It's okay. You can tell me, I won't be cross.' Mara held out her hand for John's.

'We were hopping the rocks. They were slippery. Franny fell over.' John inched his way across the room. Mara took his hand with the arm that wasn't holding Franny and squeezed his hand.

'It's okay, John,' she repeated.

'Accidents happen,' Brian added. 'I've slipped on those rocks many a time. Even with these on.' He pointed to his oddly slipper-like surf shoes. 'You were a champ. I saw you run over and help her up. You did great.' Brian grinned at John, but John was too much Mara's son, she thought. There was too much sadness in him already, and he didn't grin back like another child might. He remained cautious, ever fearful of the worst that could happen. Mara thought there would probably be nightmares about this later.

'But it might be broken…' he said, his voice wavering. Mara handed him a juice carton and a sandwich, the same as Franny, who was already looking brighter.

'Well, it might.' Mara tried to keep her voice light. 'That's why we have to go and find out. Either way, the doctor will make it better. Okay? There's nothing to worry about.'

'I'm all right, Johnny.' Franny reached out for her brother's hand. Mara suspected there was a long story coming John's way about what had happened in Franny's mind before, during and after the accident. 'It's not that bad. I think I might have strained my metatarsal. Did you know that—'

'Okay. Let's get in the car.' Mara cut her off and handed them each a chocolate biscuit. 'We'll find the hospital and then we'll… We'll have something nice for tea. Fish and chips maybe.' She made it sound as fun as she could.

'I'll carry her if you like?' Brian offered. Mara was going to refuse, but then she saw the hopeful look on Franny's face.

'All right,' she conceded. 'Thank you. I don't know what to say. If it hadn't been for you…'

'It's fine. I'm glad I could help.' He pushed his hair out of his eyes with an appealingly unsure look; Mara wondered what he must think of her, letting the children run off unsupervised. She shivered when she thought about what Gideon would say: as if he could hear her thoughts, Brian placed his wide, warm palm on her arm. 'Hey. It's okay.'

Mara felt the tears well up in her eyes again and brushed them away furiously.

'I'm all right. Really. Thank you.' She tried to smile, feeling stupid. *Keep it together*, she berated herself. *Just keep it together. Remember barrel woman.*

'Listen, if you ever want to talk, about… anything – I'm a good listener.' His hand stayed on her arm, and she swore she could feel a kind of calm radiating from it. She met his eyes; they had a warmth and softness to them she wasn't used to. She wasn't used to anyone caring for her, really, and it was almost a shock to her carefully protected self to feel that warmth from another person.

Mara helped Franny into Brian's arms, avoiding his eyes.

'Thanks. I'm fine, really.' She could feel herself pushing him away. It was as if he was the sea itself, making waves in her carefully controlled life. She realised that she was doing Abby's trick of making things into sea metaphors. *Stop it, Mara*, she thought. *They say we all turn into our mothers, but is now really the best time?*

Once Brian had Franny, Mara turned her back to him, fiddling with the pointless front door lock. Not that it mattered – the house was practically falling down and no one would be interested in looting the place, but she needed a moment. *Come on, come on,* she thought to herself, balling up her hands. She willed herself to be strong; she willed herself not to cry. She could have lost Franny. She should have watched the children more carefully; warned them not to go out on the rocks. She should have been there, and called them back. *You have to do better,* she berated herself. *It's just you now. You don't have anyone else to rely on. And you can't give Gideon any excuse to take the children away.*

She turned back to Brian and the children and smiled as brightly as she could.

'Let's get going, then,' she chided them, and followed Brian Oakley up the beach towards the car.

Chapter Eight

It was quieter than the first time she'd come to the café; today, only a few lone customers sat working at laptops, or reading books and newspapers. Jazz played in the background as Mara walked in. She'd just dropped the twins off at their school, a good forty-minute drive away with morning traffic and the twisty Cornish roads, and the café was a cosy haven from the rain outside. It smelt fantastic: a mix of rich, freshly ground coffee, cinnamon and orange, like Christmas come early. This time, she noticed details she hadn't seen before: posters and leaflets that were plastered around the counter, advertising local potters' studios, a poetry festival, rooms for hire in some of the shabby-but-still-grand Victorian terraces that lined the more inland streets of Magpie Cove. Mara shuddered at the thought of the drive to and from the kids' school every day. *Just another reason not to live here,* she thought.

The same young man that had been at the café before took her order, but the owner, Serafina – with whom Mara had had what, she reflected, was a surprisingly honest conversation – was nowhere to be seen. Mara ordered a large black filter coffee and a flapjack and took both to a small table by the full-length plate-glass window at the front of the café. It was rare that she ever spoke to strangers about her personal life – or anyone, really – yet there had been something about Serafina. She was one of those people who were so immediately warm that they melted your defences, and you didn't mind at all. She had wanted to come back and ask her what she had been about to say about Abby. Clearly, she had met Mara's mother. Mara wondered how well she knew her.

If she'd seen Serafina today she probably would also have blurted out the story of Franny falling on the rocks, not least because now she felt fine talking about it because Franny *was* fine and had survived the incident with good humour and nothing more than a twisted ankle, but, as Mara had been assured by the doctors at the hospital, no other damage. Also, if she was being completely honest with herself, she wanted to ask Serafina about Brian Oakley. The café owner seemed like the sort of person who knew things about everyone.

What did she know about the man who had not only carried Franny to the car, who had gently offered to listen to Mara, but had also ended up driving Mara's car to the hospital so that she could sit in the back, cradling Franny? Who had bought John crossword and Sudoku books to do in the waiting room before he left them there? He'd given up his time even though they were virtual strangers. And when Mara had finally driven back to the hotel with the kids in the back, she felt strangely bereft. In those short hours, Brian Oakley had stepped into Mara's life, supporting her without being asked. And it had felt right.

Mara hung up her wet raincoat on the coat rack and took out a pen and a journal from her bag, laying them beside her drink as she sat down. She took a sip of the coffee, which was as excellent as before, and poured just a little of the full cream milk the young man had added to her tray. At first, she couldn't remember his name, and was too shy to ask now. *Zeke. That was it.*

Mara uncapped the pen and held it over a clean page in the journal. This wasn't about Brian Oakley. Franny and John were fine; Franny was at school, proudly showing off her ankle with its elastic bandage and her walking stick. This was about Paul Sullivan.

She wasn't sure where to start. What should she say? It didn't help that she knew nothing about him other than that he was

Abby's son. Somewhere out there, there was a man just a few years younger than she was, who might look like her. Who was her half-brother – or even her full brother; it wasn't impossible that they might have the same father – and wherever he was now, she had to at least try to let him know that Abby had died.

She had the old address on the letters she'd found, but she reasoned that if all those letters had been sent back, then he obviously wasn't there anymore. Instead, she had looked up all the Paul Sullivans who lived in Cornwall: there were twenty-three. He might have moved away from the area completely, of course, and if he had, then there was nothing she could do. But she could at least try this: send the same letter to all twenty-three of them and see if anyone replied. What else was there to do? She wrote:

Dear Paul,

I hope this letter finds you well. If you aren't the Paul Sullivan who was adopted or put in care as a baby, then I'm sorry to have troubled you. My name is Mara Hughes, and my mother was Abby Hughes. I'm looking for a Paul Sullivan who was born in 1986 and once lived in Helston.

She paused. What to write next? She didn't know how to write the news.

Your mother is dead.
My mother is dead.

Even thinking the word *dead* was difficult; it was as if her brain skipped over it, like a patch of black ice. It was easy to slip on that word: it could easily take Mara somewhere she didn't want to be.

I'm afraid to tell you that Abby Hughes passed away a few months ago from cancer.

Mara closed her eyes and took a deep breath. She didn't want to remember those last weeks in the hospital room. The one with the lurid yellow and green curtains, overlooking a car park. She didn't want to think about the fact that this had been the last room Abby had inhabited. And she certainly didn't want to think about the way Abby was at the end – the pain she had been in.

Yes, the doctors had had her on morphine, on a drip, but it often still wasn't enough, and when the pain broke through, Mara had had to scramble for the nurse, who always took too long to come in with some extra medication Abby could have orally. It wasn't anyone's fault: the nurses were overstretched. Every time the shifts changed, Mara had to have the same conversation, bringing the new nurse up to date with what Abby already had and when.

She had sat at Abby's bedside for three weeks, sleeping in the small family room in fits and starts. She remembered exhaustedly thinking about all the other people in the world outside the hospital who were having their normal lives now: eating dinner, watching TV, laughing. It all seemed so far away from her, suddenly; she had entered a kind of limbo, outside normal life, where her only task was to watch her mother die.

Abby Hughes died on 12 June, she wrote. *She was my mother. I recently found a box of letters she wrote to you between 1987 and 2005. The last one was when you were nineteen. I don't think you ever got to read them.*

Mara felt the sorrow clench her heart again. Those last weeks in the hospital had been the worst in her life, but at least she had had Abby as a mother. Paul had never known her. And even though, at the end, the cancer had spread and spread until it was in Abby's bones and her eyes and even her brain, and she had stopped knowing who Mara was; even when she couldn't see Franny and John, and Mara had wept, holding her mother's hand, silently begging the universe for it to be over, *please let this be over,* because it was too much to bear – even with those weeks burned into her soul, Mara would never, ever have wanted to have been without Abby.

Wiping the tears from her eyes, glad that the café was so quiet, she continued writing:

> *I'm so sorry to have to be writing this letter, but I thought you should know. Abby was a complicated woman, and whatever made her give you away, I know that she thought she was doing the right thing for you. If you're the right person, I have all the letters she wrote you. I opened some, but they're all yours. There are pictures – photos of her in those letters. And photos of me! For what it's worth.*
>
> *I suppose I should tell you a little about myself. I'm a few years older than you, and I'm separated from my husband. I have twins, Franny and John. They're nine. We are moving house soon, but we would love to hear from you if you get this letter and want to reply.*

Mara broke off some of the fruity flapjack and ate it, savouring the cranberries, cinnamon and pumpkin seeds. She continued:

> *I've never had much of a family. It was always just me and Abby. So, I guess it would be nice to have a brother, or at least meet. It would be nice for the twins to have an uncle.*

Mara frowned and crossed the last line out. It was too needy. She was writing to a complete stranger. What if one of the letters got to the right Paul Sullivan, but he turned out to be a criminal, a paedophile, or just a horrible person? She shouldn't be inviting all and sundry to come and be the twins' new uncle. What was to stop the wrong Paul Sullivan answering her letter and pretending to be someone he wasn't, for some kind of heinous purpose?

Mara sat back in her chair, gazing reflectively out of the window. She'd spent some time researching how to get in touch with an adopted child, or someone that had been in the care system, and she'd done what she could. She'd added her details to the national adoption register and searched for a Paul Sullivan born in 1986, but he wasn't on record. This wasn't unusual, according to the woman she'd spoken to on the phone: either Paul Sullivan wasn't his name on his birth certificate, or he didn't want to be contacted. Adopted children could choose to be completely anonymous and not open to approach. If he'd been in the care system, then records were protected for children's safety.

As far as Mara could tell, a letter was the only option.

She signed it, then dithered about which address to put at the top if he wanted to get in touch. If it ever found him, that was. She could put the temporary address of the hotel, but that only made sense if this Paul got her letter in the next few weeks and decided to write back. If he was ever going to get in contact, she didn't know how long it might take – it might be years, or not at all. And if she was going to sell the beach house, there was no point doing that either. Yet it was her only real choice. At least, perhaps, if she sold it and a letter addressed to her arrived, she could ask for it to be sent on to her. She balked at the idea of putting her old Cedars Avenue address on it. Theoretically, Gideon could be trusted to post on her mail or keep it for her if she visited, but she didn't want to bet on it. And, somehow, she didn't want him anywhere near this part of her life.

'Love letter?'

Mara looked up to find Serafina Lucido next to her, holding a half-full filter coffee pot in one hand and a plate with some raisin cookies in the other.

'Oh. Hi. No, not a love letter.' Mara laughed nervously. 'Chance would be a fine thing, I think. Or maybe not.'

'Ha. I hear ya. Refill? On the house.' Serafina proffered the coffee jug and topped up Mara's mug when she nodded.

'Thank you, that's so kind.'

'All right if I sit down?' Serafina asked.

'Of course. It's your café.'

'Ah, but it looks as though you're concentrating very hard on whatever you're writing. I don't want to interrupt.' The café owner set the plate of cookies on the table and took one, biting into it neatly.

'No, it's fine. I've finished writing it.' Mara took a cookie: it was delicious. 'Thank you. I could do with some distraction, to be honest.'

Today Serafina wore her crimped white hair up in a messy bun with two pencils stuck through it, jeans, a 'Save the Whales' T-shirt and a blue silk kimono over the top.

'Distraction is my middle name. Well, actually, it's Cherie, but you know what I mean.' She grinned. 'You okay, darling? You looked a little upset.'

Mara tried to put a brave face on. She wasn't sure she succeeded.

'I'm fine, really. I… I lost my mum recently. It turns out she had a son I never knew about, so I'm trying to find him to let him know that she… passed away. And that I exist.' She swallowed a lump in her throat.

Serafina grabbed Mara's hand across the table.

'That's right, I remember now. You're Abby Hughes' daughter. She left you the beach house. You're… Mary?'

'Mara.'

'Right. I knew I recognised you. You were here with Brian Oakley before.' She clicked her tongue. 'Separated, aren't you. I remember now. Congratulations on getting your mitts on that one. Half of Magpie Cove's after Brian Oakley.' She laughed kindly; Mara knew she was being teased.

'I wasn't *with* him. We've met a few times, that's all.' Mara decided not to divulge the fact that Brian Oakley had also saved her daughter, driven them all to the hospital and held her hand while she waited for X-rays. Mara didn't know what to feel about him now: he was still a stranger, but a stranger with whom she'd shared a strangely intimate experience. She'd cried in front of him, briefly, out of tiredness and worry, when the kids were distracted. She hadn't wanted to cry in front of them again. He'd given her a brief, strong hug.

'I know, I know. Just pulling your leg. You did look good together, though. You're more his age, not like some of those girls that hang around him all the time. He teaches surfing down at the beach, and my goodness, the number of girls who wouldn't want to break a nail doing the washing up that suddenly want to learn to surf.' She laughed heartily. Serafina had a contagious joy about her, a way of making you feel as if she was confiding a delicious secret when she spoke to you.

'I can imagine. Oh, thanks for giving me the card for the solicitor, by the way. Aimee? I have an appointment with her tomorrow.' Mara sipped her coffee and took a bite of cookie. 'My ex keeps pushing me to sell the beach house but it's worth a lot less than it could be because it needs so much renovation, which I can't afford to do. Meanwhile, me and the kids are staying in a hotel, but that money won't last forever. I've got to find a job and somewhere permanent for us to live.' Mara explained. 'Honestly, I don't know where to start. Sorry. I shouldn't be blurting all this out to you. We've really only just met.'

'Oh, don't worry, I live for interpersonal dramas, that's why I own a café. If you didn't like people, you wouldn't last long in this game.'

Serafina regarded her thoughtfully.

'You know, if you need a job, I'm looking for someone to help me. Full-time in the café. I used to have a couple of part-timers covering the week, but one of them's an artist and she's moved to France for the winter, and otherwise I've only got Zeke and he gave me his notice a couple of weeks ago.'

'I haven't worked in a café before.' Mara spoke before thinking. *Damn, why did I say that?* She berated herself. Had Annie what's-her-name gone over Niagara Falls in a barrel before she did it for the first time? No.

''S'okay. Not much to know, apart from how to work the big coffee machine. You're a mum, so I assume you're used to waiting on people and asking how their day was?' Serafina raised a humorous eyebrow.

'I am. But what about the kids? They're at school in St Ives. I wouldn't really be able to get them and bring them back here every day.'

'Well, you can bring them here if you want. But if it doesn't work for you, I get it.' Serafina met Mara's eyes. 'Look. I knew Abby when we were kids. We were friends, though not best friends, and if I'm honest I feel bad not making more of an effort to talk to her when I saw her around those few times last year. Lot of stories round here about what happened to her at that house, and none of them were kind about Abby. I've never believed them. So, consider this a favour to your mum, if you like. But also, I've been there, sweetie. If you need help, I'm offering it.' Serafina kept her gaze and squeezed Mara's hand. 'We girls gotta stick together.'

Mara thought about the logistics. Both twins had after-school clubs a few days a week, and there was an after school-club until six where they could have dinner. It wasn't like any of them were in a hurry to get back to the hotel to eat: the options with a microwave were limited at best. She could arrange John and Franny to be in after-school club, and pick them up by six if she left the café at five. She could pay the extra cost herself.

'It might work. I could get here by nine thirty earliest, and I'd have to leave by five. Maybe four days a week? I'd have to put the kids in the after-school club, and it would be good to have at least one day they could finish at normal time…'

'No problem. Leave at four thirty, if you want. Avoid the traffic getting to St Ives. So, what about it?' Serafina nudged her. 'I could do with the help.'

'Really? You'd really give me a job?' Mara gazed around her – at the cosy café, the paintings on the walls, the slightly steamed-up windows. It was a good place. She felt comfortable here, but more than that, somehow, she felt safe. Something about Serafina made her feel that everything was going to be okay.

Serafina nodded.

'It's yours if you want it, Mara. Think about it and let me know.' She stood up and pushed her chair away.

'I'll take it.' Mara beamed. 'Thank you.'

'Great! You can start now.' Serafina went to the counter, reached behind it and threw a balled-up apron across the café to Mara. 'Put that on and I can show you how we work this monstrosity of a coffee machine.'

Mara caught the apron and followed Serafina to the counter. 'What were the rumours? The gossip? What did people say? About Mum?' she asked.

Serafina shook her head. 'Oh, mean stuff. People can be awful. So, here's where we keep all the crockery: mugs, cups and saucers, small plates, bigger plates.' Serafina opened a long cupboard underneath the countertop and pointed out its contents to Mara. 'Here's the dishwasher. Industrial grade. Never made a better purchase, honestly, we just load it up and put it on overnight. I—'

'Okay.' Mara rested her hand on the top of the dishwasher and met Serafina's gaze. 'Look, first I need to know why my mum left Magpie Cove, Serafina. She never told me. I never met my grandparents. It's clear she had some kind of awful secret and… I just want to know. She was my mother.'

Serafina pursed her mouth.

'Really, Mara. It wasn't nice. Your grandparents were very well known in Magpie Cove; your grandfather was the local bank manager and was very involved in the church and they were both very … you know, *upstanding* people. It was awful for them when Abby left because everyone said they'd driven their daughter away. Some people said horrible things about your grandfather, Abe, too.' She raised an eyebrow.

'What things?'

'I think you can guess. People are awful, like I said.'

'Oh, no.' Mara was horrified. 'Do you mean—'

'No, no. Now, I can't say what happened in that house, but Abby's parents were good people. Churchy, sure, but that's no bad thing.' Serafina shook her head. 'I really don't think that was what happened. He wasn't… a toucher, you know? He was a nice man and he adored Abby. But the rumours after she left, well… they ruined your grandparents. They left too, in the end, and the beach house went to rack and ruin. They must have died and left it to her, but I don't know when.'

'Oh.' Mara had hoped Serafina would know more than this. 'So, when was the last time you saw her? My mum? Before she came back, I mean.' Absent-mindedly, she opened a drawer and discovered the cutlery; next to it, a drawer full of clean tea towels and napkins.

'I was eighteen, a year older than she was. There was a party at the beach house. A family party of some kind. It was summer. Some of us went. It was fun. I can't remember anything being amiss. And then a few weeks after that, maybe a month, she was gone. The party was the last time I saw her. As I say, we were friends but not close. I'm sorry, honey. You thought I'd know more...' Serafina took her hand and squeezed it.

'It's okay.' Mara sighed. 'I appreciate it, anyway.'

'I know. I can only imagine how difficult things must be.' Serafina hugged her, unexpectedly. 'Agh. Families, eh?'

'Families,' Mara repeated, pulling away from the hug.

'We can keep talking about it. People around here might know more than me. You never know.' Serafina added, 'Magpie Cove is one gossipy village.'

'Oh dear. I've just become *persona non grata* at the school gates.' Mara rolled her eyes. 'I don't know if I can handle being the focus of even more gossip.'

'Well, sometimes, it can be useful.' A glint twinkled in Serafina's eye. 'You'd be surprised at what people say when they're drinking coffee with their friends.'

'Serafina! Don't tell me you listen in!'

'Oh, honey, I don't have to, half the time. They're shouting down their phones, telling someone all about the latest. I just come past and top up their coffee...'

'And the other half of the time?' Mara grinned back.

'The other half, they tell me everything.' Her new friend laughed. 'And I am sworn to secrecy.'

'Oh. So all gossip stops with you?' Mara laughed.

'Well... not all of it, hon. Yours does, of course. Goes without saying. Basically, if I like you, I'll take your secrets to the grave.'

'And if you don't like someone?'

'I'll take it about as far as the hairdresser's chair.' Serafina put her hand on her heart. Mara smiled and wiped her eyes.

'I miss her,' she said in a low voice. 'I wish she was here. I could do with her help right now, you know? She was great at talking things through with me. All this is just so hard.' She took a deep breath. 'Ack. I'm sorry. For baring my soul like this again. We hardly know each other.'

'Ah, don't think of it, my love.' Serafina handed Mara a paper napkin from the silver holder on the table. 'I'm so pleased to be able to help. Makes me feel a bit better, if I'm honest. For not being a better friend to your mum. I've missed her too, all these years. I should have gone to see her at the beach house. I dunno – I was… scared. I didn't know what to say. Now it's too late.'

'I feel like she's here. In Magpie Cove. Is that a weird thing to say?' Mara pushed her fringe out of her eyes. 'Like, I get a real sense of her here. It was her home, I guess.'

'Maybe she is here, still.' Serafina looked thoughtful. 'I think souls stay in places they've loved, sometimes. Maybe there's a saying goodbye that has to happen. Or maybe she's just with you because she knows you need her. You can bet if my kids were going through what you are, being dead wouldn't stop me either. I'd be right there with them, holding their hands. Cursing their enemies if necessary.'

Mara laughed again, through the tears. 'That's a nice thought,' she said. 'And you're right. I'd do that too.'

'There you are, then. Mothers' privilege to haunt our children. For their own good.' Serafina beckoned Mara into the small kitchenette. 'Come on. I'll show you around, and then we can have lunch. On the house for staff.'

'Serafina, you're amazing.' Mara followed her new boss into the kitchen.

'I know, darling. I know,' she replied.

Chapter Nine

Mara had been walking around the one supermarket in Magpie Cove with an empty basket for at least half an hour when she found herself standing in front of the chocolate-spread shelf, crying again.

She'd now explored the village a little further and found this place two streets away from Serafina's. As well as the usual supermarket fare, it also had an excellent fish counter, selling locally caught plaice, cod and flounder as well as Cornish brown shrimp, oysters and mussels. There was also a hand-painted sign that proclaimed 'FRESH FISH PIE – TUESDAYS' and 'ASK US ABOUT CUSTOM ORDERS'.

Get a hold of yourself, she thought now, but she couldn't stop the tears coming. She wiped at them furiously; the teenagers at the checkout had already given her some serious side-eye as she'd walked around the shop in a haze.

She lowered her head so that the friendly fishmonger, Alan – who she'd chatted to a couple of times since she'd found the shop – wouldn't see her cry, and ducked into the bakery aisle which boasted fresh scones from the small bakery, Maude's Fine Buns, that sat opposite Serafina's café. Mara had already treated the kids and herself to the scones spread with strawberry jam and a large pot of the thick, creamy yellow clotted cream you could also buy in the supermarket. It was made at a local dairy, Gordon's, and, even as someone who had lived in Cornwall all her life, Mara thought she'd never tasted anything as good.

It was the family on the standee that had started her crying: the large cardboard promotional poster that stood alongside the jars of chocolate spread. The slogan was 'Take a Family Break', and the family – mum, dad, a boy and a girl – were photographed laughing over breakfast.

'*Take a Family Break.' Done that*, Mara thought, then – *Wow, you're stupid. It's a bloody advert.*

She knew it was posed and they weren't a real family. That wasn't the point. The point was that she'd had what looked like the perfect family, and now it was over. They weren't the chocolate-spread family anymore. She wasn't the chocolate spread-mum anymore. Chocolate spread didn't tend to be advertised with pictures of single mums who roamed supermarkets, crying.

She'd just had her appointment with Aimee, the solicitor that Serafina had recommended. Aimee was friendly, comforting and reassuring. She'd pointed out that as Mara had a low-paid part-time job, then Gideon could reasonably be asked to pay her bill, and was getting in contact with Gideon's solicitor now to talk through the divorce. Aimee also thought that Gideon telling Mara that the sale from the beach house would have to cover her buying a new house for her and the kids was 'frankly, horseshit'.

Aimee had been amazing. It wasn't her that was making Mara cry. It was reality setting in. She was getting divorced. She didn't get to be part of the chocolate-spread family anymore.

Mara put two jars of the spread into her basket, then turned onto the cake aisle and added four apple turnovers, a box of cream slices, a Battenberg loaf and some chocolate tiffin. She walked straight past the grocery and meats and into the wine aisle, where she picked up four bottles of white wine, thought for a moment, put them back and then picked up a box of the same wine instead.

She was making her way to the till and rubbing her eyes – her mascara was stinging from when she'd cried – so she didn't see the man until it was too late.

He made an *oooof* sound as Mara accidentally bashed her basket into his thigh, and then dropped it on his feet.

'Oh my… I'm so sorry,' she muttered, blushing crimson.

The man removed the basket from his feet and gave it back to her, grimacing slightly as he did so.

'It's okay,' he said, politely. 'I thought you saw me.'

'No, I… had something in my eye,' Mara muttered. Then she realised it was Brian Oakley, who had taken them to A&E when Franny had fallen on the rocks. 'Oh. It's you.'

'It is,' he confirmed, rubbing his thigh. 'How's Franny?'

'Oh, she's fine. Enjoying her walking stick and telling everyone at school about her sprain. Thanks again for… you know. Everything you did that day,' Mara said, awkwardly.

He shrugged. 'Anyone would have done the same.'

Brian cast an eye over her basket.

'Big night planned, huh?'

'Just some essentials,' she said, breezily, pushing the basket behind her foot.

'Is everything OK?' He looked at her face with concern. Mara wondered how it was possible for her to have gone years wearing a full make-up and never accidentally walking into an attractive man, yet she'd done it today with panda eyes and a basket full of items that screamed 'I'M DEPRESSED AND LONELY'.

Unbelievable.

'Fine.' She fake-smiled as brightly as she could.

'Great,' he replied.

'So…' There was a silence; Mara wished someone would set off the smoke alarm so she could legitimately run away.

'So… good to see you. I just wanted to ask—' he began, but one of the young women who worked in the supermarket suddenly walked past and tapped him on the shoulder.

'Hi, Brian.' She fluttered her eyelashes coquettishly.

'Oh, hi, Sam. How are you?' He glanced from Mara to the girl and then shot her that raffish, warm look that Mara had seen him give a few girls now. *Petra was right – he was like some kind of girl magnet.* Every time she saw Brian Oakley, some young woman would turn up and flirt with him. Mara still couldn't tell if he was flirting with them back, or whether he was just really friendly to everyone. Though, it did always seem to be pretty girls, rather than elderly car mechanics or overweight milkmen, for instance.

'I'm good.' The girl, Sam, looked from Brian to Mara, questioningly, but Brian didn't introduce her.

'Well, you look great, as always,' he agreed. 'Nice to see you.'

'Take care, hon.' The girl winked at Brian, gave Mara an unfriendly stare, and walked away.

There was an uncomfortable silence.

'So… I wondered if you would like to—' Brian started again, but she started talking at the same time.

'Well, it's been nice seeing you, but—'

Mara could feel herself blushing again. *I need to get out of here,* she thought. *This is going from bad to worse.* All she wanted to do was go back to the hotel and eat her body weight in cake.

'Sorry.' Brian Oakley looked around, embarrassed.

Oh no, he can't wait to get away, Mara thought.

'I won't keep you, then. Bye!' She walked past, wishing she could leave the basket, but that would look odder still.

'Oh, okay. Bye!' he called out after her. She took a deep breath as she approached the tills and ignored the expressions on the teenage boy and girl's faces as she placed her box of wine, chocolate spread and what looked like half the cake aisle on the conveyor belt. Mara resisted the urge to look over her shoulder and check Brian wasn't following her to the till, but he had disappeared into one of the other aisles. Probably to find that girl, Sam.

Thank goodness, she thought.

Chapter Ten

Mara found herself settling into working at the café with ease. The only hard thing about it was that she was standing up most of the day, serving customers at the counter, bringing food to the tables, cleaning up and stacking the dishwasher, as well as taking food deliveries. She also helped Serafina prepare casseroles, vegetable lasagnes, Martinique coconut curry, wild rice salad and a variety of other delicious menu staples. By the end of the day, her feet were sore, but she'd taken to soaking them in the evenings in an old washing-up bowl filled with warm water and Epsom salts, *like an old lady,* she thought, *but I don't care.*

There were quiet times in the café, between pouring coffee and cutting cake and cleaning tables, when Mara could lean on her elbows and stare out of the windows at the street, dreaming. They were simple dreams: a house that didn't let the rain in, seeing the children happy, enough money so that she didn't have to worry every day about making ends meet. The job was helping with that, at least: Mara's wages weren't much, but they were something, and it meant that she and the kids could stay in the hotel a little longer. Not that she really wanted to, but at least it gave her some headspace to decide what to do next. The hotel was a small, family run place, and while it was clean and secure, it certainly wasn't anything fancy. On the first night they'd stayed there, Mara had been kept awake by foxes crying and knocking over the bins outside; the shower was, at best, a warm trickle, and the sheets, while clean, had holes in them. However, Mara had negotiated a weekly rate that was less than some of per night costs for the hotels she, Gideon and the kids had stayed at in the past.

However, the idea of having to stay in the hotel for much longer didn't exactly fill Mara with a great deal of enthusiasm. When the kids got home from their long day at school, they were exhausted and tended to watch TV until bedtime at eight. Mara read to them until eight thirty, then it was lights out. Even with Serafina letting her take food home from the café for their dinner, Mara was getting tired of not having a kitchen to cook in, or a garden where John and Franny could run around and have their friends over.

Occasionally, if she couldn't sleep, she went out onto their balcony and watched the stars, sometimes drinking a glass of wine. But mostly, she fell asleep about the same time as them, sometimes reading for a while, the interlocking door between their rooms open, listening to them breathe. It wasn't real life. They were camping out, waiting for life to happen.

The life she'd had with Gideon had been good. She would never deny that: she had a beautiful house, there were expensive holidays, her SUV and she got to shop pretty much whenever she wanted. She had never really had much of anything growing up with Abby, and sometimes she felt as though her life with Gideon was for her past self, to make it up to the young Mara. But the truth was that she had always had what she needed from Abby: love. Despite her sadness, her mother had never skimped in the love department. The fancy hotels and cars were nice, but she never cared about them all that much, because she had found out soon enough that there was little love attached to the price tag.

It had been comfortable, being Gideon's wife, to see the twins enjoy their clubs and activities – but Mara had gone from being a poor kid with a single mum, to being the wife of a rich man, and now she was back to not having much and being a single mum herself. And it was okay.

There still hadn't been any interest in the beach house, except for one stupidly low offer that she couldn't bear to accept, even though the estate agent tried to persuade her it was a good idea. Mara hadn't seen Brian Oakley since that night at the supermarket, but she had thought more than once about his suggestion that he renovate the house for a share in the profits. It was a solution, but it felt wrong to enter into such a big project with someone she hardly knew.

As often as she dreamt of the future, Mara thought more and more of the past. She thought about Abby; of being a child, of the times when Abby was happy, and the times when she had felt drowned in her mother's sadness. And she thought about Abby's death. She tried not to, especially when she was working, but sometimes it came like a wave. Had she been a good enough daughter? Had she done everything she could to help Abby? She should have put her mother into some kind of therapy: whatever had darkened Abby's past, she'd never got over it. She'd tried, repeatedly, even to the point of booking appointments for her mother, but Abby never turned up to them. When Mara had berated Abby about it, she'd stubbornly refused to talk. One day, after Mara had tried to get Abby to see a counsellor, Abby had lost her temper and screamed at her daughter. *I'm your mother, Mara. You're not mine. Stop trying to fix me.*

At the end, Abby hadn't known her. In the final days before she had stopped talking altogether and started to slip into the hinterland of dying, her spirit walking slowly into the dark, Mara had helped the nurse take her mother to the bathroom. While Mara and the nurse were holding her over the toilet, Abby had said to the nurse, *Never have children. They ruin your life.*

Mara knew Abby hadn't meant it: the cancer had taken over now, and her mother wasn't really there anymore. It was as if

Abby's body, bloated and enlarged from the tumours, was a house she was trapped in. Somewhere in a back room, Abby was confined to a bed, calling out for help, but no one could hear her anymore.

Mara couldn't think about Abby's last days too much. As if purposefully compounding her grief, Gideon had chosen the week of Abby's death to inform her that he was leaving her and 'making a go of it' with Charlotte. At that stage, Mara had hardly flinched: it was nothing compared to watching her mother die. But now, it made her sick to think of the two things together. Worse, that she had been married to a man who would do that to her. She'd slept in the same bed with him for all those years. She couldn't quite comprehend how any person with even half a heart could think that ending a marriage in the same week as their partner's parent dying was a sensible thing to do. When she told Serafina, her new boss hadn't believed her at first, and then pronounced Gideon a robot or an alien of some kind.

Serafina kept order pads and pens next to the till, and when the café was quiet, Mara had started using one of the order pads to write in. It was nothing much at first: she had been watching seagulls pecking crumbs in the street outside and started a silly story that she thought might amuse Franny: a pigeon who the villagers start to use to send messages to each other because no one is speaking to anyone else.

Then, over a few weeks, she realised that she wasn't writing about a greedy pigeon and a sullen town of people with grudges, she was writing about Abby. In her story, the pigeon became a magpie like the ones she saw and heard cawing on the beach, and the magpie was Abby's spirit. *One for sorrow*, like the old rhyme. The magpie wanted to fly home, to its real home, an island out at sea, but something was keeping it on the beach. It couldn't move on.

'You look deep in thought.'

A voice interrupted her writing and Mara looked up in surprise; she hadn't even heard the bell when the door opened, she had been so engrossed in her writing. Brian Oakley stood opposite her, smiling that same wry smile she remembered so well. Too well.

'Oh. Hi! I was just… writing something.' Mara closed the spiral-bound pad quickly. 'I thought you were away at a conference?' she blurted out, and then wished she hadn't said anything. It sounded like she was stalking him or something. 'Serafina mentioned it, that's all.'

'Surf convention in Newquay. I just got back.' He sat down at the counter.

'Coffee?'

Don't mention the supermarket, don't mention the supermarket, she thought, willing him not to say anything about her hurling her wine- and cake-filled basket at his leg and then running away.

'So. Eat all that cake yet?' He returned to the counter and sat down on one of the stools. 'When you assaulted me in the supermarket, I mean.'

Great.

'Oh. No. Yes, I mean, it was for the kids,' she explained, blushing again.

'And the wine?' He twinkled at her; *rude,* she thought.

'None of your business?' She beamed at him.

'Fair enough. You work here now, then?' Today he was wearing a blue linen shirt and dark blue jeans; his dark blond hair was a little longer than before and flicked up over his collar.

'Yes. For a few weeks now. What type of coffee do you want?' She pointed at the board behind her, wishing she'd put more make-up on this morning. Not that she needed to look nice for anyone, least of all Brian Oakley, Magpie Cove's most eligible bachelor. Mara had an innate distrust of all *eligible bachelors,* flirty men, players… any man, in fact, who seemed overly confident about their attractiveness to women. She'd always been more attracted to quieter, even shy, men – not that she'd ever had one ask her out. She had almost asked one out herself once, but had lost her nerve at the last minute. She supposed this was the occupational hazard of shy men – that they were backwards at coming forwards, and so you ended up with the ones who would at least *ask*.

Gideon hadn't seemed like a cheater when she'd met him: he was obsessed with his work and accumulating wealth more than anything. That he had turned out to be as untrustworthy as he had was pure bad luck, Mara was coming to realise. Still, she could do herself a favour and avoid players like Brian Oakley in the future.

'Cappuccino, thanks. And… what do you recommend, food-wise?'

'The brownies are good. Or I can make you a sandwich: prawn, egg, cheese, salad, ham…' She counted the options off on her fingers.

'Prawn salad?'

'White or granary?'

'Granary. Thanks.'

'You're welcome.'

Mara turned away to start the coffee, then sliced a couple of rounds from a large granary loaf.

'So, how's the house?' Brian asked, behind her. She turned back and started assembling the sandwich on a wide white plastic board; red was for meat, blue was for cheese, white was shellfish.

'Pretty much the same. The roof's not holding up against the weather too well.'

It was raining again outside. It would be Halloween soon – Serafina was holding a party at the café, which the twins were very excited about – but the approaching winter was a worry. The beach house wasn't up to harsh weather, and if its state deteriorated again, it would become almost worthless to a buyer. She didn't say any of this to Brian, but she thought anyone making an educated guess about how the beach house would survive winter in Magpie Cove would be thinking the same thing.

'Magpie Cove's famous for its high tides in winter. Been getting worse, too, over the past few years,' Brian replied. 'The wind, too. It's taken down a lot of fences, and some of the older roofs.'

'I know. It's a worry I could do without,' Mara admitted, spreading the bread with butter and again with a prawn and mayonnaise mix. The succulent brown shrimp were caught locally, and Serafina made her own mayonnaise which was lemony and rich at the same time. She handed the plated sandwich to Brian.

'That looks amazing. Thanks.' He bit into it and made an exaggerated expression of pleasure. 'Wow, that's good!'

'Serafina's secret recipe.'

'Hm. You'll have to break her pact of silence and give it to me. The recipe, that is.' He winked at her and chewed his sandwich.

'It's more than my life's worth.' Mara shook her head mock-gravely. She couldn't help it: he made her laugh.

'Listen, Mara. My offer's still open. The house renovation? No pressure, but I'm going to predict that if that roof doesn't get fixed, you're going to be looking at worse in a month or two. And that'll just cost more.' Brian sipped his coffee.

'It's a good offer. Don't get me wrong. It's just…' she exhaled, trying to think of how to explain how she felt. 'I… I don't know you, and it's a difficult time for me at the moment. My marriage just ended, and I'm seeing a solicitor about a divorce, and I've got this house that I have to sell, but it's falling apart, and I'm falling apart, and… I don't know what to do for the best,' she blurted out. *Why had she said all that? That she was falling apart?*

Brian looked worried, and though she was mortified at what she'd just said, seeing his genuine concern for her touched her heart. He cared. A person who cared about a fellow human being was nice.

'Of course. I'm sorry. I know it's a difficult time for you, with losing your mum too. I can't imagine how you feel. I just thought I could help, and…' He reached across the counter as if to touch her hand, but, instinctively, she pulled it away. 'Okay. I'm sorry.'

He got up, looking uncomfortable.

'No, I… I didn't mean…' Mara felt terrible: it had been an instinctive reaction. She didn't trust men at all right now. And she didn't trust her own judgement, after Gideon.

The bell jangled as the door opened, and Petra strolled in, as bright and red-headed and as much as like a pre-Raphaelite princess as Mara remembered her.

'Hey, babe.' She went straight up to Brian and planted a kiss on his cheek. Mara could see that, from Petra's point of view, Brian looked as if he was standing up to greet her, when in fact he was retreating from the awkward mess – which was Mara – behind the counter.

'Oh, hi, sweetheart.' He enfolded Petra in a hug and kissed her. Mara turned away, pretending to do something to the coffee machine. Not that there was any reason for it, but she felt self-conscious. 'I'm just having some lunch and then I was going to come round.'

Mara wondered what Petra did for a living that meant she was around in the middle of the day: Brian was presumably between surf lessons and carpentry projects.

'I just popped in for a takeaway coffee. I'm at a really important part of the painting, but I'm absolutely desperate for caffeine! I've been up all night.' Petra sailed across the café to the counter and beamed brightly at Mara. Mara remembered her mentioning painting before – Petra must be one of the many artists who lived in Magpie Cove.

'Oh! Are you new? Could I have a large soy latte to take away?'

'Sure. Yes, I've been working here a few weeks.' Mara smiled, took Petra's money and turned away to make the coffee. Over her shoulder, she heard Petra baby-talking to Brian and made a face. *Yuck.*

'…because Petwa weally misses Bwian. Petwa is weally lonely without her special Bwian bear.' Petra was giggling, making goo-goo eyes at Brian, who had the decency to look embarrassed when Mara turned around with the coffee and caught his eye.

'Oh, thank you so much. I'm sorry, I don't know your name?' Petra took the paper cup from Mara, immediately returning to a normal tone of voice.

'Mara Hughes. We have met once before.' Amused at the scene, Mara tried not to laugh at Brian's obvious mortification at Petra's baby talk, and hid her amusement in a cough, covering her mouth.

'Oh my lawwwwd!' Petra smacked herself lightly in the face with the palm of her hand. 'I'm so sorry. I've got that thing, you know, where you don't remember faces? Bad for an artist. Just as well I do abstracts. I do remember you now. You've got the beach house, right?'

'Right.' Mara wiped the counter down. She exchanged a subtle glance with Brian, whose expression was unreadable. Before, he'd seemed almost embarrassed by Petra, though Mara couldn't imagine why. Surely any man would be over the moon to have such a pretty girlfriend.

'How's it going with the house?' Petra sat down at the counter next to Brian and looked at his sandwich. 'Brian! Is that mayonnaise? We talked about this.' She shook her head disapprovingly. 'He's not supposed to have mayo. Or *any* dairy.'

'Oh, I didn't know.' Mara shot Brian an amused look; he gave her a frown in reply.

'Pets, I can have it now and again. But I should have said something, sure. Next time.' He explained, 'If I have too much it just gives me a bad stomach. I can make exceptions, though.'

'Bwian bear needs to wemember about his own health. Petwa bear can't be held wesponsible all the timey-wimey.' Petra put her arms around Brian's neck, apparently unembarrassed at the people around her being able to hear.

'Pets, shhh.' Brian frowned, looking uncomfortable.

'Oh, no, Bwian bear is so easily embawassed!' Petra continued, rolling her eyes.

'Petra, I'm serious. Shut up.' Brian gave her a distinctly unimpressed look; his tone was definitely not happy. 'Knock it off, for chrissake.'

'Okay, okay. Well, it's lovely to meet you *again*, Mara. I'll remember next time!' Petra gave her another megawatt beam. Petra was gorgeous and obviously talented if she was a full-time artist. What more could a man want? *Certainly not an emotionally devastated single mother of two with frown lines and visible roots.*

And if she and Brian had shared a moment before Petra had turned up, it was just the result of him being a nice person. He had reached out to comfort someone who was having a hard time. That was why everyone liked him. He was nice to everyone. Maybe more so to women, but still.

So why did she keep thinking about the moment he'd reached out for her with his wide, warm hand? And how, when he touched her, she felt safer than she ever had?

Chapter Eleven

The café was almost unrecognisable: Serafina had done an amazing job in transforming it into a haunted house for her Halloween party.

'It's amazing, isn't it?' Petra appeared at Mara's side, dressed impeccably as a sexy vampire: her red curly hair was perfect for the outfit. 'Mara. I remembered you this time! So sorry again about that, before.'

'That's all right. Nice to see you, Petra. You're looking devilishly gorgeous.' Mara grinned. 'What do you think of my costume?'

Mara twirled around to show the girl her barrel. She'd made if from cardboard and even stuffed the top with a couple of old cushions. She was pretty proud of the fact she'd even stencilled 'ANNIE EDSON TAYLOR, HEROINE OF NIAGARA FALLS' on her barrel, just like Annie had.

Petra frowned. 'I don't get it.'

'First woman to go over Niagara Falls in a barrel,' Mara explained.

'Okay... any particular reason why her?'

'Dunno. Felt appropriate.' Mara wasn't going to get into an explanation of all the ways in which her life was falling apart right now, and how the idea of voluntarily leaping into a barrel to ride one of the largest waterfalls was strangely attractive by comparison. 'Bit of a personal heroine of mine.'

'Right. That's such a good idea! I should have come as something less derivative.' Petra tugged at the miniskirt of her vampire outfit self-consciously. 'I mean, as a feminist, you're right, I should be… Frida Kahlo or someone.' She looked so disappointed with herself that Mara felt suddenly guilty for having somehow outshone her stunning new friend by turning up at a party looking like a crushed delivery package. She was also painfully aware of how dowdy she must look next to Petra.

'Don't be silly. These are my children, Franny and John. Or, Sigmund Freud and a mummy –pun intended, I think?' John had made significantly less effort with his outfit of toilet paper than Franny, who had made Mara trawl the second-hand shops in St Ives for a brown suit small enough for her; she was carrying a cardboard sign that said 'PSYCHOANALYSIS APPOINT-MENTS BEING TAKEN' and Mara had slicked back her hair and fashioned a moustache out of a snipping from a grey fake-fur coat collar of Serafina's.

'Oh! That's so clever! A *mummy!*' Petra squealed, delighted. 'You guys are amazing!'

Franny looked absurdly pleased.

'I didn't think anyone would get that. But you do have to see us together for it to work,' she said, gripping John's arm. Mara exchanged a sympathetic glance with her son.

'No, I totally get it! So clever. How *old* are you?' Petra squealed.

'Nine.' Franny preened.

'Wow. Nine! You're like some kind of genius!'

Brian, across the room, heard Petra and looked over, catching Mara's eye. He laughed, seeing her costume, and made an OK sign with his thumb and forefinger. She gave him a look that said *I would appreciate it if you would refrain from commenting on my costume* – but when she saw what he was wearing, she felt significantly less stupid.

'Wow. First woman over Niagara Falls.' He laughed as he joined the group. 'Full points for originality. Hi, guys. Cool costumes.' He high-fived John; Franny blushed. 'How's the ankle, Fran?'

'It has healed well, thank you,' Franny replied primly. 'I have regained full mobility.'

'Great.' He grinned at her.

'You know the kids?' Petra asked Brian.

'Oh. Yeah. Franny had a fall on the beach a few weeks ago. I was there surfing, so I helped out a bit. That's all.' Brian looked embarrassed again, and Mara could see he hadn't mentioned it to Petra. Why not? There was no reason not to say anything. She could see that Petra was going to say something more about it, but Brian handed her a hot dog instead.

'Vegan, Pets.' He smiled at Mara.

'And your costume …?' Mara enquired politely; she knew she had Annie's name stencilled on her costume but she was still secretly pleased that Brian knew who Annie was.

'A shark.' He grinned. 'Obviously.'

'I see.' Mara nodded gravely. 'Lucky for me I'm inside a barrel.'

'I don't know… some sharks have been known to bite through surfboards. And surfers.' He raised his eyebrows at the kids.

Franny giggled delightedly. 'Yuck! Gross.'

'So unoriginal.' Petra rolled her eyes, chewing the vegan hot dog. 'A shark. Was it the only costume left in the shop?'

'No, they had a middle-aged surf instructor with commitment issues, but I thought it was too much of a cliché,' he answered, deadpan. Mara snorted with laughter, but Petra looked blank.

'I don't get it.'

He sighed.

'You're a vampire,' he countered. 'That's not very original. And a sexy one at that.'

'What's that supposed to mean?' she asked, affronted.

'I mean, I would have expected you to… I don't know, make something cool. Be a terrifying vampire queen, at least.' He shrugged and drank from the beer bottle he was holding. Mara frowned. She didn't know Petra or Brian, but she could hear a being-polite-in-public couple's argument two miles away.

'I was busy this week, finishing a commission. My work was a bit more important than making a Halloween costume,' Petra replied, sounding annoyed. Mara didn't really blame her: Brian was acting like an idiot. 'What's wrong with being sexy, anyway? I haven't noticed you complaining before.'

Brian shrugged. There was an awkward silence.

'Well, I think Sigmund Freud might have some new clients later this evening,' Mara murmured, and put her arms around the twins' shoulders. 'If you'll excuse us, we're going to get some drinks. Serafina's made some amazing mocktails.'

She guided the kids through the crowd to the counter which she had draped in black crepe earlier. Serafina was behind the counter, serving 80s-themed cocktails: Blue Lagoons, Long Island Ice Teas and Harvey Wallbangers for the grown-ups. For the kids, she'd made jugs of virgin mojitos with lime and mint and served pineapple juice and coconut cream over crushed ice as baby pina coladas.

Serafina herself was dressed as Dorothy from the Wizard of Oz, complete with her curly white hair in pigtails and a blue-and-white gingham dress.

'Hey! You guys look terrific!' she squealed, leaning over the counter to kiss everyone on the cheek. 'Mara, would you give me a hand for a minute? I know you're not working, I just need help bringing the cake through.'

'Of course.' Mara handed the kids a baby pina colada each and slipped behind the counter to help Serafina. 'I have to say, I got some looks at the hotel when we left in all this.' She indicated her costume.

'How is it, over there?' Serafina handed her a large gateau box and picked one up herself. 'I always think of you in that poky little place with the kids. It can't be easy, living in two rooms.'

'It's okay,' Mara lied. It wasn't okay; it was really difficult, and she missed having a home. The hotel was all right, but it was weird living somewhere where they had almost no personal possessions: no pictures, no favourite vases, no sentimental trinkets. That was all still back at her old house, as far as she knew, anyway. Gideon had originally given her a month before he said he'd put all her stuff in storage. *Good luck with that*, she thought, *because I chose everything in that house.* Though he'd paid for it, so she supposed he considered things like sofas and the AI-enabled fridge very much his.

'Hmmm.' Mara followed Serafina back out to the café and placed her cake box on a long trestle table which groaned with food: sandwiches, grilled vegetable kebabs, salads, sourdough bread cut into thick slices, cheese boards draped with grapes, bowls of chips and all manner of other delicious treats. 'You know, if I had room in the flat, you and the kids would be welcome to stay. But it's just about big enough for me.'

Mara gave Serafina's shoulders a squeeze. 'Hey. You've already given me a job and listened to all my problems, Serafina. That's enough, okay? You don't need to house me and the kids as well.' She looked over to where John and Franny had found some other kids and were dancing at the far end of the café which was now the dance floor, with a DJ playing some 80s party classics. 'We're okay. It's just temporary. And, to be honest, even though it's kind of cramped, and the guy in the room next door at the moment plays his TV *really* loud past midnight, it's good to have our own space, you know? Work out who we are as a family of three instead of four. On the weekends, we stay up and watch terrible family movies from the 80s in bed with popcorn. Franny points out all the plot holes, and John always cries, even if it's a happy ending. It's okay. We're finding ourselves.'

All that was true, but it wasn't the whole truth. John often cried because he missed Gideon. Franny cried less, but she asked about Gideon all the time: *when can Daddy help me with my homework, when will see Daddy, can we go to the museum and see the paintings I like?* Gideon had found time for the kids on a few weekends here and there, but as good a dad as he usually was, he didn't seem to understand that what they needed most was regularity and routine. He'd blamed it on work, but Mara had had to explain that calling on a Saturday morning and asking her to bring them over at an hour's notice wasn't OK.

A lump formed in her throat; she took a deep breath to centre herself. *Take it easy, take it easy,* she thought.

'That's a good way to look at it,' Serafina agreed. 'You're doing so great.'

'Thanks. I don't feel like I am, most of the time, but I'm coping.' Mara watched the twins dance with Petra, who had appeared on the dance floor alone.

'Saw you talking to Brian.' Serafina followed her gaze. 'What do you think of him?'

Mara shrugged. 'He's nice enough.'

'I think he likes you.' Serafina looked pointedly across the room, to where Brian stood alone, not watching Petra on the dance floor, but staring straight at Mara. A six-foot-four surfer in a shark outfit was hard to miss. Mara caught his gaze, blushed, and looked away.

'He doesn't. He's just that guy, you know? He's nice to everyone.'

'Hmmm. He doesn't stare at everyone across rooms, let me tell you,' Serafina said archly. 'Usually doesn't have to. I've watched girls drape themselves all over him in the café. He never has to work for anyone's attention.'

Mara picked up a Blue Lagoon and drank half of it, feeling Brian's gaze on her but refusing to look back.

'Are you suggesting I'm making him work for something?' she asked her friend.

'Maybe. I think he thinks it's worth the work, anyway.' Serafina raised her eyebrow. 'If you want my opinion.'

'I'm not interested,' Mara replied. 'No way. I'm here to have a good time with the kids. Be silly. Let our hair down. They need it.'

'Absolutely.' Serafina grinned. 'Go and dance. I'm all good here now.'

'Okay.' Mara made her way through the crowd to the twins, picking up John and twirling him around.

She hugged them both awkwardly in her cardboard outfit, holding their hands and making up silly dance moves. She looked up, grinning. The party was in full swing; the café was full of locals laughing, dancing and eating Serafina's amazing food. For the first time in months, she felt happy and carefree.

As she looked across the café, noticing Brian talking to Petra, and now it seemed as though they were having a big argument. She felt sorry for the girl; Petra was really too young for Brian, and he'd been a real idiot earlier as well. He seemed to treat her like a kid, and Mara doubted Petra liked that. She wouldn't. As she watched, Brian said something, and Petra slapped his face and walked out.

Ouch, Mara thought. *I think you deserved that.*

Brian Oakley was clearly like all men: more trouble than he was worth, and his rudeness earlier had put any minor crush Mara might have had on him firmly on the backburner.

She caught his eye; he shot her a rueful look. Mara raised her eyebrow and turned away, back to the twins. They were her world now, just like they had always been. She didn't need to get involved with a man like Brian Oakley.

Chapter Twelve

Mara was working on her story at the counter; the café was quiet and Serafina was doing the accounts upstairs.

Like Serafina herself, her flat was draped in luxurious fabrics – shimmering teal satin kimono fabric billowed from ornate curtain rails in the lounge, cerise organza drowned Serafina's bedroom and multicoloured cushions littered the comfy chairs. Most of the surfaces groaned under coffee table art books, tarot cards and huge candles. She'd invited Mara and the kids up for more than one Saturday night, and Mara loved being there.

They'd watched movies Serafina projected onto a white sheet in her living room, all snuggled up on the huge, battered white leather sofa. John and Franny, up past their bedtime, had been thrilled that they were allowed to eat as much popcorn and cookies as they liked. Mara had watched them snuggle up to Serafina with a glow of thankfulness in her heart.

Serafina had, without being asked, given Mara a job, friendship and emotional support. And whenever Mara tried, awkwardly, to thank her, Serafina refused to believe she was doing anything remarkable. *You helped me out of a tight spot,* she'd insist, grinning, as if it was an impossible task to get anyone to work in the café. But one night, after the kids had fallen asleep and they'd carried them to back to the car, Mara saw longing in her eyes. Serafina had smiled wistfully and watched Mara strap John and Franny in. *I miss having children around,* she'd said. *I miss having a family.*

She'd told Mara a little, here and there, about her children, who were grown up and lived far away: one in London, one in

Australia. *Two boys,* she said. *As unalike as could be. Whatever the opposite of peas in a pod was. One's like me, the traveller – Australia, Sao Paulo, Barcelona. He's a citizen of the world, doesn't like to be tied down anywhere for long. The other one, he's off building his empire. He gets that from my dad.*

The beach house was still on the market, and there had been next to no interest in it. Gideon had texted yesterday and told her that he was going abroad for a month for work, but if the house wasn't under offer by the time he got home, he'd take over the sale. Mara was trying to ignore the thought. She knew he could do it if he wanted – they were still married, and Gideon would think nothing of calling up the estate agent and informing her that he would be the new contact for the sale, not Mara. She would have to stop him, and the idea both filled her with dread and a newfound wicked delight. Just like Annie before she went over the falls.

A woman had approached the counter and Mara put her pen down, looking up with a smile.

'What can I get you?' she asked. 'Lovely cakes today, just in from the bakery. The vegan gateaux are amazing.' She indicated the four-layered chocolate and lemon cakes that were slathered in vegan buttercream. Franny and John called them princess cakes. They'd sampled all of them, naturally.

'Just a tea, please.' The woman smiled back, but it was combined with a curious look. 'Are you Mara? Mara Hughes?'

'I am.' Mara reached down to the shelf below the counter for a ceramic teapot and placed it on a tray. 'Have we met?' A trickle of caution twinged in her stomach for a moment: what if Gideon had hired this woman to watch her? She had no idea why he would do something like that, but it wouldn't surprise her either.

'No, we haven't. But I'm a friend of your mum's. From a long way back.' The woman held out her hand. 'Simona Gordon. I knew Abby when we were kids. We were inseparable, once.'

'Wow. You heard I was working here, then?' Mara filled a small ceramic jug with milk and placed it on the tray. 'Sorry. Do you want milk? Or we have oat milk, almond milk, lemon…' she trailed off. It had happened more than once now, this experience of people knowing who she was because of Abby. It was odd: not unpleasant, but it always felt like it put her on the back foot and made her instantly anxious. Would this woman know why Abby left Magpie Cove as a teenager?

'Milk's fine, thanks. Yes, Serafina told me. Word gets around, somewhere like Magpie Cove.' Simona had a warm, bright-eyed, animated face that Mara liked immediately. 'I hadn't seen Abby for years. Serafina had, apparently, but I had no idea she'd been back to the beach house. I hadn't seen her since we were seventeen. Long time ago now.'

'But if you were friends, how come you didn't keep in touch?' Mara frowned, pouring hot water onto the tea leaves in the bottom of the teapot.

'I wanted to, but she just disappeared one day, and that was that. Her parents didn't know where she'd gone. No letter, no phone call. Just gone.' Simona took the tea tray and handed over a note to pay. 'I was hoping you could tell me what happened. Abby Hughes has been a mystery in Magpie Cove for years, for those of us who remember that far back.'

'She ran away and had me. She passed away recently.' Mara avoided Simona's friendly eye contact.

'Oh, I'm sorry to hear that. 'Course, your grandparents, Abby's mum and dad, they're gone now. Died some years back. I'm so sorry.'

Mara felt a wave of sadness wash over her. 'It's okay.'

'It's not okay, my love. Not okay with you, not okay with me. She was too young. I would have liked to see her again.' Simona paused. 'As I say, one day she was here, the next day, she was gone. She didn't tell me anything. I mean, I know she and her folks had some ups and downs, but we were teenagers. I hated my parents then as well.'

'But you didn't run away pregnant. That must have been the reason. She had me at that age. Seems too much of a coincidence otherwise.' Mara had a sudden thought. 'Wait. She must have had a boyfriend when you knew her. That must be my father.' Her eyes widened at the sudden possibility of finding out something she had never believed she'd know. 'Do you remember who it was?'

Simona shook her head, and Mara felt her brief hopes deflate.

'She didn't have one that I remember. She wasn't really into boys, even. Or girls. It was just like… I don't know. She just didn't want to be involved at all. Some people are like that, or they get interested in sex, relationships, much later on. I suppose I thought she was a bit of a late developer at the time. So it seems so odd that she would have got pregnant then.' Simona sipped her tea, thinking. 'Weird. I mean, her folks were like all our parents then… I don't think they would have been thrilled if she got pregnant as a teenager, but at the same time, I can't imagine them throwing her out. They were good people. It must have been her decision to leave. Strange.'

'Abby had a lot of secrets.' Mara blinked back tears. She wondered if she'd ever know everything about her mother. She decided to hold back from telling Simona about Paul Sullivan. Somehow, it seemed disloyal. Yet, she liked Simona, and talking to her made her feel closer to her mother.

'Listen. I'm not working on Sunday, and I was planning to go to the beach house with the kids. Would you like to come? Maybe being there might spark some memories – it would be great to know anything you can remember about Mum. If you want to, of course.'

Mara hoped she wasn't being too pushy, but she imagined what it would be like, being at the beach house with someone who had, presumably, been there before it had got so derelict. 'I mean, you would have visited Abby when she lived there, when you were kids? I need to do so much to the house, and it would be great if you could even just tell me what it used to look like. It would help in restoring it.'

Mara didn't mention that she only wanted to restore it enough to sell it, and that it was probably a lost cause anyway because there was too much to do in the next month, before Gideon got back.

'Wow. The old house. That will be weird, but okay.' Simona frowned. 'You've got kids?'

'Twins. John and Franny.'

Simona shook her head in wonder.

'That's so strange. I can't imagine Abby being a grandmother.'

'Well, she was. A good one, too.' Mara felt a deep longing for her mother, then. Simona must have caught the expression in her eyes, because she squeezed Mara's hand kindly.

'I bet she was. Okay, well, I don't work on a Sunday either, so that suits me. I'll meet you there, when? Mid-morning?'

'Mid-morning is fine.'

'All right. Here's my card if you want me before then.' Simona handed her a baby pink card with gold text that swirled 'Simona's Salon: Unisex Stylist'. 'And, you know, if you're renovating that house, you should really speak to Brian Oakley. He did all the fixtures and fittings at the salon a couple of years ago. Really professional, great job, he made me bespoke units, shelving, everything. Not expensive, either. Serafina knows him.' She waved her hand at the front of the shop counter which acted like an unofficial bulletin board for everyone in Magpie Cove. 'His number's bound to be on there.'

'Oh, I ... I've already met him.' Mara cleared her throat and tried to look natural, although she immediately wondered why she should have to make an effort to do so. *It's nothing remarkable, to have met the local handyman,* she thought, trying not to blush. Simona waved her hand in a kind of salute.

'Oh, good. Brian's lovely. That's settled then!' Simona got up and put her coat back on.

'Well... I don't know that it's settled, exactly—' Mara protested, but Simona had her coat on and was waving goodbye.

'See you on Sunday!' she called out.

There was nothing else for it: if she only had a month left before Gideon started really applying the pressure, then she was going to have to resort to emergency measures. The house wasn't going to sell without a thorough renovation.

Well, I guess I need to call Brian Oakley, she thought, getting her phone out of her pocket: she'd slipped his card into a flap at the back of her phone case.

She took a deep breath and pressed the call button.

Chapter Thirteen

Simona sat next to Mara on the porch, companionably watching the orange autumn sun set over the sea as they drank tea from a thermos Simona had brought with her. It had been an unseasonably warm Sunday for early November, and the kids had been desperate to come and play at the beach. Mara watched a lone magpie circle the beach house, and it made her think of the story she was writing. It was fanciful to think that the magpie represented Abby's spirit, but she still had the feeling that her mother was around, somehow. That she hadn't moved on: there was something keeping her here. Mara knew if she told anyone, they'd probably think she was mad. Serafina might understand, maybe.

'It's going to be okay, you know.' Simona caught Mara's eye as she followed the magpie with her gaze. 'The divorce. The kids. They'll be okay. They're good kids.'

'You don't know that. That they'll be okay, I mean.' Mara sipped her tea; behind her, the beach house creaked in the light wind. Brian had been very enthusiastic about the development on the phone, giving her all sorts of ideas. If it wasn't done, she might as well kiss the house goodbye altogether – one bad storm might ruin it if she was unlucky, and Mara Hughes didn't feel particularly lucky right now. If she was doing the roof, it made sense to do the house up completely. It was just that it was such a big step to make with someone she still hardly knew… 'They are good kids, though. Thank goodness.'

She'd texted Gideon to let him know what she was doing. He hadn't replied, but it wasn't up to him to approve it or not; she just thought she should keep him informed, and explain why it hadn't sold yet. If she made him see that she was in charge of what was happening with the beach house, then he might back off. And if he didn't, she'd tell him to.

'That's your work that's made them good.' Simona chided. 'I know all about it. I've got three boys. My goodness, they were a handful growing up. Mud. Sarcasm. Video games. Years when all three of them just grunted when they wanted to communicate. But I was always firm and fair, and now they've miraculously turned into pleasant young men. One of them's even engaged.'

'You must have the patience of a saint!' Mara laughed, imagining three muddy-booted, wisecracking boys. She now knew that Simona, as well as running her hair salon in town, worked on a farm with her husband, a burly, bearded mountain of a man called Geoff. He'd dropped Simona off earlier and briefly unfolded himself from a mud-splashed Range Rover. Simona was tiny, but Mara got the instant impression that she was nonetheless the unchallenged queen of the household.

'Goodness, no. My work kept me sane. I used to cut hair at home in the kitchen before I bought the salon. And the farm kept the boys out of the way, once they were big enough. They were driving the tractor by the time they were ten, Geoff had them cleaning out the pigs well before that, sitting with him up in the hay baler, that kind of thing. Being outdoors is the best thing for kids.' Simona pointed to John and Franny, who were collecting shells and stones and making them into some kind of pattern on the sand. 'Now that you've got the beach house, the kids are going to really love it. They'll thrive out here.'

'They do love it. I don't know if I can cope, though. On my own. I'm used to having Gideon to…' she broke off. 'He was… is… great with the kids. Sometimes I think they don't think I'm as fun as him, you know? He'd take them to do cool trips and activities on the weekends. I'm knackered after a week's work and organising them and their endless school requirements. Not to mention the beach house. I can't be Fun Mum as well.'

Simona set down her cup and put her arm around Mara's shoulders.

'I know, sweetheart. But you can do this. I promise you. And if you need a babysitter, or a hug, just yell. I'm happy to have the twins up to the farm anytime. They'll love it. Or just you, if you need a coffee. Or something stronger.'

Mara felt the warmth from Simona's arm around her.

'That would be great. Thank you.' *Perhaps it would all be okay. Perhaps she could start to hope.*

'Point is, as long as they know they're loved, they'll be fine. Geoff worked long hours when they were little, especially. Some weeks I hardly saw him. It was hard, and then it was hard in a different way when they got older and wanted to challenge him. You know, as the alpha male.' She rolled her eyes. 'Fortunately, Geoff might look like a tank but he's as soft as butter.'

Mara smiled. 'You're lucky.'

'I am. Who's that?' Simona shaded her eyes from the low sun and looked up the beach to the slip road. A car had drawn up and parked, and a man had got out and was heading towards them.

'Just someone out for a walk, I suppose.' Mara watched him as he made his way over the sand to them. He didn't have a dog, which was the usual reason anyone else had been at the beach while she and the kids were there, apart from the occasional surfer like Brian Oakley, of course.

But the figure drew closer, and Mara sat up straighter, putting her cup down as he approached the porch. Without knowing why, a feeling of unease had spread in her chest. She looked to see where John and Franny were; they were safe, sitting on a rock now, casting pebbles into the sea.

'Can I help you?' Mara looked up, shading her eyes as he approached. He was about her age, dark-haired, medium height and with a slight build and wearing black jeans, trainers and a faded black Pac Man sweatshirt: boyish, she supposed. He didn't look particularly threatening, but the way he was looking at her made her feel strange.

'I'm looking for Mara Hughes,' he said. He seemed nervous. Simona exchanged a glance with Mara.

'What for?' Simona asked before Mara could say anything. He turned his gaze to Simona, who stood up.

'I… want to talk to her.' His expression remained serious, unreadable. Mara looked for the children again, standing up next to her friend. She could feel Simona's protective instinct and was grateful for it, but if this was some kind of messenger from Gideon, then she would have to take responsibility.

'Well, she's not here right now,' Simona breezed. 'I'll give her a message, though, if you like?'

The young man was staring at Mara. *He knows who I am,* she thought, fear clutching at her. She stayed quiet. In the distance, the magpie chattered suddenly. What was it again? *One for sorrow?* She swallowed hard.

'She's not here?' he pointed at Mara. 'Who are you?'

'This is my friend, Abby.' Simona lied with ease. 'I'm Simona Gordon. Who are you?'

He frowned harder, looking intently at Mara. 'You're not Abby.'

'How do you know who I am?' Mara replied shakily. His stare was so intense.

'Because I'm Paul Sullivan. Abby Hughes was my mother. And she's dead,' he answered smoothly, his eyes not leaving Mara's.

Chapter Fourteen

'What?' Mara stared at him as the words sank in. 'Paul? You're Paul Sullivan?'

He reached into his jeans pocket and took out the letter Mara had agonised over writing that day in the café, weeks ago. 'Oh... I can't believe you got that.' She watched him unfold the envelope, which looked as if it has been folded and refolded several times.

'I got it,' he replied, a little grimly. 'You're Mara, then?'

Simona opened her mouth to interject, but Mara shook her head.

'It's okay, Simona.' She held out her hand and he took it briefly, with the most perfunctory of shakes.

'It's nice to meet you. I... I didn't really think you'd ever get my letter. I wrote to twenty-three different Paul Sullivans, but I didn't think...' she stammered, glad that Simona was with her. She had also sent a copy of the letter to the address on Abby's letter, just in case. Paul's manner was cold and distant; he didn't smile as she was talking, didn't nod encouragingly or do anything else to indicate that he was friendly.

'No. I... um. It's all been a bit of a shock, if I'm honest.' He hung his head for a moment, and Mara saw his uncertainty under the icy manner. It must have been hard getting her letter. Turning up and meeting his long-lost sister, harder still.

'Do you want to sit down?' Mara gestured to the split wood of the porch, but Paul shook his head.

'I won't stay long. I just wanted to make contact. Meet you. See the house.' He looked beyond Mara to the shambling beach house behind her. 'So this is it, huh. Her house?'

'She grew up here. I didn't know about it either until she'd…
passed away.' Mara swallowed, trying to keep her voice steady.
'Listen… I don't know why she did what she did. Left you. It
must be… I don't know. I can't imagine how you feel…' she
finished lamely. He grimaced and scuffed his foot in the pebbly
sand where he stood.

'Not great, that's for sure.'

'So… you were… adopted?' Mara wrapped her arms around
her body, holding onto herself. Simona, sensing that Paul was
probably reasonably safe, quietly walked over to where the children
were and started talking to them; her low voice was a comfort
in the background. It was getting colder; they'd have to go back
soon. Mara realised that the magpie was now nowhere to be seen.
She wondered what that meant, before berating herself that it
didn't have to *mean* anything. It was just a bird.

'Yup. Lois and Joel adopted me when I was a baby.'

'They lived where you live now?' Mara asked, wondering if she
was being too inquisitive, but also needing to know. Needing to
see this part of Abby's story that had been hidden.

'Yes. They died. I inherited the house. I'm the one in Helston,
if you were wondering. Seeing as you wrote to twenty-three
people.'

Mara thought for a moment.

'Helston? But that was the address all the letters were returned
from.'

'I don't understand.' Paul looked blank.

'I had that address from letters Mum wrote – to you – but
they were all returned unopened. You were there, all that time?'

Paul looked more confused. 'That's where I've always lived.
Are you saying… she tried to write to me? When I was a kid?'

Mara nodded.

'And they never told me?'

'I guess not.' She winced. She could see the realisation dawning on his face, and the pain that accompanied it. 'I'm so sorry. Were they um… good parents?' Mara asked, carefully.

'No,' Paul snapped. Mara noticed more things about him now: he had the kind of black stubble that would appear every day even with shaving. He had dark eyes, like Abby, with long lashes.

'Okay.'

There was a silence. Mara wanted to ask more, but they'd only just met, and it was obvious that Paul didn't want to tell her. Not right now.

He sighed and leaned forward slightly, resting his hand on the wooden frame of the porch.

'Look. I didn't come here to talk about my crappy childhood, okay? This Abby… did she leave any documents, any proof that I'm her son? A birth certificate?'

'I don't know. Not that I've found so far, but I can look again. I… I found the letters, and I just thought… I wanted to find you. If I could.'

He looked away at the sea; the tide was flat on the sand, and the sun had set now. His face was partly in shadow as Mara stared at him.

'Okay. Well, if I'm her son, then half of this belongs to me, right?' He tapped his hand on the wood he leaned against, still refusing to meet her eyes. 'She owes me that much. For abandoning me. She kept you. You had her, all these years. I never will. So, the least she can do is give me half of what she left.'

Mara's heart sank.

'You can't be serious…' she whispered. He met her eyes, and she saw tears there.

'Why not? Isn't it fair? Pretty much nothing in my life has been fair until now. You don't want to know what those people did to me, Mara. Abby – she left me to them. She threw me to the wolves—'

'She didn't know! She couldn't have known. She wanted to know you… the letters… I mean, I don't have them with me, but I'll show you, another day.'

'I don't want to see them.' Paul turned away.

'What?'

'I don't want to see them. It's too late.' There was a catch in his voice. Mara reached out, tentatively, to touch his arm, but her hand hovered in the air; they were strangers and it was strange, comforting him, even though he was Abby's son. Her hand dropped back to her side.

'Paul, I—'

'No, there's nothing else to say. Okay? I'm sure you're a really nice person, and maybe Abby was a good person, but I… I just can't get beyond what she did. I shouldn't have come here.'

He wiped his eyes and walked away.

'Paul!' Mara ran after him, but he wouldn't stop. She caught sight of the kids watching her from across the beach; Simona had her arm around John, whose face was a picture of anxiety. Franny stood slightly apart from them, watching Mara closely and twisting her hair around one finger.

She turned back to Paul, and called his name again, but he carried on towards his car. Awkwardly, he raised his hand in a wave before getting in and driving away.

Well, there goes my brother, Mara thought. *So much for long-lost reunions.*

Chapter Fifteen

'So. What are we doing today?' Simona held out an orange gown for Mara to put on and settled her in front of the mirror. A small tray with a full coffee plunger, cup, milk and a biscuit sat on the table in front of her.

'I think it needs tidying up at the ends, and my roots need touching up.' Mara ran a hand through her hair self-consciously. It had been ages since she'd thought about having her hair done, or any kind of nice pampering for herself.

'We can most definitely do that.'

They were alone in the salon. After their chat at the beach, Mara had decided to take Simona up on her offer and come and see the salon. She'd popped in before work the day before and made an appointment for her lunchbreak today. The salon had three stations with the same comfortable brown leather chairs, mirror and table combos, with several tall green ficus trees in baby pink planters, and glossy green trailing plants in macramé hanging pots. Coral pink rock salt lamps sat on repurposed wooden crates, and a retro-style radio played a local oldies station.

'How are the twins?' Simona asked, adjusting the volume of the radio down. 'I have this on loud when it's just me in the salon. I usually have Nic or Leni in, but neither of them work Wednesdays. Wednesday's my day to let loose and sing to all my favourite country classics.'

'Oh, well, don't stop singing on my account. They're fine. At school.'

'So they're still at their old school? You haven't thought about moving them to the one here?' Simona tucked a towel around the top of the robe.

'No, not for now, anyway. I want them to stay there for as long as they can. My ex, Gideon, he pays the fees, and I'm hoping he'll continue to pay them. If he doesn't, then I'd have to move them, but I don't think it'll be a problem. And I want to maintain some consistency for them, anyway.'

'Makes sense. I dunno… I just wondered whether you'd be looking to settle in Magpie Cove.'

'I'm not sure. My plan was to buy somewhere around St Ives. Keep them at the same school and near to their dad.' Mara shrugged. 'Though I do like it here.'

'Well, Magpie Cove is no St Ives. But maybe that's no bad thing,' Simona mused. 'So, that was some drama the other day on the beach, with your brother turning up out of the blue.' She poured steaming coffee into Mara's cup. 'Milk?'

'Oh, I can do it. Thanks.' Mara stirred milk and some sugar into the cup and took a sip. 'I know. I was so glad you were there!'

'I had no idea Abby had a little boy too. I guess when you lose touch in your teens, you really don't know a lot about a person.'

'Ha. Believe me, even when you know someone their whole life, there's no guarantee.' Mara rolled her eyes.

'Well, it was so dramatic! I wouldn't have missed it. I told Geoff about it when I got back and he said, imagine if that was one of our boys? If they'd lost us and then found out they had a secret sister – well, I don't think they'd deal with it that well at first either.'

'I suppose so,' Mara mused. 'I feel bad about contacting him at all. Maybe I should have just left it, you know? Let sleeping dogs lie.'

Simona turned away to a cupboard filled with boxes of hair colour and took out a few, holding them up against Mara's dark brunette hair. 'Hmmm, well, you could. You've only got a bit of grey coming through, by the way. It's not that bad.'

'I know, but every time the colour washes out, there's more of it.'

'Fair enough. The good Lord wouldn't have given us organic, non-ammonia hair colourant if he didn't want us to use it. How's this one?' She showed Mara the colour. 'It's a little darker than your natural colour but I think it'll work.'

'Looks great.'

'So. Did you hear any more from Paul after the weekend?'

'No. I don't know what to do for the best, if I'm honest. Leave him alone, or pursue a relationship, somehow? He was so angry. I don't blame him.'

'Hmmm. It's a tough situation for everyone.' Simona cocked her head to one side and regarded Mara in the mirror. 'Have you ever had highlights? Just a suggestion, but I think you could really take some dark gold in this. We could put a fringe back in – it looks like you had one a while back?' Mara nodded. 'Yeah. And make the most of that natural wave you've got. It could be very subtle sun-kissed glamour. Like Cindy Crawford in the 90s. Or Jennifer Lopez. Look.' Simona handed her a couple of magazines.

'Do you think I should get in contact with him?' Mara wasn't really looking at the pictures: she was thinking about Paul. She had wanted to find him, and she'd found him. Now that she'd made contact, was she willing to cope with the reality of who he was?

Although she was feeling settled in the new daily routine, there was an alarm at the back of Mara's mind that felt like it could go off at any time, like a smoke detector with a low battery which would beep every now and again to let you know it needed attention. She liked Magpie Cove. She liked working at the café and she even sort of didn't mind living at the hotel: it was, at least, her space. But at the back of her mind there was always the worry that it was all going to fall to pieces, just like her old life had. There had been no warning. What if Paul was another force that would pull her life apart again?

'Well, you opened the box. You wanted to find him enough to – what? Write letters to every Paul Sullivan in the West Country?' the hairdresser asked.

'Yeah.'

'Right. So, now you found him. It seems kind of unfair to leave him hanging. The lad's confused, Mara. You would be too in his position. I'd give it another try with him. I think Abby would have liked that.'

'You think so?' Mara turned around in her seat to look Simona in the eye. 'I don't have his number or anything, though. Just his address.'

'I do think so. Maybe it's because of my boys, you know? But I'd hate to think of them alone, in the same situation, like Geoff said. I mean, I don't know any more than you what went on. Why she had him adopted. But we both know that you don't give up a baby without some real heartbreak attached. He's her son, regardless of why she gave him up. I think she's out there, somewhere, in spirit, watching all this. I think she'd want you to know him. If you've got his address, you can pay him a visit.'

Mara turned back to the mirror and stared at her reflection again. She wasn't really spiritual at all; she didn't have any particular beliefs about what happened after death. But there was something that rang true in Simona's words; she did feel as though Abby was still around. Like she was waiting for something. Maybe she was still in Magpie Cove. Was she waiting for Paul and Mara to become friends?

'I suppose I could. It'd be a bit strange, turning up unannounced, though.' She frowned.

'Worst case, you could take his number then and arrange another time. I think it's worth a try.' Simona pursed her lips. 'Otherwise, won't you always wonder? If you never see him again, if he decides he doesn't want to make the effort to see you, then that… I dunno. Seems a shame, my love,' Simona reflected. 'To have come this far.'

'No, you're right. I'll go to his house. Try and talk to him.' Mara couldn't cope with the idea that Abby's spirit would be displeased if she didn't at least try to reach Paul again. She'd heard of spirits not wanting to move on because of unfinished business – mostly in melodramatic TV dramas – but the thought had been put into her mind now and she couldn't quite let it go. What if this was one of those occasions?

Mara looked at the pictures in the magazines. 'Can you do this? Like, lighten the ends, like this one?' She pointed to a picture of a celebrity she didn't recognise, a brunette with long, artfully mussed loose ringlets that started dark brown and ended up a subtle gold. 'If I'm going to turn up at Paul's house, I feel like it would be nice to look kind of… together.' She rolled her eyes. 'I can look smart and organised, even if I'm a mess inside, right?'

'Oh, definitely. Life's always easier when you've got your hair done and a good pair of knickers on, in my experience.' Simona twinkled at her. 'Let's make you look even more gorgeous than usual!'

'I might have to take a long lunch.' Mara looked doubtfully at the clock in the salon; they'd already been chatting for twenty minutes and Simona hadn't even started her hair yet.

'Ah, I forgot you were on your lunch break. Fine. The ends will take a bit longer than a roots job… We'll do the cut now, and I'll do the colour tomorrow, if you can have an hour and a half? I'll ask Serafina for you, if you want?' The hairdresser winked at Mara as she misted her hair and started combing it out.

'No, that's okay. It'll be fine.' Mara laughed. 'Though I appreciate the support.'

'Gotta stick together, us girls.' Simona tapped Mara on the shoulder. 'Though fortunately Serafina is well aware of the restorative power of hair and beauty. Like Dolly Parton says in that movie, *Honey, time marches on and eventually you realise it's marching across your face.* Or your hair. Both, in fact.' Simona affected a Southern drawl so convincing it made Mara laugh out loud.

'Simona?'

'What?'

'Do you think you can make me look like Cindy Crawford in the 90s?'

'We'll have a bloody good try, my love,' the hairdresser replied.

Chapter Sixteen

Mara was wiping down the empty tables in the café when her phone rang. It was Aimee.

'Mara?'

'Yes. Hi.' Mara sat down in one of the empty chairs and took a deep breath.

'So, I've spoken to Gideon's solicitor. He's issued the petition. I'm emailing you the details now. If you agree to everything – mostly the suggestions for who looks after John and Franny, and the financial settlement – then we can reply within seven days to accept it or not. I've had a look, and I think we can make some suggestions. You don't have to accept his.'

Gideon was wasting no time. He was away working, or so he said, and yet he was still on top of all this.

'Okay,' Mara said. 'What has he said?'

'You'll see the details in the email, but basically he's proposed that he sees the kids every other weekend. His financial settlement offer isn't acceptable, in my opinion. And his ideas about having half of the beach house are laughable. I think we should push back.' Aimee sounded confident.

So, it was really happening.

'Okay,' Mara repeated.

'Look through everything and I'll call you back tomorrow, and we can agree a response,' Aimee suggested. 'All right? Don't worry, Mara. This is all perfectly normal. His solicitor will have advised him to go in low. It's just what I'd expect.'

'Right. I'll look at it.' Mara couldn't think of what to say. Anxiety churned in her stomach.

It was clearly a day for bad news. She'd been in a daze all day because, that morning, she'd dropped into the beach house before work and found a letter on the doormat. It was from Paul, and it had cut her to the quick. She read the letter out to Aimee over the phone now.

'Oh, jeez. Okay. Send me a copy of the letter, okay? You don't need this right now. Don't worry, Mara. As an adopted child, he doesn't have any legal claim to your mum's estate. It's going to be okay.'

Mara laid her head on her arms and stared up close at the texture of the stripped pine table.

'He doesn't have a legal claim?' she asked Aimee, looking at the letter. In it, Paul had written, *I think you should do the decent thing and give me half.*

'No. Once his parents adopted him, he became able to inherit from them and not Abby,' Aimee repeated.

'Do you think he knows that?' Mara looked at the letter again.

'Maybe not. The letter isn't from a solicitor, so I assume he hasn't taken legal advice. I think this is all coming from him.'

'Right. But I do feel bad for him, he is her child after all.'

'That's a whole other thing. If you want to give him something that belonged to Abby, that's up to you. You don't have to, though, is what I'm saying. By law.'

Barrel, falls, plunge… I'd take Niagara over this, Mara thought.

The irony was that he would never have known about the beach house if Mara hadn't wanted to give him some kind of closure – if her stupid, naïve heart hadn't broken when she'd read those old letters of Abby's; if she hadn't tried to find the recipient of those sad, unanswered missives into the unknown. She had tried to give Paul something – a link to his family, an answer to the question

Abby's abandonment must have seared into his soul. And what did she get in return? Another man that wanted to take one of the only things she had left.

Mara screwed up Paul's letter in her fist in a sudden rage. Gideon, Paul, they were the same. Why did they think they were allowed to get away with torturing her? *Ugh. I am sick and tired of men*, she thought. *Maybe I can go and live on some kind of women's commune where everybody is nice and eats cake and plants lovely vegetable gardens and we have monthly moon rituals and community sing-songs and I could train to be a medicine woman, and no one would ever be mean or unreasonable. It's not much to ask.*

She sighed and put her phone back behind the counter and went to serve a couple of surfer girls that had just come in and were waiting. She wanted to tell them, warn them, *Don't get older. Don't get married and have kids and believe the dream girls like you get sold: that all your problems will magically disappear as soon as that wedding ring goes on. That it's your destiny, that you're supposed to settle down and not travel, have adventures, meet fascinating people, be a citizen of the world. You might like being married, but you might not, and then one day you'll be thirty-something years old, taking a call from your solicitor in the café you work in and trying to figure out if you're a bad mother for taking your kids away from their father who they adore but who you can't stand.*

But another part of her wanted to say to them, *You'll love those children more than you'll ever love anyone else; you would die for them in a heartbeat, you'd be happy to do it because you love them so much. I hope you know that love one day.*

But Mara told them neither of those things: just took their order and watched them as they sat down at a table, talking and laughing. As she made their coffee, she listened to their giggles, and it made her smile. She had always wanted to be that carefree. Maybe, just maybe, it was still possible.

Chapter Seventeen

It had rained earlier, but now the weather had brightened enough for the kids to have their first surf lesson.

'Are you warm enough?' Mara fussed around the twins, zipping them up in grey-and-red wetsuits and helping them on with the same kind of wetsuit slipper-shoes as she'd seen Brian wear.

'We're fine, Mum. Ouch. My hair's caught.' Mara released her daughter's ponytail from the wetsuit zip and offered her a drink of water from a sports bottle. Franny refused.

'Mum! Stop fussing!'

'I just don't want you to be dehydrated,' Mara protested.

'We're going in the SEA, Mum,' Franny argued. 'We will *literally* be the most hydrated we could ever be.'

'You know that's not what I mean.' Mara shook her head and exchanged a look with Serafina, sitting next to her, who stifled a laugh. 'Don't encourage her. She loves an audience.'

Serafina snorted.

'Sorry. But I think they'll be fine. Brian's a good teacher.'

'Ready?' Brian came out of the sea, carrying his surfboard, his dark blond hair dripping and plastered to his head. Mara looked away from his toned physique which the wetsuit couldn't help but highlight. Why did he always make her feel like they were at the prom and the most handsome boy in the room had asked her to dance?

'Ready!' the twins shouted, excitedly.

'Okay. Let's go!' Brian held out his hand. 'Surf team high five!' They slapped palms, whooping. 'Okay. Your mum says you guys are both good swimmers, right?'

'We are excellent swimmers. We can both swim a mile and we're proficient underwater,' Franny explained in her usual formal manner. 'We've had lessons since we were four.'

'Excellent. That's what I like to hear. But we're going to start off on land, okay? Surfing takes time. You've got to take it step by step. We're going to start with popping up on the board on the beach, and then we'll go in the water.'

'Are we going to be using a board like yours?' John asked.

'Not yet. I've got some lighter boards you can use. They're called foamies. Perfect for your size.' Brian pointed further down the cove to his small surf shack which stood at the other end. 'We can go and choose one each.'

'Not a proper one?' John's face fell. 'I'm big enough!'

Brian mussed his hair.

'I know. Believe me, John, you're going to ace this. But we have to do everything in the right order, so when you get to a full board, you're ready for it. Okay?'

'Okay…' Mara could see that John was disappointed. She gave him a wink.

'You're going to have a great time, sweetie,' she reassured him.

Brian turned to Mara. 'We'll be about an hour. Depends how much they can do, or want to do. First time can be pretty tiring.'

'No problem. We'll be here.' Mara shaded her eyes, looking up at him. It was a brisk autumn day, but the sun had taken that moment to come out and it was in her eyes. 'How's the work on the house going?'

'Pretty good. I can show you around after, if you want?' He gazed over at the beach house, which was maybe fifty metres from where Mara and Serafina were sitting on the sand. Luckily, they'd brought weatherproof picnic blankets.

'That would be great. I'm glad you're looking after it now.'

'So am I.' He looked back at her and then screwed up his face in concentration.

'Did you change your hair?' he asked.

Mara ran her fingers through her newly highlighted dark gold curls. 'Oh. Yes. Just fancied a change, that's all.'

'Suits you.' He gave her that relaxed grin she suspected most of the eligible women in Magpie Cove had seen at one time or another. Mara felt drawn into his blue eyes. She liked the laughter lines around them. *Stop thinking about his eyes,* she rebuked herself.

'Okay. We'll see you after. They'll be hungry, I expect,' he added.

'We have food.' Serafina opened a cool bag she'd brought with her.

'I see.' Brian raised his eyebrow. 'Save me a sandwich?'

'We'll see if you deserve it!' Mara grinned. 'I'm paying you to wear the twins out. Not an easy task, let me tell you.'

'I'm up to it. At least save me some cake. I know Serafina will have brought some.' He raised his eyebrow.

'Maybe.' Serafina closed the top of the cool bag. 'Off you go. We want to gossip about you now.'

Mara blushed, and was instantly mortified. She cleared her throat and opened her handbag, pretending to look for something.

'Okay, okay, I'm going.' Brian caught up to the twins, who were already racing towards the surf shack. Mara watched as they went in and came out a few minutes later carrying smaller blue and yellow boards.

'So.' Serafina reached into her cool bag and handed Mara a sandwich in a paper bag. 'I brought you prawn mayonnaise. I know you like that. And ham and cheese for the twins.'

'Oooh. Thanks, Serafina. I'm starving.'

'Thank you for inviting me down to the beach. I need a reminder to get out sometimes.' Serafina slung a thick tartan wrap around her shoulders. 'Chilly, mind you.'

'Bracing.' Mara grinned, taking a bite of the sandwich. 'I brought a thermos of coffee.' She noticed the magpies were back: three of them this time, chattering from the roof of the beach house. *Three for a girl? Was that right?* she wondered for a moment before turning her attention back to her friend.

'Perfect.' Serafina accepted a steaming mug and wrapped her hands around it. 'How's it going with Aimee? I feel like we never get a chance to talk at work.' The café had been busier than usual because of an art show in town.

'She's really great. Reassuring.' Mara took another bite of the sandwich and watched as the twins placed their boards on the sand and concentrated as Brian demonstrated crouching next to his and then jumping onto it and standing up. 'Sorting out the settlement feels like it's going to be tough.'

'Well, I guess that's the nature of the beast. You're safe in her hands, though. Have you heard any more from this half-brother of yours? I've been meaning to ask you about that. So mysterious!' Serafina reopened the cool bag and extracted a biscuit. 'I will leave some for the kids, I promise,' she added, looking guilty.

'Right. Well, I told you he just turned up on the beach the other week?'

'Yup. How did he know where to find you?'

'I wrote to him. I only found out about him when Abby left me the house.' Mara sipped her coffee. 'Anyway, my letter found him. But now he says he wants half of the sale.' She tilted her head towards the beach house. 'Even though Aimee says he's not legally entitled to it.'

'So it's not a problem, then. You can tell him where to go. Not that it looks like it's worth having half of right now.' Serafina looked it up and down. 'I didn't really appreciate how bad it was. Brian's got his work cut out.'

'I know. Anyway, I don't want to tell him where to go. I wrote to him because I wanted to make contact.'

'It's just a shame that he's turned out to be a bit of a dud, then.'

'I guess,' Mara conceded. 'I could really do with some more family of my own. I hoped… well, I don't know what I hoped.'

'You want me to read your cards?'

'What?' Mara watched as her friend reached into her voluminous pink suede handbag and pulled out a pack of tarot cards. 'Oh… um… you do that?'

'Sure. Been doing it for years. Unofficial agony aunt of Magpie Cove.' Serafina unwrapped the cards from a green silk scarf.

'How does it work?'

'Ask a question.' Serafina shuffled the cards.

'What kind of question?'

'Anything. Will Paul turn out to be a friend or foe? Will you ever sleep with Brian Oakley? How will your divorce go? That kind of thing.'

'Serafina! I am not going to sleep with Brian Oakley!' Mara hissed, though the kids – and Brian – were way too far away to hear.

'That's what you think.' Serafina twinkled at her.

'That's what I *know*,' Mara retorted. 'Fine. Tell me about Paul.'

Serafina handed the pack to Mara.

'Shuffle, and think about the question,' she instructed. 'Then cut the pack.'

Mara did as she was told. Serafina picked up one half of the deck and dealt three cards.

'Oh. Okay. He's wounded. Heartbroken.' She pointed to the first card, which was a heart pierced with three swords. 'That's why he's being like this with you. But he's actually a good person. Steady and quite sweet.' She pointed to the card in the middle, a man with dark hair like Paul, mounted on horseback. 'It's going to be all right with Paul. You'll be friends.' She pointed to the last card, which featured three people raising cups to each other in a toast.

'Oh. That was surprisingly short. I thought you were going to… I don't know, tell me a long story about my past life as Joan of Arc or something.'

Serafina laughed.

'No Joan of Arc for you, sweetie. Want to ask something else?'

Mara looked at the cards for a moment. Part of her wanted to ask about Brian Oakley, but it was stupid. It was all a game, anyway. It didn't mean anything.

'I don't know. The divorce, then. Gideon. Will it go smoothly?' Mara shrugged, wanting not to seem too intrigued. Serafina shuffled the cards and Mara cut the pack in two again.

'Hm. It's disorganised. Going back and forwards about things.' Serafina turned over the first and then the second card. 'This is him. The Emperor. Powerful guy. Rich.'

'Oh!' Serafina frowned as she turned over the third card. 'Oddly, though, there's something unexpected coming. A choice of some kind.' She frowned and turned over another card. 'Huh. You have a choice between him and someone else.' She gave Mara a meaningful look and then gazed out to sea. Mara followed her eyes; the twins had now moved into the shallows and were taking turns lying on their boards and trying to get to their feet with Brian's help.

Mara rolled her eyes. 'Stop matchmaking, Serafina. Honestly.'

'The cards don't lie,' her friend crooned. 'Look. All I'm saying is that things with Gideon might not be as cut and dried as you think.'

'I guess we'll see about that.' Mara raised an eyebrow. 'I want it to be cut and dried. I'm ready to cut, dry and vacuum pack that marriage.'

Serafina giggled.

'Everything comes clear with time.' Her friend shuffled the cards back into the pack and returned them to the red velvet bag she'd taken them out of.

'How long have you been reading the cards?' Mara asked, wanting to change the subject.

'Long time. I learnt when I was twenty, or something. I rebelled against my parents and got a job at a travelling funfair. We went all over Cornwall and Devon too. I was kind of like a Girl Friday. The woman that managed the fair taught me. Practice over the years made me pretty good.'

'You worked in a funfair?' Mara laughed. 'What did being a Girl Friday consist of?'

'Oh, anything. Taking money at the gate. Minding the dodgems. Handing out sacks for the Helter Skelter. That kind of thing.'

Mara finished her coffee. 'You're full of surprises.'

Brian came running up the beach, followed by the twins.

'Hey! John tells me you like the water,' he panted. 'We're pretty much done here. Want to come in?'

'Oh, please come in, Mum!' Franny ran up behind Brian and enveloped her mother in a damp hug. 'It's so fun!'

'Don't be silly! I haven't got a wetsuit on!' Mara stood up and kissed her daughter on the top of her head. 'You had a good time, then?'

'I love surfing. Can we come every week?' her daughter answered excitedly.

'If it's okay with Brian.' Mara hugged John, who was red in the face but grinning from ear to ear.

'Of course. We can set a regular time.' He winked at the twins. 'But I think Mum needs to dip her toes in at the very least.'

'Brian, I am not going in the sea, so you might as well not bother persuading me!' Mara put her hands on her hips.

'I see,' he nodded gravely. 'Well…'

Without warning, he picked her up in his arms and ran down to the water's edge, the twins running behind, giggling.

'Hey! Put me down!' Mara cried out, wriggling in Brian's grasp, but he held her firmly.

'I promised the kids,' he murmured apologetically, and stopped when he was ankle-deep in the water. 'They made me do it.'

Franny caught up to them and wrestled Mara's trainers and socks off while Brian held her above the water.

'Frances Thorne! Leave me alone!' Mara yelled, but she was finding it hard to keep a straight face, especially when John ran up and started tickling her bare feet. 'Okay, okay! No tickles! I'll get in!'

Brian lowered her gently so that she could stand in the water; she pushed up the legs of her skinny jeans so they were at her knee.

'Aghhh, it's cold!' she yelled. John splashed her, flicking water with his palm at Mara.

'Hey!' Mara giggled and flicked water back at her son with her toes. 'Not fair. You've all got wetsuits on!'

John laughed as he jumped out of the way.

'Can't catch me!' he squealed.

Franny sloshed a huge scoop of water at Brian, who gasped theatrically and feinted at Franny; she screamed in delight and jumped further into the waves.

'Don't make me dangle you head-first in the waves, Fran!' he yelled.

'You wouldn't dare!' Franny yelled back, adopting a regal pose.

'Oh, wouldn't I?' Brian raced after her as Franny ran through the shallow tide line, giggling. Mara grabbed John and mussed his hair with her wet hands.

'Got you,' she laughed.

'You're all mad!' Serafina called from the beach, her hands on her hips.

'You're next, Serafina Lucido!' Brian yelled; he and Franny exchanged a glance and raced up the beach after Serafina, who squealed and ran to the beach house.

Mara watched with John; she was having more fun than she could remember in what felt like forever. It was good to see the twins laugh and be silly. More than that, it felt good to laugh herself; it was as though it freed up something in her chest that had been tight for too long. She hugged her son again snugly.

'I love you, Johnny,' she whispered in his ear. She could feel the tide shifting the sand under her feet, and John's weight as he leaned on her.

'I love you too, Mum,' he whispered back. 'I'm sorry we got you all wet.'

'Don't be sorry, sweetheart,' she reached for his hand. 'This was fun.'

'It was, wasn't it?' John beamed up at her, and she felt that tightness in her chest loosen even further. 'It was Franny's idea, though.'

Mara laughed.

'I'm not at all surprised,' she said, as they walked out of the sea and onto the beach. 'But I don't mind. I don't mind at all.'

Chapter Eighteen

'Well, I think I've made a good start.' Brian Oakley hitched up his jeans, shading his eyes from the setting sun. He'd changed after the surf lesson and joined her on the porch of the beach house. Serafina was inside, looking around with the twins. John and Franny wanted to show their new friend everything, including the hole in the roof.

'How long before it's watertight?' Mara hugged her coat around her.

If she was very, very honest with herself, she was happy to get to spend some time with Brian again. With Gideon and Paul wanting to pull her to pieces, it was nice to be with someone like him. At least he seemed to care about repairing the house. Putting something back together rather than ripping it apart.

And there was a kind of quiet, happy hum of energy between them whenever they talked – she wondered if he felt it. Was that what people meant when they said *chemistry*? She wondered for a moment whether he and Petra were still an item after their argument at the Halloween party. And then hated herself for thinking it. It was none of her business.

'You know what I mean. Secure, I guess.' She smiled carefully. Her trust of men was at an all-time low right now, not that it had ever been that high. At one time in her childhood she remembered being actually afraid of men; playing at her friends' houses, she'd quailed when dads and brothers strode in, owning the space taking up room with their loud voices and jokes, no matter how kindly. She remembered overhearing Abby explaining to the mother of one of her friends – she didn't remember who – that Mara didn't like men at all. *I don't know why*, Abby had said, *maybe it's because it's just us at home. Who can blame her though, right?* and she'd laughed, and the other mother had laughed too.

Who could blame me, given the current men in my life? Mara grimaced. *I'd be happy if the world was full of women being kind to each other. No men at all.* But of course, that ban would have to include John, her sweet, huggy boy who knew her heart as well as she did. Who made her laugh, who would kiss her solemnly on the forehead and once on both cheeks at night and say something terribly old-timey like *goodnight, Mummy, my dear friend.* It was enough to make her mist up just thinking about it.

John was one of the good ones; he wasn't his father's son, and, if there was a John with his little-old-man personality and his old soul of a heart, there were other good men too. She knew that. She did. It was just that sometimes, it was hard to remember.

'Security is important.' Brian took a sip of tea from the flask. 'I mean, you never know. You wouldn't want kids climbing in, squatters, that kind of thing. Not least because someone could do themselves a serious injury.'

'Squatters? I'd never even thought about that.' Mara looked worriedly through the open front door. 'In Magpie Cove? Really?'

'Well, it's unlikely, I'll give you that. People are pretty nice, sure, and thankfully if anyone heard about people needing a roof over their heads, someone would help. It's that kind of place. But a place like this left alone for too long... it's a worry, that's all. So, I'm happy you called on me to fix it.'

'You were worried about the house?' Mara cocked her head to one side and frowned.

'Yes.' He refilled the tea in the flask lid and offered it to her; she shook her head.

'I've had too much coffee as it is.'

'No working bathroom. I gotcha.' He grinned, and Mara blushed. 'No, I just… it sounds weird. I like this old place. Houses… sometimes, they have a soul, you know? I just feel protective of it. The house. When things are broken, I want to fix them.'

'You're in the right job, then.' Mara looked away. Her heart had softened, listening to him. She was suspicious of her feelings, which had only ever led her to Gideon. And Brian Oakley was a flirt, a playboy, beloved by everyone and loyal to none.

'Yeah…'

There was a silence. She could feel him looking at her, but she kept her head turned away. She wasn't going to give him the satisfaction of falling all over him just like every other woman in Magpie Cove seemed to do. *You're not getting me under your spell,* she thought. *Stick with your twenty-year-olds. They haven't lived long enough to know what men like you are all about. Or to see through your painfully obvious 'fixing broken things' references. Even if that is something I actually like about you.*

'So I heard there was food?' He lowered his head to look into her eyes, a friendly smile on his lips. It was that same warm, raffish look, but she had to admit, it was quite nice when it was directed at you. *Like some sort of friendly terrier,* she thought, despite her previous thoughts. *Well, you're not going to fall for his charms, so what harm can it do?*

'We saved you some. The twins have already scoffed theirs,' she explained. 'They were ravenous! D'you think they enjoyed the lesson?'

'They seemed to. They were great. Happy to give them more time if they want it. So, what is there to eat? I'm famished.' He rummaged in the cool bag. 'No champagne? Disappointing.'

'No candles either, I'm afraid.' Mara raised her eyebrow. 'You know. For romantic lighting.'

'Oh. Shame.' He chuckled.

'Well, there's sandwiches, as I said. And chocolate biscuits for after. You'd never keep a flame lit in this weather,' Mara chattered, to cover up her embarrassment. Why had she said the thing about the candles?

'Right you are.' He followed her through the front door, which she closed behind them. 'Sorry about the mess. I will clean it thoroughly when I'm done, it's just working on the beach, it's unavoidable.' He bent down and started sweeping some of the muddy sand on the floor away with his hand, but Mara stopped him.

'Don't worry. The main thing is that it's getting fixed.' Her fingers traced the back of his hand, and she pulled them away self-consciously.

'Sorry,' she muttered, and stood up.

'I brought some beers.' He reached into his bag and brought out two beer bottles. He snapped off the top of one of them with a bottle opener on his keyring. 'Want one?'

'Oh. Thanks, I guess I could have one.' She took it from him and he opened the other bottle. They were nice and cold.

'I left them in the wet sand when we were doing the lesson,' he explained.

'Of course.'

There was a comfortable silence; they both listened to the twins chattering excitedly with Serafina upstairs.

'So, tell me about you.' She took a sip of the beer.

'Tell you what about me?' he asked, unpacking the cool bag and opening a sandwich bag. 'Ah, I love Serafina's sandwiches. Awesome.'

'Anything. I don't really know you that well, so...' she trailed off. 'I feel like you know more about me. Divorce, kids, et cetera.'

'Surprising appreciation for women in barrels?'

'Right.' She grinned. 'Oh. Remember, you're not supposed to have mayo. They probably have mayo in them.'

'Oh, shut up. That was embarrassing.' He cringed.

'I think Petra Bear was only looking out for Brian Bear,' Mara said, straight-faced.

'Ummm. Okay. Are we doing this?' He gave her a pained look. 'Please. I hate that baby talk and she just does it on purpose to annoy me.'

Mara raised an eyebrow. 'Well, it definitely worked.'

'Can we not talk about Petra, please?'

'Fine. Tell me the story of your life instead.' She took a long drink from the beer bottle.

'OK. Lived here all my life. My dad's still alive, but not Mum. He lives here. I drop in and see him every day.' He took a bite of the sandwich. 'Damn, I'm starving.'

'That's nice. I'm sorry about your mum.'

'Thanks. She passed when I was a teenager. Long time ago now.'

'Doesn't make a difference when, though. I don't expect to ever wake up one day and be over my mum's passing. Are you?' She watched his face.

He sighed and took a drink of beer.

'No. It was tough. Especially it being in my teens, I think. You need a mother then. We were close. Very alike. Dad says that's why I've never had…. Oh, I shouldn't say it.' He looked uncomfortable and shook his head. 'Doesn't matter.'

'What? Never had what?'

'Never had any trouble finding… female company.' He gave her an embarrassed look. 'He says it's because I'm like her. Good at talking to people. Making them feel relaxed with me.' He shrugged.

'I would have thought that a teen boy losing his mother at a very formative age would explain why you haven't settled down, rather than anything else,' she replied. 'No, I mean – there's obviously some kind of trauma there around relating to women. Otherwise a man your age wouldn't be spending your time chasing twenty-year olds.' She took another long drink from the bottle and closed her eyes for a moment. She hardly drank beer, and remembered now how much she liked it.

'Um, wow! Say what you really think, why don't you?' He laughed. Mara blushed.

'Sorry. I didn't mean to be so... personal. That's just what I'd think, as a mother. That's all.'

'Maybe you're right, Mara Hughes.' He smiled softly, picking the paper wrapper from the outside of the beer bottle. There was a silence.

'Where is your house, anyway? I hardly know where anything is around here, mind you,' she asked, to break it.

'Oh, I'll have to give you the grand tour of the village. Good use of a spare twenty-seven minutes.'

'Great. I'd love that.'

'I've got a flat in one of the terraces overlooking the beach.' He pointed behind them. Mara had spent quite a bit of time staring up at the once-grand houses there.

'Oh! They look nice. I haven't been inside one,' she explained needlessly. *Well, obviously. You don't know anyone, apart from Brian, Simona and Serafina, you idiot,* she berated herself.

'I'll include it in the tour.'

'Okay. What else?'

'What else what?'

'You were telling me about yourself.'

'What else do you want to know?' He bit into the second half of the sandwich.

'Favourite colour?'

He laughed.

'Blue. Unoriginal. Sorry.'

'Favourite ice cream flavour?'

'I'm dairy intolerant, so as long as it's soy, anything.'

'Oh. Of course. Favourite... number?'

'Oh. Definitely eight,' he said, pretending to be serious. 'You're all about the important stuff, huh?'

'For sure.' Mara giggled.

'Okay. Enough about me. Tell me about your week. And your favourite colour.'

'Red,' she answered.

'And your week?'

'Oh, you don't want to hear about it.' Mara rolled her eyes. 'Middle-aged housewife drama.'

'I doubt that. And, unless I've misunderstood the situation, you're not a housewife. Or middle-aged, come to that.' His blue eyes twinkled.

She took a spare sandwich, unwrapped it and gave him a droll stare.

'Listen. You might as well not bother laying on the charm. Save it for your surf girls.' She took a bite: it tasted like home-baked ham with a layer of tangy pickle on soft granary bread. The bread had been hand cut in thick doorstep-style slices. 'Mmmm.'

He coughed, halfway through taking a drink.

'Glad to hear it. My... surf girls?'

'Come on. You know what I'm talking about.' Mara took another drink of beer.

'I'm not sure that I do, but let's leave that for a minute. Tell me what happened.' He ate steadily, keeping his eyes on her face. He was a strangely comforting presence, Mara thought, though perhaps it was the beer.

Before she could say anything, the twins thundered down the stairs with Serafina trailing them.

'Mum! Serafina says she'll take us to the café for ice cream. Can we go?' Franny asked. 'Please?'

'Did you finish your sandwich?' Mara frowned, looking into the cool bag. 'You need to eat real food, not just sweets all day.'

'I ate the whole sandwich *and* a banana. So did John,' Franny argued.

'Oh. Well, only if Serafina doesn't mind. Do you want me to come too?' she asked her friend, but Serafina made a dismissive gesture.

'No, no. Catch up about the house, you've probably got a lot of building things to talk about. I need to check in at the café anyway. Just come and get them when you're ready.' She winked and ushered the kids out of the door.

'Serafina? Can we have dinner at the café?' John asked as they were halfway out of the door.

'Of course, sweetie.' The woman handed the twins their coats.

'Do you have lasagne?' Franny asked.

'Can we have chips?' John added.

'Can we have baked potatoes with tuna and with chips on the side?' Franny gushed.

'You can have whatever I've got in, kittens.' Serafina chuckled.

'Guys, please don't harangue Serafina about food!' Mara called after them, but they ignored her. 'OK, I'll see you later?' she called, weakly. She turned back to Brian, who was grinning.

'Don't laugh. They're like locusts.'

'They're growing kids.' He chuckled. 'So, you were going to tell me about your terrible week.'

'Where do you want to start? The fact that my husband – no, my ex-husband – filed for divorce on Wednesday? Or that, in the same week, I met the half-brother I never knew I had – and now he wants half of this place too?' She took another bite of her sandwich. 'Oh. And there's the fact that nobody wants to buy this place. And if I don't sell it by the time Gideon gets home, he's threatening to take over the sale and… I don't know. Sell it for a pittance.' She looked out of the window onto the sea, which was a dark grey in the fading light outside. The wind had picked up and had started blowing around the house, whistling here and there like a ghost.

'Okay. You win.' He raised his eyebrows. 'I'm sorry. I didn't mean to joke. That's… okay, that's a pretty bad week.'

'Yup.'

'So, your ex-husband, he wants this place? I suppose he thinks he's entitled to half of it.'

'Honestly, I don't think he really wants it. Basically, he just wants me to sell it as soon as possible because, in his mind, that means I can buy a house to live in with the kids and let him ride into the sunset with Little Miss New Boobs.'

'Is that her real name?'

'As far as I'm concerned.' Mara twisted her wedding ring. It still wouldn't come off.

'If you own the family home together, you get half of it if it's sold, but usually the mother and the children would get the house. If he wants you out, he's obligated to buy you out. The beach house doesn't come into it, surely?' Brian frowned, playing with the half-peeled label on his bottle. 'It doesn't sound very fair.'

'He wants me to sell it fast, and if I do, then he won't ask for half of it. He's suggested a pretty crappy custody agreement, and he doesn't seem too keen in giving me half of our house, either. The one in St Ives,' she added. 'I have a solicitor. She's good. But in the meantime, it doesn't stop him being a pain in the ass.'

'I think he's threatening you because he wants to scare you and get off with a free pass. He's liable for maintenance for the kids and for you. Especially if the reason for the divorce is his infidelity. He's full of it.' Brian shook his head.

Brian had already finished his beer bottle and placed it back, empty, on the table. 'I've been there, divorce is expensive and messy. And it sounds like your ex isn't exactly focused on getting a good deal for you or the kids.'

Mara groaned and put her head in her hands.

'Ugh. Everything is terrible.'

'You'll get through it. I did. And you seem a much more capable person than me.'

'Well, I am a woman.' She looked at Brian through her fingers, smiling archly.

He returned her grin. 'Natural advantage.'

'So, you were married?' A marriage didn't fit into her idea of him.

'A long time ago. School sweethearts. Married at twenty. Loved each other. We wanted a family, but it turned out that I wasn't able to give her that.' He looked away at the sea through the window.

'I'm sorry.'

'Don't be. It just wasn't meant to be.' He shrugged. 'If we'd have met later in life, if she'd had kids already, maybe it could have worked. But in the end, I knew if she stayed with me, she'd end up resenting me. Children were so important to her. I mean, to me too. So, we split up.'

'You could have adopted?'

'Maybe. But she didn't want to.' He shrugged. 'We were young. It seemed the best thing to do to let her have her own children. That was really important to her. She was adopted and... you know. She wanted a family with people who looked like her. It's understandable.'

'What about sperm donation? You could have done that.'

'We had the free IVF cycle we were allotted on the National Health, but we couldn't afford any more cycles. When we realised it was me that was the problem, Lucy suggested sperm donation, but...' He sighed. 'I refused. I was young. It felt like she was trying to emasculate me, I suppose. I already felt bad enough that I couldn't be a man, you know. To me it was all about a threat to my masculinity. I couldn't give her a baby, I couldn't do the one thing I was supposed to be able to do, to prove I was a man. I was an idiot. I should have said yes.'

Mara murmured, 'That's rough. I'm sorry.'

'Water under the bridge. I guess I wasn't supposed to be a dad.' He gave her a half-hearted grin. 'Must be hard, being a parent. Especially when it didn't work out – that whole 2.4 children, roses-around-the-door thing.'

'Yeah. I just feel like I've failed them. They had a family, and now they just have me.' She closed her eyes and tried to steel herself not to cry, not again. She felt like she was always crying these days, and she really didn't want to cry in front of Brian Oakley. She thought of Annie in her barrel, but it didn't cheer her up like it normally did.

Brian leaned over the table and took her hands in his. His palms were warm; his fingers were dry, hard, the skin at the nails slightly cracked.

'Hey. Come on, now. It's going to be all right. You've just lost your mum, too. You just have to take all this a day at a time. And this half-brother. He's the least of your worries right now.'

'But it was me that wanted to find him. I found all these old letters Mum had written him. She abandoned him when he was a baby and I don't know why… so when I found them, I… my heart just went out to him, you know?' She glanced up into his eyes, and he nodded, still holding her hands firmly. 'I can't imagine how that must feel. How she must have felt, to…' Mara shivered. 'When I think of giving away John or Franny, I just… I can't imagine what must have made her do it. How terribly frightened she must have been to do it. But I don't know what of.'

Brian slowly let out his breath.

'Hmm. I can't imagine it either. She must have been young and scared. I guess without much support. Was she close to her parents? Your grandparents?'

Mara choked back a tear.

'I don't know.' She shook her head. 'I don't know anything about them.'

The wind had grown stronger outside, a strong gust rattled the windows.

'It's really coming in out there.' He stood up and went to the window. 'Looks like a storm. We shouldn't stay too long.'

'No, I should be getting back to the twins. They'll have eaten Serafina out of house and home by the time I get there.' Mara felt sad. Talking to Brian was turning out to be the best part of her week so far.

'Take a biscuit with you.' Brian came back to the table and started packing their little tea up into his bag and Mara felt another twinge of disappointment. What had she expected, that they'd spend the whole night here, talking by candlelight? Or that they'd make love by the light of a flickering fire, on a fur rug, like a scene in a terrible romance novel? She hardly knew the man. And she would never do anything like that. Though, as soon as she had the thought that she wouldn't, she felt a little sad.

'You know, I don't… I mean, your comment about the surf girls earlier…' he said, touching her arm gently as she stood up. 'I don't know what you've heard, but people like to gossip.'

'You have a girlfriend, though. Don't you? Petra?' Mara met his gaze with her own level stare. She might have been fooled once, but it wasn't going to happen again.

'Yes.' He returned her gaze. 'Aren't I allowed to have a girl-friend?'

Now it was her turn to look away, embarrassed.

'Of course. I just meant—'

'Nothing wrong happened here, Mara. We just talked. I'd like to be your friend.' He reached for her hand again, but she kept both hands by her sides.

'I saw you at the party. It looked like you... broke up. Not that it's any of my business.' She stumbled over her words.

'Oh, that. Just an argument. We didn't break up, but... you have to understand that things with Petra are very... casual,' he said, not meeting her eye.

'What does that mean? She's good enough to sleep with but nothing else?' Mara snapped.

'No, that's not what I said. Petra—'

'Oh, don't bother.' Mara turned away, not understanding her feelings. *Or, understanding them too well*, she thought. *I like him, and I don't want to be just his friend. And I think he knows that, yet he's going to try and play me along.* 'Men like you make me sick. That girl obviously adores you.'

He blinked in surprise.

'I make you sick? And who are "men like me"?' he demanded.

Mara regretted her words, but she wasn't going to take them back. *My days of kowtowing are over, my friend,* she thought. She glared at Brian.

'You know what I mean. Is Petra even the only girl you're seeing? Every time we meet, another twenty-five-year-old appears and you flirt with her,' she muttered.

'It's Petra who wants to keep things casual, if you must know, and I'm happy with that arrangement. But you're right. It isn't any of your business. And it certainly isn't any of your business if I do some harmless flirting here and there. I'm a surf coach. If I know a lot of girls that age, it's because I teach them, that's all.' He stood up and started tidying up the sandwich wrappers and the beer bottles. 'Not because I'm... emotionally traumatised, or something.'

'You're right. I shouldn't have said that, earlier. I've got to get the kids.' She buttoned up her coat and opened the front door and strode away from the house, up to the car. She might as well drive it up to the café and then head back to the hotel from there.

'Mara?' he called after her, but she wasn't going to stop. She was angry, mostly at herself. She'd managed to turn a professional relationship between her and Brian into something undignified; somehow, it had got way too personal in there.

'Lock up, will you?' she called over her shoulder. Above the wind, she could hear a magpie cawing and chattering. She looked up: it flew down from the top of the roof and squawked above her loudly, flying in a loop before returning to the beach house.

'Abby, just go!' she shouted angrily at the bird, before she could stop to analyse what she was doing. 'If that's you, just tell me what you want!' Her voice disappeared on the wind; she could see the storm sitting above the sea like a nightmare, tendrils of dark rain reaching down into the sea.

She didn't know what she expected to happen, but nothing did. The bird sat huddled on the roof of the house, and she felt immediately stupid. *What on earth was she doing?*

She ran to her car as the rain started to splatter her clothes, her hair; by the time she had made the short run to the car, her long dark plait was already wet.

Chapter Nineteen

Mara knocked on the door of the small house and waited. Here it was, the place that Abby had sent all those letters to, and heard nothing. Had she ever driven here like Mara had done today? Along the twisting coastal roads that led inland, slowly, to wider roads, like a puzzle that gradually became clear? Had she driven past the old Cornish tin mines, through the small slate-roofed villages, sometimes with a pub or post office, but often just a row of four or five houses along the road, nestling together against the wind?

Helston was bigger than Magpie Cove: it was full of the standard Cornish tourist stuff – pasty shops, fudge stalls, a Cornish museum inside a stately building, built of grey Cornish stone. There was a popular tourist railway that Mara had taken the kids on a few times. You could have a cream tea in the train carriage whilst the steam engine puffed its way through the lush Cornish countryside. Mara drove through the town and out to the other side, where her satnav led her to a small semi-detached house in dark brick with dark wood doors and windows in a close that felt somehow suffocating.

Like Simona had suggested, she was making an unannounced visit. Mara thought, if the worst happened, then at least she would have seen Paul again and seen where he lived. If she could get his phone number or an email address, then they could gradually build a relationship. She wasn't under any illusions about the fact that it would be difficult. That was okay. She was prepared to take it slowly.

Paul Sullivan opened the door. Like the day at the beach when they'd met, he was dressed in black jeans, though today she could see he was wearing Tom and Jerry socks with a hole in the toe of one foot. He wore a red hoodie unzipped over a *Star Wars* T-shirt. His expression registered surprise, then became guarded.

'Oh. It's you. I didn't ask you to come here.' He stepped half-behind the door, as if it would protect him from her.

'Don't shut the door. We need to talk.' Mara kept her voice even, trying to keep her anxiety out of it. 'Please.'

He tutted but opened the door, revealing a cramped hallway.

'Okay. Come in. But I've got to go to work soon.'

'Thanks.' She followed him into the house, which had a slightly musty smell; it needed airing out.

'What do you do? Your job?' she asked politely as he walked into a sitting room and sat on the edge of one of the sofas. Both looked as though they'd been there since the 80s, judging by the style, and the smell of long-ago cigarettes. Mara perched cautiously at the edge of hers, mirroring him.

'I manage a bookshop in town.' He was staring at his hands, refusing to meet her gaze.

'That's nice.' Mara felt like the stuffy room was going to choke her. 'You like *Star Wars*?' she pointed to his T-shirt.

'Yeah.'

There was a silence. Paul was acting like a sulky teenager. Mara reminded herself that she had just turned up unannounced; he wasn't prepared. *Though he was prepared enough to turn up at the beach house with no notice*, she thought. *So we're quits.*

'What's your favourite *Star Wars* film?' she asked.

'*The Empire Strikes Back*. Obviously.' He stared out of the window.

'Oh. I quite enjoyed the prequels,' she said, airily. He stared at her in derision.

'You have to be kidding.'

'I find the history of the Clone Wars very interesting,' she replied, straight-faced.

'Next you'll be telling me Jar-Jar Binks is your favourite character.'

She raised an eyebrow. 'Oh, I love him.'

'You're having me on.' He crossed his arms over his chest.

'Of course I am. I'm not a total idiot. More of an Ewok fan.'

'Right.' He gave her a slightly less frowny look. 'So did you come here to talk about *Star Wars*?'

'No. Just trying to get you to talk to me.'

There was another silence.

'This has come out of the blue, Mara. You've got to understand that.'

'I do understand. It's weird for me too. It was just me and Abby all those years. I had no idea you existed.'

'Well, I did,' he said.

'Do you have a family? Or…?' She looked around her for signs of children, but there were no framed photographs, no toys, none of the general mess that followed John and Franny around.

'No, just me.'

'You lived here as a child, then? When… when Abby wrote the letters to you?'

She had found him, this brother, and she wasn't going to let him go without a fight. *You will talk to me. This is too important,* she thought, trying to keep herself feeling fierce, though she was scared as hell.

'Yes,' he snapped. 'When she abandoned me.'

'I know.' Mara replied, softly. 'I had no idea. Until she died and I found the letters. You have to believe me.'

He looked up, meeting her eyes. His were as dark brown as Abby's; he even had her soft eyelashes.

'I believe you. But it doesn't change what she did. And why she kept you and not me.'

'I know that. But she must have had a good reason for doing it. I don't know what, but...' Mara trailed off.

'You mentioned the other day that your parents... they were difficult?' she said softly. She wanted to know more about him.

'I mean, they adopted me, but they made my life hell. I guess they thought adoption was a good way to get themselves a punching bag for free.' He shook his head, picked up a Rubik's Cube from the dark wood coffee table next to where he was sitting and started to turn it around in his hands, instinctively shuffling the colours around, first one way and then the other.

'What do you mean?' Mara got the sense that Paul wanted to talk, but he obviously wasn't used to discussing his feelings very often. Least of all to a total stranger he'd just realised was his sister, she supposed. Was he implying that his parents had abused him? Her stomach turned at the thought of anyone doing that to a child.

'You wouldn't understand.'

'Try me.' Mara leaned forwards. 'I'm not going anywhere.'

'I don't want to talk about it,' he muttered, like a surly teenager, playing with the cube.

Mara thought for a moment about how she would talk to John to make him open up. Franny was different: she was more logical in her emotions, and better at holding forth – sometimes at length – presenting her views to the world. John, though cuddly and affectionate, sometimes needed drawing out slowly. If something was really bothering him, he was more likely to talk to you whilst you were distracted with something else: digging the garden, building Lego, attached to a task of some kind. Mara sat back on the couch, looking around the room.

She took a different tack, ignoring Paul's obvious discomfort. 'I'm surprised you haven't redecorated.'

'What?'

'The décor. It's a bit faded, isn't it? I'd have probably, you know…' She looked around her, assessing the room 'Stripped this paper off. Painted it white throughout. Got some new furniture in.'

'Oh. Umm, well, I…' he trailed off. 'I don't earn that much at the shop.'

'But you don't have a mortgage, I take it? You don't have to pay rent here?'

'No, but—'

'So you must have some disposable cash every month? You could go room by room. I'd help you.'

'Hang on… what are we talking about? I was trying to tell you about my parents—'

'But you said you didn't want to.' Mara got up, briskly. 'Come on. Show me the rest of the house.' She crossed the room and stood at the door, hand on her hip. 'I'm waiting.'

She had obviously taken him by surprise, because he followed her without comment.

'What's upstairs?' she asked.

'You really want to see it all? You're, like, weirdly intrusive.'

'Yes,' she said brightly. 'I am your sister, after all.'

'It seems kind of soon to be acting like we even know each other. But, whatever, fine.'

Mara followed him up the narrow stairs which were covered in yellow carpet with bright orange flowers. She winced at the Seventies design. It was pretty worn through, too, like everything in the house.

Upstairs, there were three bedrooms that led off a small square hallway.

'That was my parents' room. I did strip that one out and turned it into vinyl storage,' he said, indicating a room lined with two large shelving units that held row upon row of vinyl records.

'Wow. You're a collector?' Mara went in to look more closely. 'Can I flip through?' Every album was encased in an identical plastic sleeve. She had been into music more when she was younger, but like most things, she'd slowly veered away from it in her life with Gideon.

'Sure.'

He watched as Mara discovered picture discs, novelty fold out sleeves and Seventies psychedelia albums with dreamy artwork.

'Wow. Paul, these are awesome.' She beamed at him, standing in the door, watching her. 'Hey! Mum had this one!' She pulled out a Big Brother and the Holding Company LP. 'She used to play this all the time. She loved Janis Joplin.'

'This is really rare. Look, it still has the hype sticker attached to the shrink wrap. It's from 1967, the Mainstream record label.' He took it from her gently and held it, looking at the cover for a minute. 'She listened to this?'

'Yes! We had that exact album.' Mara turned it over and read the track listing. 'Oh, my goodness, I'd forgotten all about these songs. "All is Loneliness". "Women is Losers". She used to sing that one.' Mara shut her eyes and tried to remember the tune. She sang it a little. 'Like that?'

'I don't know. I've never played it.' He slid it back onto the shelf. 'I buy them as a collector.'

'You should listen. It's amazing.'

He looked uncomfortable. 'I don't really know Janis Joplin's music…'

'Oh, damn. We've got to change that. She had the most amazing voice. Raw. Powerful. Full of heartbreak. She's always singing about being unlucky in love and choosing the wrong man and being heartbroken. And drunk. I guess Mum could relate,' Mara said, thoughtfully.

'Well, that's pretty much it. Bathroom, my bedroom, study.' He pointed at the other doors leading off the hallway. Mara poked her head in the study which was set up as a gaming den with a huge adjustable leather chair in front of a massive screen, and a wall of games in their cases. She pretended not to see the posters featuring female characters from various fantasy games, all of whom had tiny waists, big breasts and were dressed pretty impractically for fighting zombies or colonising Mars.

I guess he doesn't get out much, she thought.

Mara followed Paul back downstairs and along the corridor to a small kitchen that overflowed with half-empty bread bags, empty beer cans and crisp packets. She wrinkled her nose at the musty smell which, in here, was tempered with gone-off milk.

'I wasn't exactly expecting company,' Paul muttered, his hands in his pockets.

'Hmmm. This would look lovely with lighter cupboard doors, you know,' she said, brightly. *And a damn good clean*, she added, in her mind.

'I can't afford a new kitchen,' he said. 'Anyway, look. I don't need you to make over the house. It's fine as it is.'

Mara looked him up and down. 'I think you're living in this house and it's full of ghosts. If you keep living here like this, it's going to break you. It can't be healthy being in this house on your own, stuck in front of that huge screen for hours on end.' She realised she sounded as if she was talking to Franny and John, but she couldn't help it. Paul was her little brother. She felt oddly protective of him.

'You don't know the first thing about me. Who are you to come in here and make crazy statements like that? Jesus. I'm late for work. I never asked you to come here. Why are you even here, anyway?'

'Because, you're my brother. I want to get to know you.'

'Like hell. You just don't want to give up the beach house,' he retorted.

Mara leaned on the fridge.

'That's not it. I just think, if we got to know each other, we could come to some kind of agreement. I want to know you. I don't have much family apart from the kids now. I'd like a brother.' She held out her hand for his, but he shook his head.

'I'm sorry. You seem… well, a bit bossy, to be honest. But I'm sure you're okay. I just… I don't do family.'

'So, what? You're just going to live here in this mouldering house, stuck in the 1970s, alone? Forever?'

'Sure. What's it to you? We don't know each other. Go back to your kids and have a nice life,' he snapped again.

'Damnit!' Mara stood up and turned to the sink, instinctively picking up the rubbish strewn around the countertop and putting it in the bin. She opened cupboard doors, looking for some kind of cleaning product. In the cupboard under the sink, she found some washing-up liquid. 'I don't have a nice life to go back to. I'm getting divorced, I'm working in a café to pay the bills and trying to repair a huge hole in the roof of that beach house you want half of – which, by the way, is a total wreck that no one wants to buy. My husband Gideon's run off with his assistant and, oh, let's see, my mother just died and my newly discovered brother is being a total idiot.'

Mara started running hot water into the sink, pushing the dirty cups and plates in it already to one side. *Well, I've got to say it,* she thought. 'Look. I don't mean to be rude, or anything, but… your letter?'

'Right…' His voice was level, not giving anything away.

'My solicitor says you don't have a legal right to the house. Because your parents adopted you – you don't have a claim to Abby's estate.'

'I know. I researched it after I sent the letter. I was angry.'

'Oh.' She didn't know what to say. 'So…?'

'So, forget it. I was angry. I *am* angry, but it's not your fault.'

'It doesn't mean you can't have something of Abby's. The letters are yours, for one. And I'd be happy to give you some of what I get for the house. It feels right. I think Abby would have wanted that.' Mara shrugged, watching the sink fill up with soapy water.

'Maybe. Let's see how we get on, I guess. We hardly know each other.' Paul smiled tentatively at her. 'Sorry I was kind of a dick about the beach house.'

'It's OK.'

'Are you doing my washing up, then?' He gave her a quizzical look. 'You know I can do that for myself, right?'

'Theoretically. Though I don't see any actual evidence of that,' she replied tersely, and turned around in surprise when she heard him laugh. 'What?'

'Okay, okay. You're strange, Mara.'

'I am not strange. I just can't stand dirty dishes.' She turned back to the sink, and started washing the plates. 'Make some space on the drainer, for goodness' sake.'

He came to stand next to her, shifting his weight uncomfortably. She pointed to the plates that had been put on the drier but still had streaks of food on them.

'Those need doing too. Put them in the sink.'

'They're clean!' he protested.

'They are not clean,' she insisted. He sighed and put them in the sink then rummaged in a drawer for a tea towel.

'I do have to leave for work soon. I wasn't lying.'

'Fine. I'll come back.'

'To finish the dishes?'

'No, idiot. To spend more quality time with you.'

'Oh. Right.' He took a clean plate from her, wiped it dry and then, following her raised eyebrow, slotted it into a nearby cupboard.

'Okay,' she replied, levelly. There was a silence for a few moments, as they washed the dishes companionably.

'Mara?' Paul asked.

'Yes?'

'You think I could just replace the cupboard doors in here?'

'I think it would make it a lot brighter.' She smiled.

Chapter Twenty

'That wind last night must have done it.' Brian was frowning, looking up at the beach house roof. There had been a heavy storm the night before: as she'd watched it roll in from her hotel room, Mara had had a bad feeling about it. It looked like she had been right to think the worst: the hole in the roof that Brian had already started patching was now much, much worse.

'What in the... it's gone. The whole left side...' Mara didn't know what to say. Brian had called whilst she was driving back from Helston, but she'd been negotiating a winding lane at the time and hadn't answered. She hadn't even intended to come to the beach house, but she still had a few free hours and thought she'd check in on Brian's progress before she picked the kids up from school. Serafina had given her the day off; the café was closed because of a leak under the sink.

'I'm sorry, Mara. Like I said, it was a matter of time.'

'Is it... fixable?' she stammered. What was a down-at-heel beach house was rapidly turning into a ruin. If she wasn't choking back tears, she would have laughed. Honestly, what else was going to go wrong? If it was happening to anyone else, she would have refused to believe her own run of bad luck.

'Everything's fixable, but...' he paused and looked at her. 'You know what I'm going to say.'

'More money.' She shook her head. 'I don't have it.'

'Would your husband front the repairs? You said he wants you to sell it.'

And that was another thing: Gideon was due home this week.

'Oh, no. Gideon. No. I doubt it, anyway.' She sat down on the pebbles on the beach, not caring that it was freezing cold.

'It's really that bad?' Brian asked, and then shied away at her expression. 'Okay, okay! I get it.'

'Let's just say he's not the helpful type, unless it's about the kids. He's usually reasonable on that front at least, although in the custody arrangement he's proposed he only takes them every other weekend.' Mara rested her head on her fists and stared at the house in frustration. 'Oh, bloody hell! Why can't anything go right? Just once!'

'So… um, should we carry on? Even though this adds to the development costs?' He looked at the almost roof-less house. 'I'm still in. If you are.'

'I don't see what option I really have. We've got to do the repairs and make it sellable. Just do what you have to do to keep costs down, and we'll manage. You can still go halves on the expenses?'

'He looked sideways at her, her chin in her hands. 'I can do that. Don't let Abby's house disappear. It's your heritage, your history, after all.'

Well, now that it's in even worse condition than before, it wouldn't be worth anything to sell anyway.

She met his eyes. 'You're right. There's no point letting it go to ruin.'

'You're sure? I don't want to railroad you into carrying on with the development if you think it's a lost cause. Sell it as it is if you want. It's your choice.' He touched her arm gently, then took his hand away as if he wasn't sure whether he should. 'You need to do what's best for you and the kids.'

'But if I let it go, I couldn't pay you for what you've done already.' She shrugged. 'No. This is the best thing.' She forced a positive expression onto her face, even though it felt as though all her dreams of the best thing were very far away. Instead of the best thing, she had a small number of second-best options available to her, and if she didn't at least try to get one of these, they too would disappear to be replaced with less and less palatable options.

Someone should tell kids that this is what happens when you grow up, she thought. *Not dreams, not nightmares, but a series of disappointments. I understand Annie and her barrel more and more every day.*

'What about your husband?'

Mara took in a deep breath and made herself think about Gideon; grimly, she made herself see all of this from his point of view.

'He's going to check in with me when he gets home. I doubt he'll leave it to his solicitor, that's not his style. I'll be honest. What else can I do? The house hasn't sold, it's been damaged in a storm. The plan for the renovation hasn't changed. Just… got a bit more expensive.' She avoided Brian's eyes and stared out to the sea. There was a silence.

'You know, I know it doesn't feel like it now, but maybe this happened for the best. You and Gideon, I mean.' Brian hunkered down next to her and stared out to the shoreline, following her gaze. Mara snorted.

'It definitely does not feel like that,' she muttered.

'I know. When I split from Lucy, my wife, it broke my heart. Even though we were young, even though I knew it was the right thing to do. But I still hated it. I didn't want to get a divorce. But then, one day, you find yourself sitting on a beach with someone, just talking, and not wanting the person you broke your heart over for all those years. You realise maybe if you'd stayed with Lucy, or one of the other ones that you tried to find the same feeling with, then this could never have happened.' His tone softened and Mara turned to face him, confused.

'What do you mean?' She frowned.

He met her eyes for a moment and paused. Mara saw something in his expression, something in the way that he was looking at her, but it was so foreign that she didn't recognise it for a moment. Then, she realised, and was taken aback. He was flirting with her. Worse than flirting – he was actually making a move on her. He was serious. 'Nothing.' He looked away.

'What do you mean?' She wasn't going to let this pass.

'Nothing. It doesn't matter.' He smiled vaguely which infuriated Mara.

'You're still seeing Petra, I take it?' she asked icily.

'Yes, I am,' he replied, in a measured tone.

'Right.' She stood up. 'Then why are you saying these things to me? I'm going home.'

'Mara, please don't go.' He stood up too, looking uncomfortable.

'I'm not one of your girls, you know,' she said. 'I've told you before. I'm not interested in… in… men like you. We can restore the house, that's fine. But if you think I'm going to fall for some line you've used on a million women, you've got another think coming. I'm not a desperate divorcee. I'm not…' she searched for a phrase, but her mind had gone blank, 'some *fancy woman*,' she ended, lamely.

'Is that what you think? I like you, Mara.' He stood up next to her. 'I was… I don't know, I was being stupid. I'm sorry if I offended you. We're friends – I just… I promise I'll keep it all business from now on.'

Something in her heart fell a little flat at that thought, but she held her chin high and her shoulders back. She wasn't going to let Brian take advantage of her just like Gideon had for all those years. She wasn't going to be a fool for anyone again.

Mara pushed the fact that she had no real idea *who* she was to the back of her mind. She'd work it out, and in the meantime, she had to keep things strictly professional with Brian Oakley. There were years and years ahead of her to fall for someone, if that was indeed something she even wanted.

'Fine.' She held out her hand awkwardly, and he shook it.

'Friends, and business partners,' she replied curtly. 'You know, I'm not comfortable with you doing this work without a formal agreement. I'll have my solicitor draw something up. Just so we know where we are. Now that I have one, I might as well use her.' She met his eyes assertively. 'I don't need any more drama in my life right now.'

'All right, then,' he said. 'We'll do it your way. I just want you to be comfortable with this. And in the meantime, I'll start costing up the repair and we can work out budgets, order of work for the rest of it, that kind of thing.'

'All right.' Now she felt awkward but was unsure what to do about it. *It's better this way,* she reassured herself, ignoring that stubborn twinge in her heart that wanted to guarantee her that it wasn't; that the best thing to do right now, before it was too late, would be to walk over to Brian Oakley, take his face in her hands and kiss him hard.

'Well, keep in touch.' She turned away and walked to the car. *If you know anything,* she berated herself furiously, *it's that you have terrible taste in men. This isn't the time, Mara. It really isn't the time to start to have feelings for this man. Not when he's seeing someone else AND seems to be involved with every other girl in town.*

As she drove away slowly, she looked down onto the beach: at the house, almost skeletal against the early November sky. She was glad that it would come back to life again. She just hoped that she too could *live* again one day, not just exist, holding it together, day to day. To live again – to wake up happy in the mornings, perhaps for the first time – that would be something.

Chapter Twenty-One

'So this guy knows what he's doing?' Paul grunted as he stepped carefully backwards, towards his front door. He was at one end of the orange-brown sofa, and Mara held the other. 'Right… right… okay, put it down here.'

They deposited the sofa in the hall – there was just enough room for it. Paul swatted at the dust that flew into the air as the weight of the old chair hit the hallway rug. Mara wiped the sweat from her forehead.

'I think so. Everyone in the village seems to rave about him. You should have done this a long time ago,' she added.

'I guess so.' Paul sat on one of the sofa arms and took a deep breath. 'I mean, you could just sell it. Without the renovations.'

'Paul, you know what little interest the house has had. The condition is just going to get worse over the winter if we don't do it up now. And at least then it'll sell.' She stood with her hands on her hips. He'd called a couple of days ago when she'd been writing and asked her to come over to talk more. He'd phoned late, then apologised for not realising the time. He'd been playing a computer game and suddenly wanted to speak to her.

The story she'd been scribbling in spare moments, here and there, was lengthening, becoming something real. She felt as though she could see it, like a film, and all she was doing was writing it down: it didn't feel like imagination as such, or a conjuring the story out of nowhere, which is what she had always assumed writing would be like. Serafina had loaned her a laptop and Mara had started writing at night in the hotel after the kids went to sleep.

The images nagged at her as she worked and as she warmed up the twins' dinner; as she tested them on their spellings or held their hands while she walked them up to the school gates. And all the time as she wrote, she was thinking about Abby; that somehow, her spirit was caught in Magpie Cove. There were sea birds that circled the old beach house as if it pulled them to it; as if there were some important treasure inside it. The birds didn't want to let the house go; they wouldn't want it knocked down; it was part of their landscape.

And Abby was in that house, as knocked down and ragged as it was. She had lived in it as a child, and Mara knew – knew, deep in her bones – that Abby had unfinished business with it. She didn't know what, but something bound her mother to the beach house. Like the birds circled the house, Abby was still there, walking its creaking boards, and she would walk it until... what? Some kind of resolution was found. Mara had no idea what.

'Well, the thing is... I've agreed with Brian that he'll get half of the sale proceeds when it's done. It's almost without value as it stands. At least after he's put it back to what it was, it'll sell. Maybe for a lot more with the original features put back in,' she explained. She'd had her solicitor draw up the paperwork like she'd said she would. Brian had signed it immediately and handed it back to her with glee. He was already refitting new wooden sash windows he'd made especially and had organised a contractor to come in and repair the electrics. As well as that, he was working round the clock to rebuild parts of walls that were falling down.

He'd shown her pictures of a beach house he'd found online he was basing the new work on. There would be a new stone hearth in the kitchen with a smart black-wood burning stove sitting against the light grey stone and whitewashed wood-panelled walls, a terracotta tiled floor and shiny silver appliances. Even though Brian was now putting in half of the renovation money, it was still more than she'd planned, but he assured her that he could find things at cost price or better – he'd already found the floor tiles at a reclamation yard, and a beautiful old Belfast sink for next to nothing.

As if in a strange kind of universal synergy with what was happening at the beach house, Mara had arrived at Paul's house that day to find he'd stripped off the wallpaper in the lounge and the hall.

'You were right.' He looked at the walls in the hall. Already the house seemed brighter without some of its sad history; stripping it away was like an exorcism. 'This place needs an overhaul. And… I apologise again for being so rude to you, before… well, I suppose it was the shock. Finding out about you and Abby. I didn't know how to feel about it. But none of it was your fault, so I'm sorry about that.'

'It's okay.'

Paul stared at the wall and took in a deep breath.

'Mum and Dad had the adoption papers upstairs, in the wardrobe. I mean, I knew I was adopted, I just never wanted to know any more about it, you know?'

Mara watched his face as he talked. His eyes were Abby's, and it gave her a simultaneous yearning and joy to look at them. Every day Mara searched the faces of the people she walked past in the street or the customers at the café, looking for Abby. When she found someone with the same colour hair or a similar tilt to her head, she stared at them, drinking in that small moment of recognition. She supposed that it was normal to feel that the person you'd lost was still around, that she would walk around a corner at any moment or that she was in the next room. It made her feel odd that Paul, a relative stranger, had Abby's eyes.

'What? You're looking at me funny.' He frowned.

'No, it's just… you have her eyes. It's weird, but nice at the same time.' Mara smiled, though she didn't know how she felt. Half of her wanted to cry, half wanted to hug him, just to be in some kind of closeness to Abby.

'Oh. I didn't know.' He looked uncomfortable.

'What were you saying? About the adoption papers?' Mara prompted him. It was awkward; she didn't want to make him feel bad again.

'Just that her name is on them. Abigail Hughes. She was my mother. Father, unknown.' He looked at his hands in his lap. 'And I never knew her. Now it's too late.' His voice broke. Mara thought briefly – *should I do anything?* She worried that he might not want her near him, but her instinct took over and she climbed over her end of the sofa and made her way unsteadily to where he sat on the edge of the couch.

'Paul. I'm so sorry.' She wrapped him up in a hug and let him cry on her jumper just like she would John or Franny; her hand made circling motions on his back. 'I know. I'm so sad for you too. But at least we have each other now. Okay?'

'Okay.' His voice was muffled; they sat together on the couch, legs scrunched up onto the ancient sofa cushions because there was nowhere to dangle them over the side.

'I listened to the record,' he muttered, blowing his nose.

'What record?'

'The Janis Joplin one. Big Brother and the Holding Company. You said she had it.'

'Oh, right! What did you think?' Mara sat up a little.

'I liked it. Like you said – raw.'

'Yeah.'

'She died really young. Drug overdose. She was twenty-seven,' Paul added.

'Another victim of the Sixties, I guess. So talented, though,' Mara replied. 'You should listen to her other albums. Mum could sing. She had a nice voice. Not like Janis, obviously. But she could carry a tune.'

Paul nodded, thoughtfully.

'What else did she like? What was she like?'

Mara reflected for a moment.

'She was kind most of the time, sometimes impatient. She was young, you've got to remember that. She had me at seventeen, you when she was, what, twenty-one, I think? So even when I was a teenager, she was in her thirties. She liked music. She'd dance sometimes. She was quite spiritual, she read a lot of books about healing and prayer. But she was mostly shy with people. She didn't have boyfriends or anything when I was growing up. I think she'd been scarred by whatever her earlier experiences were.' Mara reflected for a moment. 'She had a lot of sadness in her. She tried her best, but our life was… insular.' She sighed. 'I used to envy kids with real families. Who were loud and opinionated. Messy. We were small, quiet. She was sad. I think a lot of that rubbed off on me.'

'I'm sorry. That was hard.'

'I never knew my grandparents or any family. Not my dad, whoever he was. She never told me that. It was always just her and me. She didn't want me knowing about them. I don't know why.'

'Seems like she was full of secrets.'

'She was. It's something to do with that house – what happened when she was a child there. But I don't know what.' Mara paused, unsure how to describe what she felt about the house. 'It's… haunted, somehow.'

He gave her a look. 'Haunted? Like, ghosts?'

'Not literally. Well, I don't know. It might be. I just meant, secrets, unfinished business, that kind of thing.'

'Ah.' He picked at a piece of wallpaper still stuck to the wall. 'I guess when someone dies with as many unanswered questions as Abby, there's going to be a certain degree of... discoveries, afterwards.'

'I guess. Why were your adoptive parents so awful?' Mara asked again. 'Maybe I can help.'

'You can't help. They're dead, anyway.' He looked around him.

'You can tell me.' She took his hand. 'It might help.'

He sighed.

'They were just terrible people. Dad was an alcoholic. He hit Mum regularly, and me, when I got old enough. Sometimes I wouldn't even need to say anything. You'd just look at him the wrong way and you'd know about it.' He shook his head. 'I have no idea to this day why they even wanted a kid. They fostered some other kids before me – you get money for that. Maybe they didn't understand that you don't get any money for adopting until it was too late.'

'I'm sorry.'

'That's okay. Well, it's not, but you know what I mean.'

'But your mum was good to you?'

He shrugged.

'In the sense that she didn't hit me, sure. I think she was just trying to survive, though. She didn't intervene if he was... you know. She stayed out of the way. For a long time she hardly spoke. It was like she was a ghost. Speaking of them, as we were.'

'Why do you still live in the house? Surely it's got too many bad memories,' Mara said, looking around her. 'You could sell it. Move on.'

'I don't know. I'm just... stuck here,' he said. 'There's no mortgage, like you said.'

'You'd still have no mortgage if you sold it and moved somewhere smaller,' Mara prompted him. He squeezed her hand.

'Maybe. For now, help me make this room look like it isn't 1974?'

'Deal.' She grinned. They were still sitting on the sofa in the hallway. 'What're you going to do with this?' She patted the sofa cushion.

'Leave it outside and hope someone will take it?'

'You can't leave a rotting sofa outside your house.'

'It's not rotting,' Paul remonstrated. 'It's just a bit…'

'Dusty? Smells of cigarettes? May house a family of mice?' Mara interjected. 'Get me my phone. It's in the lounge. You're going to need a skip.'

'Are you serious?' Paul climbed off the sofa and disappeared into the lounge, returning with Mara's phone. 'Someone might buy it. Some vintage furniture enthusiast.'

'Paul. Come on. No one wants this in their house. It's carcinogenic.'

'It's not that bad.' He sniffed it, and then made a face. 'Ugh. Okay, you may have a point.'

'We can do a big clear out. You can easily fill a skip. You'll feel better, I promise.' Mara searched for a local skip hire company and found a number. 'I'm calling it.'

'Fine. Not like I could stop you. You're like the bossiest person I've ever known,' Paul humphed. Mara finished the call and gave Paul a big grin.

'Done! Now, let's get back in there. I've never wallpapered before, so I hope you have.'

Paul laughed.

'Never. But we'll work it out. How hard can it be?'

Chapter Twenty-Two

Mara let out a sigh of pure contentment as she smoothed the pristine new white bed sheets down with her hand and stood back to admire her handiwork.

When she had first seen this room, it had been dank and unloved; the hole in the roof had meant that the filthy, sandy walls dripped with water, and rubbish that had blown in from the beach littered the floor.

Now, after seven weeks of Brian's ministrations – and with the help of a small crew of builders, and an electrician and a plumber, all friends of his – the house had been transformed. It was almost ready to go up for sale again. Mara had invited the agent to come around in a week's time and she and Brian were working frantically at putting the finishing touches on the place.

The master bedroom had been the last room to come together, but now its repaired white-painted walls and a newly laid scrubbed pine wood floor made the space feel clean and fresh, and Brian had replaced the window which looked out over the beach. It was almost Christmas, but Mara had still flung the window open and leaned out to breathe in the cold, salty air. Downstairs, Brian was testing out the new log burner, and the delicious scent of wood smoke gusted in suddenly from outside.

Mara hardly recognised it: what had been a cold, flaking, damp shell was now a cosy haven. Brian had done a thorough job with the weather-proofing and clever new glazing which reduced the sound of the crashing waves outside, but still let in enough sound to be soothing.

Together, they'd chosen warm lighting and simple, stylish brass standard lamps that glowed against the rustic white walls of the lounge. Here and there, Mara had chosen beautiful details: a large oil painting of a choppy sea scene framed in a burnished gold frame that Serafina had loaned her from the café; a pair of tall, ornate candlesticks with thick white candles stood on top of the new mantelpiece, and inside the grate, she had sourced some Moroccan blue-patterned tiles for the main fireplace you saw when you walked into the house.

In the bedroom, she'd continued the mostly white palette, but the new, king-sized bed frame was an ornate dull gold, bought from a local antique dealer. He'd told her it was French. Mara supposed she could see that, in the broad sweep of its curved back and the curlicue design on the headboard. She adored it as soon as she saw it. The sheets were new, thick white cotton, completely plain apart from a small broderie anglaise pattern. The only other adornment in the room was a white pottery bowl full of grey-black pebbles John and Franny had collected from the beach, and golden yellow irises and blue cornflowers on the original fireplace tiles, which both Brian and she had wanted to keep.

Mara stood, looking at the bedroom. It was so beautiful: she wished it was hers, but she had to keep reminding herself that the house was going to be sold. As much as she loved it – the newly painted wooden panelling on the walls, the renovated porch which she'd dressed with a wicker rocker, refreshed hanging baskets trailing winter green leaves – she had to sell it and move on to the next part of her life.

She turned around at the sound of steps on the wooden stairs and smiled as Brian put his head around the door. Mara gestured to the room.

'What do you think?' she asked, shyly. He raised his eyebrows.

'Wow. It looks beautiful, Mara.'

He came to stand beside her, inspecting the finished paintwork, casting his eye appreciatively over the room. He pushed his tousled dark blond hair out of his eyes. He wore a simple dark blue T-shirt and paint-spattered jeans, but Mara felt her stomach flip watching his muscled arm tense and his shirt rise up just enough to show a glimpse of his toned, brown stomach.

'Thank you.' She looked away quickly, not wanting him to see where her eyes had strayed. 'It's really all down to you,' she added. 'I could never have done this without you suggesting we do it together.'

Brian put his arm around her shoulder, casually giving her a squeeze.

'Hey. You've worked as hard as I have; you painted almost all the rooms, found the new furniture and managed to look after the kids at the same time.'

'Actually, they probably think Serafina's their mum now. They spend way more time with her than with me at the moment.' Mara laughed. In fact, Serafina had given her a week's holiday from the café to work on the house full-time to get it ready for sale, and watched the kids as well, with help from Simona, who had taken them up to the farm for a few days and taught them how to milk cows, make holly wreaths and all manner of other farmhouse wonders. Mara suspected that John had his eye on learning to drive the forklift.

Brian's arm stayed around her shoulders. They stood looking at the room in silence for a moment, Mara's laughter fading comfortably. Brian smiled down into her eyes, and she looked up into his, smiling back. His gaze was soft, and Mara knew what she read in them. Her stomach flipped again. Did he really want her, or was this another easy conquest for Brian Oakley, Casanova of Magpie Cove?

The moment lengthened, and the silence became heavy. Mara cleared her throat, unsure of what to do next. She knew what she wanted to do. She wanted to reach her hands up into Brian's hair, touch the back of his neck; she wanted to kiss him and feel his hands around her waist.

'Mara.' Brian's voice was soft, and he pulled her to him gently, so that they stood even closer. As if he had heard her thoughts, his hands found her waist; she drew in a breath, a thrill of excitement flushing her cheeks without warning. Up close, he smelt just a little of the smoke from the wood burner. Her name in his soft, deep voice was more than she could resist. She let go of all her misgivings and surrendered to the moment, closing her eyes as he bent his head and kissed her gently.

Mara hadn't kissed so many men to make her an expert by any means, but when Brian's lips touched hers, she felt a connection she'd never experienced before. It felt so right, so natural, to be kissing him, that part of her wondered how she had ever kissed anyone else. It had never been like this with Gideon – that was for sure. But she didn't want to think about Gideon now. She wouldn't.

Brian's arms wrapped around her as he kissed her gently; she pressed up against him and returned his kiss, feeling an unexpected fierceness take her over. For a moment, Brian seemed to step back, surprised at her response, but after a second he returned the fire in her embrace. Suddenly, they were all over each other. Mara felt all the pent-up anger in her come bubbling up, and the frustration of wanting Brian but not letting herself submit to his flirting. Her body had taken over, and it wanted him. She wanted him. And it was more than that – she needed somebody to hold her, to love her. It had been so long; she craved another person's touch.

They fell onto the bed, kissing, their legs entwined. *Mara, Mara,* Brian repeated her name in between kisses, on sighed breaths as they rolled around on the bed. *Like teenagers,* Mara wondered, though her thoughts were hardly her own. She dove gratefully into the passion that had engulfed her because it meant she didn't have to think at all; she could just follow her body. It knew what she wanted.

Brian was pulling off his T-shirt, and Mara fumbled with the catches on her dungarees. She pushed them off impatiently and caught Brian's eye.

'What?' he gasped.

'Wait. Are you still with Petra?' she asked. Her heart fell at the thought; she couldn't be with Brian like this if he was still involved with someone else. She'd kissed him without thinking.

'Don't worry about that. We're not seeing each other anymore.' His eyes travelled hungrily over her.

'Oh. Right.'

He sat at the end of the bed with an odd expression.

'What?' she asked, breathlessly. 'You want me to put these back on?'

'No, no, I… I'm very into the dungarees off thing. I just… I don't know, is this happening too fast for you? I don't want to push you… You know.'

He looked so delicious, bare-chested and propped up on one shoulder on the bed that Mara paused to drink in the sight for a moment. Normal life could wait. Everything could wait, and suddenly nothing was going too fast for her.

'You're not pushing me to do anything.' She pulled off her white T-shirt and he took in a deep breath, then pulled her to him and kissed her deeply.

'Okay,' he breathed, and Mara closed her eyes in bliss as his kisses traced the line of her neck. 'I've wanted you for so long, Mara. So long,' he murmured, as he caressed her. His warm hands travelled lower, and she took in a deep, delicious breath as she felt them on her breasts, her hips. Time slowed, and neither of them noticed as the winter sun set over the calm sea, and night came.

Chapter Twenty-Three

Gideon opened the front door to Mara's old family home in St Ives abruptly; she jumped at the loud creak of the hinges. Once, she would have expected it, but she realised with some shock that the house not only wasn't hers anymore, but that she didn't think of it as such. She'd lived here for eleven years. Called it home, thought of it as home, opened letters addressed to her past self in the hall, carried shopping into the kitchen along the long hallway. She had been pregnant here, climbed the stairs in those late days, sciatica in her legs and the weight of the twins in her swollen ankles. She had played games of hide and seek here, hosted parties for Gideon's work friends who talked to her like she was an idiot while they ate the food she'd made for them; she'd baked birthday cakes and chocolate chip cookies, sung songs, done all the right things.

She took a deep breath in: it smelt different. Blank, impersonal. She had always liked to keep a scented candle near the door, a scent diffuser, perhaps some cut flowers. But now, though it was tidy – Gideon had obviously kept their cleaner, Marcella, on – it didn't feel like a home for anyone.

He embraced her stiffly, and the unexpected closeness of his perfectly shaved neck to her cheek made her recoil. Her breath, carefully measured as she'd stood at the door, grew light and fast.

'You're looking well, Mara,' he murmured before he let her go. Discomfited, she looked around her. She coughed; she started to feel lightheaded and made herself take in some deep breaths: *in through the nose, out through the mouth, in, out.*

Why was she even here? He'd called the night before, and she'd really wanted to refuse to come around at the late notice, but it just happened to be a night that Serafina had offered to take the children so that Mara could work on the beach house. Serafina had also dropped a few heavy hints about her spending so much time with Brian, but Mara hadn't given her any details. It was reasonable: they had a house to flip.

It was too soon to talk about whatever was happening with Brian. Last night, they'd made love again in the big white bed, up under the eaves, with the window slightly open and the sea crashing outside. And it *was* making love: this wasn't casual for her, and she was pretty sure it wasn't for him, either. She found herself thinking about a future with him in it. Watching sunsets. Dancing in the kitchen, drinking wine, eating dinner, laughing. Growing old together.

I'm out of control, she thought, and she knew she shouldn't think of it as anything other than it was, *just sex, that's all it was,* all it could ever be with a man like Brian Oakley. Yet there was a nagging voice at the back of her mind that said, *But what if – what if this is different, what if I'm different, what if I'm the one that changes a man like that. What if he isn't what I think he is?*

It was emotional suicide, thinking that way, though. She knew it; she'd watched enough daytime TV. Love rats never changed. Playboys. Womanisers. He'd admitted as much to her last night. They'd been lying naked next to each other, afterwards. She'd asked him, *How many women have you been with?* He'd rolled over to look at her solemnly. *Why is it important?*

It's important to me, she'd replied, returning her stare.

I'm not a monk, if that's what you want to know. I don't know. Somewhere between one and more than one.

She followed Gideon into the kitchen. So many times she had been out of breath in this house, for no reason other than

Gideon kept her off-balance, kept her searching for the thread of what she'd been going to say in response to something, but he had already moved on, moved the goalposts of whatever discussion-entering-an-argument it was. The panic had got to her, made her breathless. She had even gone to the doctor about it, and he'd told her to do relaxation exercises. Did she have a stressful job? *No,* she'd replied, her knuckles white, gripping the edge of doctor's couch. *Not at all.*

How many times until I can't breathe anymore? she thought as her eyes flickered over the kids' school photos on the wall: their carefully chosen frames, harmonious with the tasteful wallpaper. Nothing too showy, but carefully expensive, so that visitors would know as soon as they walked in that Gideon had money. And it was Gideon's money. Not theirs. Never theirs.

'Drink?' He held up a wine glass. A bottle of chilled Pinot Grigio was open on the marble island. Gideon sat comfortably on one of the six chrome high-bar stools that stood at perfectly spaced intervals around it. He wore a pinstripe business suit; baby blue shirt, cufflinks. His shoes were still on, but he'd taken off his tie and unbuttoned his top button.

Other women had often told her how lucky she was to have found such an attractive husband. Mara regarded him dispassionately now. Gideon was conventionally good-looking. His brown eyes appeared soft because of his naturally long eyelashes, and he had the kind of strong chin and pin-up preppy good looks that a lot of women went for, especially down here in Cornwall where an old-school businessman was more of a rarity among the artists and the surfers.

He was one for all the accoutrements: tie pins, pocket handkerchief, matching shoes and briefcases. On the weekends he wore pressed chinos and a monogrammed sweater, or a polo shirt in the summer. She mentally compared him with Brian Oakley, who she'd never seen in anything other than T-shirt and jeans, paint-spattered work clothes or a wetsuit.

But it was the small details that really separated them, if you didn't look at their clothes but their faces. Brian was dark blond, tousled and blue-eyed, where Gideon had that clean-cut businessman look that some people liked. Brian's eyes were patterned with laugh lines where Gideon's were carefully smooth. Brian's smile lit up his face, and he had a naughty twinkle in his eyes that Mara thought of as his *come-to-bed* look. Having been on the receiving end of that look, Mara knew damn well it worked, too.

Gideon had no twinkle; he sometimes had a flat, amused look, which Mara knew wasn't amusement, but a look Gideon used in public to appear affable. Brian made jokes, made her laugh, could be silly and sang along with the radio while he worked – and, Mara had noticed, he sang especially loudly with power ballads and love songs. Gideon enjoyed silence in the house. At parties he played staid classical music or, occasionally, let his hair down with Dire Straits.

'Just a glass of water. I'm driving.' She smiled politely. He wasn't above telling his solicitor that she'd driven home drunk and was therefore an unfit mother.

'Fine.' He went to the cupboard, selected a tumbler and ran it under the cold tap. 'It's good to see you, Mara.' He handed it to her; his fingers met the back of her hand. 'I've missed you.'

As soon as she'd seen his number on her phone, Mara's stomach had clenched, and had stayed that way ever since. She'd come partly because she happened to be free, but really it was to get it over with. She knew that Gideon wouldn't leave her alone until he had what he wanted.

'You said you wanted to talk about the beach house?' She took in a breath and sipped the water. *Wine would have been good, but still.*

'Yes. I talked to the estate agent. She says it hasn't had any good offers.'

'No.' Mara watched his expression which was unexpectedly warm. Something was wrong here. He nodded at her encouragingly. Gideon was never encouraging. She wondered briefly if this was how he was at work, or with Charlotte. Or, as Serafina and Mara both now called her, Miss New Boobs.

'So?'

'So what?' She balled her fist under the table. *If you want this, you're going to have to take it. I'm not giving you anything, you slippery bastard,* she thought, and the thought gave her strength. Since the separation, Gideon seemed to have forgotten that it was his fault. His affair. His betrayal.

'What do you think? About the beach house? If we can't sell it?'

Mara decided to ignore the *we* for a moment. She met his gaze.

'It's looking really good, actually.' She felt herself blushing, uncomfortable talking about Brian, and looked away.

'I see.' She could feel Gideon watching her.

'It's my house, Gideon. I'm going to finish the renovation and then I'm going to sell it. But my solicitor says you don't have any rights to it anyway. So I don't see what there is to talk about.'

'I agree.' He topped up his wine glass.

'You agree?' Mara blinked.

'Of course. I never said otherwise.' He sipped his wine. Mara eyed it carefully, wondering how much he'd had before she got there. It was hard to tell with Gideon; he could drink a lot without it showing.

'But you said…' Mara felt her chest getting tight; she realised she was slipping into her old habit and took in a deep breath and let it out slowly. 'You said you wanted me to sell it quickly so I could afford a house for me and the kids, and if I hadn't done it by the time you got back from your work trip…' She paused, confused. *What was going on?*

'I know what I said, but it was all emotion, Mara. My time away has made me see things more clearly.' Gideon stood up, put his wine glass down and came over to where she stood, on the other side of the kitchen island. He stroked her arm softly.

'Emotion?' Mara couldn't help repeating the word; it sounded so ridiculous.

'Yes. Emotion. I realised I'd made a terrible mistake.' He had lowered his voice, and now his face was close to hers. 'I'm sorry. I know how awful I've been to you. It's just that… I love the kids. You know I do. But you and I had drifted apart and I didn't know how to pull us back together. I've been an idiot.'

'Gideon, what are you saying?' Mara stepped backwards, her heart beating hard in her chest. It wasn't excitement or desire; this was panic. Her hands felt clammy.

'I want you back, Mara. You and the kids. This can all stop now. I've been stupid. I admit it.'

Mara felt as though she was in some kind of odd performance – a puppet show or an amateur dramatics production, or the nightmare she'd had where she'd forgotten her lines in the school play. She stared at Gideon with her mouth open.

'What about Charlotte?' she managed to whisper.

He had the good grace to look embarrassed.

'She was a mistake. You have to forgive me, Mara.'

'A… a mistake?' Mara knew she was repeating him, but she couldn't really take it all in. What was he saying? That all the nights she'd spent crying were for nothing? Uprooting the children from their home was for nothing? The way he'd spoken to her? She felt a righteous anger simmering in her heart; her throat felt thick with all the words she wanted to throw at him.

'Charlotte… she left.' He returned to his wine and sat back down on the bar stool.

'So you thought you'd pick up again with me. Is that it?' Mara put her glass down on the table and shook her head. 'You've got some cheek, Gideon. You made your bed. You lie in it.' She turned to go.

'I'm not going to pretend I'm not in the wrong, Mara. And I know I've hurt you. I know. But I can be better, I promise. I can spend less time away. I can come home to see the kids before bed in the week like you always wanted me to. I miss them. I can... I can be sweeter to you, Mara. I didn't appreciate you when I had you. Please.' His voice broke as he hung his head.

It was so thoroughly out of character that Mara could only watch in amazement as a tear rolled Gideon's cheek.

'Gideon, you must know it's too late. I... I've got a new life. Finally. A life of my own.' She forced the words out. Despite it all, his tears had undone her. She had never seen Gideon cry. But suddenly, here he was, behaving like a human when the kids weren't around, and she didn't know what to do.

She turned away to hide her confusion.

'Please, Mara. Please! If not for me, then for John and Franny. The children shouldn't grow up without a father. You of all people know that. And I am a good dad. I love the twins.'

'I know you do, Gideon. So why did you ask for custody every other weekend? You can have them much more regularly if they mean that much to you. But I'm not coming back.'

'I was... anticipating Charlotte's needs. She – we – wanted quality time together. I was wrong.'

'I'm so sorry to have thrown a spanner into the planning of your convenient life,' Mara replied tersely.

'I know, I know. The twins need me. Children *need* a father,' he repeated. 'You know that. Think about what you're doing to them.'

'What?'

Mara spun around on her heel. Dismay turned into a raging disbelief.

The rage rose up her throat now, and everything that had been suppressed, thick in her throat, came roaring out like the sea in a storm.

'Don't you dare. Don't you *dare* talk to me about our children. You weren't thinking about John and Franny when you were sleeping with your assistant. You didn't have one iota of thought about your children and whether they'd grow up without a father when you threw me and them out of their FAMILY HOME, you lying, self-deluding— I'm sorry you're sad, Gideon. I really am. We were sad too. But you know what? Life moves on. And John and Franny are just fine without you.'

He was staring at her as if she was a total stranger, which, Mara supposed that she was. She certainly hadn't stood up to him like that before either. *I guess I've learnt a few things about myself since I left this house*, she thought, taking in a deep breath and feeling her heart slow back to its normal beat. *I can breathe again. Maybe for the first time in twelve years.*

'You don't mean that,' he stuttered. 'You can't—'

'What did you think, Gideon? That you could ask me here, give me the regretful daddy routine, and everything could just go back to normal?' she shouted. The rage felt good. It felt freeing. But at the same time, behind the rage, there lay a doubt. Gideon was a great father, and Mara knew what it was like to grow up without a dad. It was hard. The twins had missed Gideon terribly, no matter how well they'd adjusted to their new life.

There was also Gideon's money, and everything it bought. The kids had always had a life of after-school activities: horse riding, sailing, rugby, art classes. They had had regular holidays, the latest toys, special tutors if they needed it. They had had every opportunity so far.

Without Gideon, without being part of that family unit, Mara knew all of that would be so much harder for John and Franny to attain. And what kind of mother did it make her if she denied them any single one of those things? Why shouldn't they have those things if they could? And what was a few more years of unhappiness on her part as payment?

'No... I just... I don't know, Mara. I want you and the kids back. That's all.'

She choked back tears, thinking of Brian. The night before she had snuggled up to his chest, his arm lazily around her. The smell of his skin was so perfect – nobody's skin had ever smelt as right as his, not counting the children, who just smelt right to her too. *Like the way you know a good melon*, Serafina said, quoting some old movie or other. For the first time she felt happy, safe, accepted and – perhaps – loved by someone. Someone who was helping her literally rebuild her life. She didn't want to give that up. And who would want to give up the best sex of their life?

Yet, her heart knew. She didn't want to know, but she did. But she wasn't ready to let it go just yet.

She let out a long sigh. Her shoulders slumped.

'Let me think about it, Gideon. Okay?' She met his gaze. There was something in his eyes; not triumph, exactly, but it was his old look. *Did you really think he'd changed?* she asked herself. Perhaps he had, a little. But nobody changed that much in a few months.

If you go back, you go back to everything that made you weak, she thought. *He might be crying now and telling you he wants you. How long until another Charlotte comes along? Another comment that makes you feel small? Another argument, another way to belittle you?*

But the twins. She bit her lip. She loved them so much. She knew she would give away so much more for them. Even more than what Gideon was asking.

'Sure. Think. Take all the time you need,' he offered, his head in his hands.

When they were still together, she would have pecked him on the cheek before she left to go anywhere: it was habit more than anything. Instead, she picked up her coat and handbag and wondered what to say.

'I'll be in touch,' she muttered, and walked out.

Chapter Twenty-Four

'Penny for them.' Serafina deposited two large cake boxes on the counter next to where Mara had been staring into the distance, thinking.

She was biting her nails, wondering how to tell Brian that she was going back to Gideon.

She didn't want to. Of course she didn't. Not for herself.

It was John and Franny, always them. They came first, and Gideon had been right. Did they deserve to be without a father when it was possible for them to have him all the time? No. They deserved everything possible, and Mara knew, deep in her bones, that possibilities were the best thing she could give them. They loved Gideon. And seeing him part-time wasn't the same as living in the same house.

'Oh. It's nothing.' Mara ran her hands over the flaps on the box, knowing by now how to open them and take out the gateaux inside without disturbing their icing. She recognised the six-layer mocha gateau in the first box, and a Black Forest Gateau in the second.

'With you, it's never nothing.' Serafina gave Mara one of her best inquisitive looks. 'Come on. Spill it.'

'Gideon,' Mara breathed.

'Oh, heavens. What's he done now?' Serafina rolled her eyes.

'He wants me back. Us back,' she corrected herself, expertly sliding the mocha gateau onto one of Serafina's cake display plates and undoing the protective plastic around the outside. 'He's finished with Charlotte.'

'Finished with Miss New Boobs? You're kidding.'

'I am not kidding.' Mara gave half a smile, despite her mood.

'Wow.' Serafina shook her head. 'I did *not* see that coming.'

'Well. She left him, apparently. Which may have changed his plans somewhat.' Mara raised her eyebrows, concentrating on the cake. She carefully placed a tall glass dome lid over the cake and reached under the counter for another one to display the Black Forest cake.

'Jeez. She spent all his money already, huh?'

'I doubt it. He's probably got a secret vault hidden under the house. Like a bloody Bond villain.'

Serafina laughed. 'My, my, Mara Hughes. You've changed.'

'Have I?' Mara asked. She didn't feel so different, especially after last night. Gideon just expected her to go back to how everything was before, and the scary thing was that she could imagine doing exactly that. She knew how it would go. She knew what to say, how to make herself small again. The old Mara was waiting for her like an old dress. Waiting to be worn again: uncomfortable and horribly comfortable at the same time.

'Yes!' Serafina cackled delightedly. 'The old Mara would never have said something like that. And here you are, bitching about your ex-husband like the best of us. I'm so proud.'

'That's nice,' Mara replied distractedly. 'The thing is, he's not my ex yet. I have to go back.'

'You *what*?' Serafina stared at her. 'What do you mean, go back? To that idiot? You can't be thinking straight!' The café was busy: it was a Saturday morning and the December sun was bright. Mara felt several sets of eyes turn on her.

'Serafina, please,' she murmured, and turned her back to the counter.

'I thought… Mara, you can't go back to him. Why would you go back? Not now! You've come so far!' her friend exclaimed.

She looked up at the customers who were not-so-subtly listening in. 'Hey. Private conversation. Eat your cake.' She flapped her hands at the people sitting at the counter and beckoned to Mara to come with her into the kitchenette.

'What happened? I don't understand why you'd consider that.' Serafina folded her arms over her chest anxiously.

Mara chewed the inside of her cheek, wanting to explain, but not knowing where to start.

'Is it the kids?' Serafina asked, and tears welled up in Mara's eyes. She nodded, unable to speak.

'Oh, sweetie.' Serafina enfolded her in a hug. 'They'll be okay. They've been so happy just with you. You can give them everything they need: love, laughter, hugs. A place to live, when you sell the beach house. Anyway, they'll still see him. You can get shared custody.'

'I know.' Mara snuffled into her friend's shoulder. 'But it's everything I can't give them. It's the… stuff that comes with being the 2.4 children family. You know. The chocolate-spread family.'

It was hard to explain. Mara felt her throat close up with emotion, but what she wanted to say was: *When Franny's concentrating on her maths homework, I want her to know that she can go to medical school. When John sits on the sofa with his favourite coloured pencils and disappears into his own little world, I want to be able to assure him that, one day, he can go to art college if he wants to. And that, hey, a friend of your daddy's has a space at his magazine or his design studio for when you want to get some work experience. And when the other kids go on ski trips, I don't want them to be the ones that miss out because I can't afford it.*

She knew it sounded terrible, on one hand: so many children would never have those opportunities anyway. And she knew that John and Franny would have good lives, regardless. She'd raise them right. She loved them so much that it felt her heart would burst every day when she saw their beautiful faces. And there was every likelihood that Gideon would still fund those things for the twins – but what if another Charlotte came along? Worse, what if a new Charlotte came along and wanted to start a new family with Gideon? John and Franny would get pushed aside.

Mara had known a life without privilege, and though she and Abby had managed, just managing wasn't what she wanted for her children. Having a baby so young meant Abby hadn't ever had the time – or the support, having left her family – to get an education and build a career for herself. And Mara, shy as a child, had had none of the money or connections Gideon took for granted. She'd done all right at school, and got loans to go to university which Gideon had paid off when they got married. She and Gideon had met at her first job. He was the boss' nephew and destined for great things. She was a junior secretary, at a time when they were secretaries *and not bloody Executive Shag-when-you-like Assistants*, she thought angrily, and on her third week at the job, he'd asked her out. At the time, she couldn't believe her luck. In that way, she supposed, she hadn't been that different to Charlotte after all.

'I want the best for John and Franny. Not just what I can give them,' she snuffled, blowing her nose on a paper serviette Serafina handed her. 'He's right. I can't deny them their father.'

Serafina looked unimpressed.

'He was awful to you, Mara. Okay, he's a great dad. But at some point, the kids are going to notice how he talks to you. It sets an example. Is that how you want John to talk to women when he grows up? Is that what you want Franny to think love looks like?'

'I know. But he says he'll change.' Mara heard herself saying it and couldn't even believe the words coming out of her own mouth.

'I think we both know that's horseshit.' Serafina placed both of her hands on Mara's shoulders and held her at arm's length, looking into her eyes. 'Believe in yourself, Mara. You're a fantastic mother to those kids. They don't lack for love, and in terms of their futures, they'll make that for themselves. Kids will do whatever they want to, regardless of how many horse-riding classes and trips to the South of France you inflict on them. My kids? One of them manages a hedge fund. The other one's been backpacking for the past six years. They both went to the same schools. State schools, by the way. Couldn't be more different. They did fine, because I always made them believe they could achieve whatever they set their minds on. Same for John and Franny.'

'I know that's true. I do. But…'

'You didn't have it, growing up. The money.' Serafina paused thoughtfully. 'I know. But it's not everything, Believe me.' Her friend looked thoughtful for a minute. 'I had it, you know. Once. I grew up like that. Pony club. Golf club. Cars, exclusive holidays, gated communities. Didn't make me happy, though – and my parents certainly weren't happy. My dad, bless him, died of liver disease at sixty. He was an alcoholic.'

'Oh, no. I'm sorry.' Mara took her friend's hand in hers and squeezed it. 'What about your mum? You never talk about your family.'

'It's okay. Oh, she's terrorising the staff in an exclusive care home not far from here. I go and see her sometimes, but she doesn't recognise me anymore. I only found happiness with Trevor. Gave it all up for him.' She chuckled dryly. 'Mama and Papa didn't agree with me falling for a Jamaican car mechanic. Never mind raising two mixed-race children.' She raised an eyebrow. 'They were different times, to some extent. But this isn't about me. It's about you. What I want you to know is that their life didn't bring them joy. And you know if you go back to Gideon, it won't bring you any joy either. You know that.'

'I just… it's hard to explain. I feel like if I don't give it a try, then I won't be doing the right thing. I won't be fair to the kids.'

Mara looked into the café. A line was forming at the counter. 'We have to go back.'

Serafina waved her hand.

'They'll wait.' She shook her head. 'I just want you to be really sure about this, Mara. Because everything you've told me about Gideon is a flashing red light. That man will not bring you joy. And do you really want John and Franny growing up, thinking that's what marriage looks like? Hiding in the background, in your *Stepford Wives* dress and pinny? I don't think so.'

Mara pursed her mouth. It was uncomfortable, but true. She didn't want to admit it about herself. And she didn't want to think about herself like that either.

'And what about Brian?' Serafina pressed her further. 'I know something's going on. He really likes you.'

Mara's heart ached.

'I don't know,' she muttered. 'It's just… we've slept together a few times. I doubt it means much to him.' She knew it was a lie as soon as she said it. She'd seen his eyes when they made love. There was desire there, but there was tenderness too. She had always assumed it was something that only happened in films. It wasn't real. Or, if it was real, it didn't last.

'Mara, I've seen the way he looks at you. Why can't you believe he likes you? I mean, *really* likes you. It's obvious. He's not seeing Petra anymore either.'

'I know. He told me.'

'So?'

'So, that doesn't mean he has real feelings for me. And I don't know what happened between them – she might have finished with him and I'm just a distraction.' Mara wanted to believe that Brian cared, but also Serafina was such a romantic. She was forever matchmaking people in Magpie Cove.

'Oh, you're impossible! Mara, what about the beach house?' Serafina followed her back out behind the counter, where Mara started taking orders, smiling apologetically at the people in the queue.

'I don't want to talk about this right now,' Mara said out of the corner of her mouth. Serafina started the coffee beans in the grinder and set the milk to steam.

'So, what? You're going to go down there and tell Brian about Gideon?'

'I have to,' Mara replied, trying to concentrate on what people were saying to her. *A cheese and ham panini, two chocolate muffins, three slices of the Victoria sponge, two teas, three lattes.* Details were easier to concentrate on.

'He has feelings, you know. And I know you do. For him,' Serafina hissed.

'I do not. He's nice, that's all!' Mara argued, knowing that she was being disingenuous – normally, people didn't have mad, passionate sex with people just because they were nice – but she didn't want to be open about her feelings for Brian. She hadn't even admitted to herself how she felt about him, never mind anyone else. 'And it's a business arrangement, anyway. If it got a bit messy, then all the more reason to… to… re-establish boundaries.' Mara handed a woman her change and waited for the next customer in line.

Serafina came to the counter and handed various coffees to the waiting customers with practised ease.

'The boundaries you should be establishing are the ones with your cheating, manipulative, cold-hearted ex-husband,' she told Mara sternly. 'Not with the man who's made you smile more times in the last weeks than I bet you have in years. Just think about that before you do anything rash,' she warned, and reached around Mara for a hug. 'Abby's not here to tell you this, so I'm telling you, okay? Listen to someone who knows.'

'I know. I have. But I've decided. And…' Mara put her hand into her pocket and placed an envelope on the counter. 'I'm giving you my notice. There's no point driving here every day and having the kids in after-school club if they don't have to be.' She tried to breathe steadily, but tension clenched at her stomach. It was horrible doing this. Serafina had been nothing but helpful and supportive. 'Please, Serafina. I know what you think. But I have to do it. Okay?' She imagined Annie Edson Taylor walking resolutely to the top of Niagara Falls, where the barrel waited for her. *Over I go,* she thought. *Win or lose. Live or die. I have to do it.*

Serafina picked up the envelope, a pained look on her face.

'Mara, is this really what you want?' She put the envelope in her pocket without opening it. 'I'll hang onto this for a while. Think about it some more. I'm begging you.' Serafina hugged her again. 'And in a week, if you still feel the same, then, fine. I'll probably need you to work two weeks' notice.'

Mara accepted the hug and rested her head on her friend's shoulder.

'Of course.'

Now, at least that horrible part of her day was done, and there was only one more awful conversation left to have. Her heart sank when she thought of telling Brian about Gideon, but she still knew it was the only thing she could do.

Chapter Twenty-Five

'When did you decide?' Brian stood on the new porch of the beach house, gazing at her like a confused child. He held a spirit level in one hand which dropped, forgotten, to his side.

'Last week. I'm sorry,' Mara replied. She had looked him in the eye when she told him: it was the least she could do, she felt, and, anyway, she was allowed to go back to Gideon. She hadn't promised Brian Oakley anything. But she still felt awful, especially standing on the newly refurbished porch on which Brian had added an upcycled white painted wooden rocking chair, angled perfectly so that she could sit in it and look out over the side of the beach where shingle gave way to white sand. There was even a reclaimed dining table and chairs that sat on the porch, as if a family lived there. As if they would all sit down happily for dinner later: Brian, Mara, the twins. Only, that was a family that could never be.

'When did you see him?' He was frowning. 'After we…?'

'The night after. He was back from his work trip. He called and said it was important.'

It sounded pathetic, that she would go to Gideon as soon as he asked her to. Mara wanted to explain, that with Gideon, things only got worse if you made him wait. That she had wanted to get it over with, and then he'd dropped the bomb on her that he wanted to get back together. But Brian turned his back on her and stood staring at the front door of the beach house, the spirit level in one fist.

'The night after we… were together,' he said, flatly. 'I thought that meant something to you.'

'It did.' She tried to explain. 'We didn't… it's not like that. Between me and Gideon.' As if she could compare making love with Brian with anything she'd ever done with him. But it seemed too intimate to say that; if she tried to explain, it felt like it would make it worse.

'Well, what is it like, then?' He turned around and she saw how hurt he looked. 'Mara, we've got this whole house… I thought… I don't know. I thought you could see a future with me. I never said it, but…. Maybe I *should* have said something.'

'I'm sorry.' She repeated. 'It's not you. I just have to do this.'

'Why? I don't understand. He left you!' Brian kicked the top wooden step that led up to the porch from the beach.

'I just have to, okay? Please don't make me explain,' Mara begged.

'Don't make you explain? I think it's fair to want an explanation!' he shouted. Mara felt her own heart break a little more. They stood there in silence.

'Fine. What about this place, then?' He wouldn't look at her. 'We agreed. Half and half.'

'I know we did. That's still the agreement. Nothing has changed,' she said, and he laughed nastily.

'Of course it hasn't. How silly of me.'

'Brian, don't be like that,' she pleaded, then caught her tone. *No,* she thought. *You don't have to plead.* 'Well, actually, you can be however you like. I expect the work to be finished and it'll still go on the market next week. My intentions are still the same when it comes to the sale. You don't have to worry.'

'Well, I'm *so relieved* nothing has changed,' he repeated her sarcastically, and Mara took in a breath. It was exactly what Gideon would have said, in exactly Gideon's tone. She felt the sand shift under her feet. Was this who Brian was, all along? Was this who he would have become, sooner or later? In which case she was better off knowing it now.

She stepped down, off the porch and onto the sand. Unlike the sunny day before at the café, today it was grey, and a light drizzle made her hair wet. Franny ran up to her to give her a handful of shells.

'Thanks, darling.' Mara was grateful to have somewhere else to look.

'Can I give them to Daddy tomorrow?' Franny asked guilelessly; Mara had told the children they were moving back home. They were happy at the thought of having their own rooms again, but Franny had said, *In a way, I'm going to miss the hotel, Mummy.* Mara knew what she meant. The hotel, while basic and cramped, had been theirs. A kind of sanctuary. It wasn't much, but it had been her space to think. She'd written most of a book there. Could she say that about her years at her sparkling house in Cedars Avenue?

'Of course,' Mara replied, instead. 'Go and get your brother. We have to do some things in town.' There weren't really things to do – Magpie Cove was mostly closed on a Sunday, but it was a chance to get away from Brian. She didn't know what else to say, and she wasn't going to give him any more of an opportunity to be crappy to her.

'Mara…' Brian sighed, but she smiled brightly.

'No. It's fine. I think it's best if I go.'

'Please don't. I'm sorry. It's just a shock. Please, stay and talk. I'll make tea.'

But she shook her head. This was already too hard, and staying would only make it harder.

'I've got to go. I'll call you in a few days about the house. Keep you updated.'

'Please.' He looked crestfallen.

'I can't, Brian. Okay? I can't anymore.' She felt her voice wobble and her eyes brim with tears.

'Okay.' He looked away from her. 'I'll see you around.'

Mara returned his nod and walked to where the sea met the shore; John stood there, skipping stones.

'Did you break friends with Brian?' He looked up, his face pale against the darkening sea. 'He looks sad.'

Mara looked back at the beach house. Brian stood with his back to them again, but she could read the dejection in his body language as well as John could.

She didn't know what to say, so hugged John tight.

'I guess we did break friends, sweetheart.' She kissed his head and waved at Franny.

'Franny's gonna be angry. She loves Brian,' John lamented. 'She was hoping you'd get married.'

Mara laughed abruptly, shocked by the suggestion.

'Oh. Well, I don't think that's likely, I'm afraid,' she replied, trying to keep her voice bright. 'Come on. Let's head off.'

'She also thinks we're going to live in the beach house,' John continued, as they walked up to the car, Franny racing to catch them up. Mara heard her calling goodbye to Brian. 'I told her it was going to get sold, but she doesn't believe me.'

'Hmm. I guess it's hard to change your sister's mind about anything,' Mara observed, steeling herself not to look back. Sadness washed over her again. What was she doing? She was finally starting to be happy. Why throw it all away?

For the twins. It's all for them, she thought. *I can do this. I'm strong.*

They got to the car and climbed in. Franny launched herself into the back seat with her brother.

'Brian looks sad,' she reported.

'Mum and Brian broke friends,' John informed her, gravely. Franny kicked the back of her mother's seat in annoyance.

'Ugh. I can't believe it! Mum! Brian's really nice. You're so stupid,' she huffed.

'Frances Thorne! Apologise!' Mara shouted at her daughter, her emotions getting the better of her. 'You will never call me stupid! I am your mother! I am an adult and you are a child, and I will choose who I am and am not friends with!'

Franny recoiled, shocked. Mara never usually lost her temper. 'Sorry,' she muttered, and started to cry. 'But I like Brian!'

Franny had loved him ever since he saved her on the beach that day, Mara knew. She sighed and rested her head on the steering wheel for a moment while she composed herself, then got out of her seat and went to Franny, undid her seatbelt and gave her a huge hug.

'I know,' Mara whispered. Franny started to cry in earnest, and Mara held them both. 'I know,' she repeated, her heart breaking, deeper and deeper.

Chapter Twenty-Six

Mara's old house in St Ives felt alien to her now.

It had felt odd before, when she visited, but now that she and the kids had moved back in, Mara felt unmoored from reality. Not least because Gideon was acting like nothing had happened. They'd come back the night before: there was no point in delaying anything. This morning, he'd gone off to work at his usual six thirty, leaving her with a peck on the forehead. She hadn't really slept. The bed felt wrong.

Did you sleep with her in these sheets? Mara wondered, as she rubbed their familiar thickness between her fingers. Had they even been laundered since she'd left? She assumed so, but who had been here to wash, dry and press them? Marcella didn't do laundry.

After Mara heard the front door close, she screwed up her eyes and rolled into a ball in the bed. Why was she here again? *For the children, for the children*, she reminded herself, biting the inside of her cheek. In her almost-sleep she'd seen half-dreams sweep across her eyelids like an old-fashioned sepia film: Brian holding her hand as they lay in bed, listening to the sea on the shore. In the dream, her telling him, *I love you, please don't ever let this end – please.* Remembering them, she wanted to fade back inside their happiness.

Yet, here they were. Mara rolled out of bed and made herself stand up and open her eyes. She would be a good wife. She would make this work. The children would be happy. She would try her hardest. And she would keep her dreams to herself.

After dropping the children at school, walking them in to the class and then having a patronising meeting with the interfering headmistress, who spoke in woolly terms about 'family values' and 'the virtues of unity', she drove to Magpie Cove. Gideon had seemed surprised she'd found a job, and had raised an eyebrow when she'd explained that she'd given in her notice and was working her final two weeks at the café.

After work, she went to the beach house. It was sale week, and Brian had finished all his jobs. She intended to do some artful dressing here and there and give the place some finishing touches.

She knew he wouldn't be there, and she was relieved. She didn't want to face him, though that was difficult. They'd have to see each other, but she wanted to minimise contact as much as possible. She didn't want to hurt Brian any more than she had to, and, if she was being honest, she didn't want to hurt herself either. Seeing Brian would be hard. She packed away the *why* it would be hard for another time: she was used to closing her emotions in a box and slamming down the lid.

Instead, Mara busied herself in the beach house, unpacking a box of accessories she'd ordered online and admiring them: a Turkish-style woven rug in washed-out blue and brown tones for the floor of the sitting room, a few cushions that matched the clean whites and gentle blues of the decor. She arranged the dining table outside with two bronze storm lamps with thick cream candles inside, and strung twinkly fairy lights up the wooden columns.

She folded up a warm tartan blanket on the seat of the rocking chair, then stood with her hand on the back of the chair, gazing out at the sea. It was a chilly December evening, but the forecast said that the weather was going to be bright all week. The heavens were smiling on them for the sale, it seemed, but Mara still felt sad. She wanted to keep the house, but there was no way of doing that now, not with the investment Brian had put into the renovations. It was all his own money, and he'd taken the risk as much as she had. There was no way that she could ask Gideon to pay Brian what she owed him; he would never do that. It had to sell, and now, it looked like it would. The estate agent had been in touch and said she had plenty of keen buyers ready to view it: she'd start bringing people around the next day.

Upstairs, in the master bedroom, she stared at the bed. It had been washed and remade – by Brian, presumably. She ran her flat palm over the white sheets and returned, in her mind's eye, to the last time she had been here.

No. She couldn't think about that now.

The wardrobe door was slightly ajar; she went to close it, but there was something blocking the way. She tried to push the door closed, but it wouldn't go all the way.

Mara opened the door and saw that the problem was a cardboard box. She frowned, and squatted down to look at it. Opening the top flaps, she realised as soon as she looked inside that this was the box that had come from Abby's solicitor, and contained the returned letters to Paul. She frowned. Had she even bothered looking at what else was in it? She reached her hand in; there were some random items – a couple of old teddy bears that she assumed had been Abby's. They were, by now, very sorry for themselves. Mara put them aside to take home and repair.

Collected in a scuffed gift box, there were some bits of jewellery Mara remembered Abby wearing from time to time: a handmade glass-bead necklace, a brooch with some of its diamante chips missing. There was a school pin with the school crest and motto: *Sine labore nihil*. Mara racked her brain, trying to remember her schoolgirl Latin: something along the lines of *nothing without work*.

She pursed her mouth, sadly. What had Abby's hard work done for her, in the end? It broke her heart when she thought about Abby's careful scrimping and saving. She had still died with more or less nothing apart from this house – this broken-down, damp house that it had taken so much effort to rebuild. Mara had been at her mother's bedside as she died, but there had been no one else. All her life, Abby had avoided being loved by anyone apart from her daughter.

Mara had begged her, once she was in her teens, to at least be open to the idea of meeting someone. If Abby had had a boyfriend, even a husband, Mara would have worried less about her; the pressure would be off her as sole carer, sole source of love. She so wanted Abby to be happy. She wanted someone to look after her, to cherish her mother. And yes, though it wasn't the most important thing, perhaps someone to help with a bill here and there, perhaps even take Abby on holiday. Nothing earth-shattering, not a millionaire boyfriend or caviar for dinner and champagne in the fridge. Mara loved her mother: she just wanted Abby to have what everyone else seemed to have.

The normal things. She had always felt like a freak, growing up without the normal things. Without holidays, even cheap ones to the seaside with vouchers from the newspaper like the neighbours. Without chocolate bars, except for a treat. Without new clothes, only hand-me-downs from the neighbours or clothes from jumble sales. Books, they had borrowed from the library. Mara was a frequent visitor.

Mara had found someone with money and connections. Gideon might be cold to her sometimes, but, nevertheless, she had the normal things. John and Franny had the normal things, and more. Her children had never wanted for anything, and Mara valued that. The fact that she herself had never wanted for love, affection and belief from Abby was something she pushed to the back of her mind. John and Franny had the normal things, and that was all that mattered. The fact that their mother regularly fantasised about plummeting to her death in a barrel over Niagara Falls was, maybe, not something to think too hard about.

At the bottom of the box, her hand closed around something, and she brought it out. She turned it over in her palm. It was a pink plastic-covered notebook, plain on the outside. It had seen some wear. Mara opened the cover curiously.

Inside, Abby's handwriting covered page after page. Here and there, ink blobs obscured words. There were pages where Abby had scribbled things out, written in scrawled capitals. Some pages looked as though they had been ripped out.

Mara's eyes widened as she realised what she had. Looking through the pages, she saw dates. The entries seemed to cover a number of months from 1979 to 1980. She had been born in 1981, when Abby was eighteen. The last pages were written less than a year before.

Mara sat down on the wooden floorboards with her back against the wall and started reading. The first few pages made her smile; they were the diary of a typical sixteen-year-old – boys Abby had a crush on, arguments with her friends, sleepovers and stolen cigarettes. On one page, Abby would swear that Peggy was her best friend in all the world, and on the next, it was Simona. Mara traced over Simona's name in her mother's handwriting with her finger. She would have to show Simona these; she thought for a moment how thrilled her friend would be to see them.

But then, something changed. Towards the end of the book, Abby's diary entries grew more sparse. And on one page, she had written:

They can't know. They already assume I sleep around. Their words. They would never believe me.

Mara frowned and turned back to the pages before, but they were inconclusive. She reread the entry before more closely.

18 July

Family party at the beach house. Ma fixed everything up real nice. Plan is, we'll steal some beers and head off down the beach to get away from the parents. They're so dull, even though they think they're so perfect. Just because Dad runs the bank, he thinks he's the boss of the town.

Mara frowned again and turned the page, but there were several pages ripped out after that. Had something happened at this family party? Why would anyone think that Abby slept around? There didn't seem any mention of sex in the journal at all, never mind with more than one person, and Simona had said Abby never seemed that interested in having a boyfriend…

There was a long gap again in the dates before Abby wrote anything again, and Mara gasped as she read what came next.

I've started to show. I have to go. No way they'll ever listen or understand. I don't know where. Just away. He's everywhere. He cornered me once more after the party and made me do it again, but since then I've been able to avoid him. I'm seventeen now, so I guess I can cope. I'll get a job after the baby comes. Sim would tell me to get rid of it, but I can't. I'm too scared.

If they ever found out, they'd kill me. It would wreck their image in this stupid town – like anyone cares! But people do care very much about their reputations here – especially a certain friend of my dad's. Ugh… the thought of him makes my skin crawl now. I cannot believe he forced himself on

*me. He said I'd been teasing him for months. I don't know
what he means! I hardly even say hello when I see him, he's
always so creepy…*

Abby had scribbled out the rest of the page. Mara looked up
from the book, disgusted. Had someone assaulted Abby at a family
party? It seemed to be someone she knew, she alluded to a friend of
her father. Mara shivered. If that was true, then her own father was
a rapist. How on earth had Abby managed to look her in the face
every day and see him looking back at her in her daughter's eyes?
Mara touched her face self-consciously. What parts of her were his?

She felt sick.

'Oh no.' Mara put her head in her hands. 'Abby, I'm so sorry.'

Reading on, she found Abby's description of the part of
the story she already knew: Abby had run away from home at
seventeen, pregnant, and managed to get a council flat. On the
day after Mara was born, Abby wrote in her diary:

*I am a mum. I will name her Mara, like the sea. It was
never the sea's fault, none of it. It was the thing I loved most
in that house. Listening to the waves at night.*
  I love Mara, despite how she got here.
  I will make sure she never has to see any of those people.
  I will love her like they clearly never loved me.

Mara started to cry. It was so, so sad. 'Abby, why didn't you
tell me?' she sobbed aloud to the room. 'I wish I'd have known. I
wish…' But what she wished for was gone. She wished for Abby
so that she could hug her and tell her it was okay. That she had
been so brave. That she loved her.

Wiping her eyes, Mara read on. Abby wrote in fits and starts,
here and there, in between caring for her new baby. She wrote

that she wanted desperately to see her friends, but that she deliberately avoided it – that she couldn't risk her parents finding out where she was.

Because if they know, then they'll come here to get me, and Dad will tell me it was all my fault, and neither of them will believe me if I tell them who it was that did this. But worse, if they know, then he will know, and he'll come and find me, I know it. And I won't be safe, ever.

And so she was lonely, terribly lonely, in a one-bedroom council flat, where it was baking hot in the summer with windows that didn't open properly and freezing cold in the winter because they didn't close all the way either, and there was no central heating, just an electric fire that Abby could only afford to have on for a few hours a day.

There were a few more diaries in the box. Mara pulled them out and flicked through them. She thought suddenly of Paul. There was a lot here about her young life with Abby, some of which she could dimly remember. But what if there was something here about Paul? Why Abby had given him up?

She looked through the books until she found one with entries dated from 1985.

I'm pregnant. I didn't mean for it to happen, but Dave says he'll stand by me. He'll move in. Maybe we can be a proper family at last? I want that more than anything.

Dave must have been Paul's natural father. Mara scanned the earlier pages in the book for details about a Dave – she had a hazy memory of a man they'd known around that time, but she couldn't remember anything of him. Nothing substantial, just a presence. In 1985 Mara would have been four, coming up for five by the time Paul was born in 1986. She knew that whoever he was, Dave hadn't stuck around. She found the answer to why he left some pages on from the first mention of being pregnant.

He's married. I can't believe it. I'm such a bloody idiot.

He says he's going back to her. Gave me some money for an abortion even though it'd be on the National Health. But I can't have one. I just can't do it, I'm too scared, I've heard horror stories, and I know it's every woman's right to choose and everything, but… Oh, what am I going to do? Please help me. Please. I can't bring up another child alone. It's too hard. I don't have the strength for another baby and we have no money. I only just managed not to go over the edge last time; I truly fear for my sanity this time. I just managed to pull myself out of the pit, and then I get pregnant again…

Mara turned the pages, reading. Tears rolled down her cheeks. Now she knew for sure that she and Paul didn't share a father… and at least Paul's father had been having a relationship with Abby at the time.

Mara asked me why my belly is getting bigger. I didn't know what to say, so I said that I'm growing her a bunny rabbit to have as a pet. I almost cried but I kept it together.

The social services say they'll take the baby away for adoption right after the birth. I never have to see him. They asked if they should take Mara too, if I couldn't cope then maybe I shouldn't have either of them. But I said no. They can't take her. I told them that the baby's father forced himself on me, but that I didn't know who he was, even though it was Mara that happened with – well, partly. I didn't tell

*them about my dark times. If I did, they'd definitely take
Mara too and I can't bear to be alone. They watch you like
a hawk when you're a single mother. Any slip, any mistake,
they're always watching for it.*

*I want to see my baby boy, but I know I can't, or I'll
never let him go. At least they've agreed that as part of the
adoption that I can write to him, so he'll know something
about me. Maybe when he's older, he'll write back? In the
future, I don't know, maybe even they'll agree to let me see
him now and again? It's breaking my heart. My little boy.*

Mara closed the book, a huge weight of grief in her chest. The
tragedy of it was too much to bear. That whoever had adopted
Paul had agreed to Abby being in contact by letter, but that he had
obviously never read them. For whatever reason, Paul's adoptive
parents had – what? Changed their minds? Or never intended
to comply in the first place?

She remembered the rabbit: she called it Snowy, a huge white
rabbit with lop ears they'd had for years. She'd forgotten believing
that Abby had grown it in her tummy, but of course that had
been what Abby had told her: now, she remembered. A lie, a
kind lie, but a constant reminder for Abby of what she'd lost.
Abby always seemed cross and short-tempered after that, and
Mara remembered wondering whether it was because she didn't
like the rabbit. She remembered Abby being sad, but she hadn't
realised the extent of her mother's depression. That she'd hidden it
from the authorities, fearing that Mara would be taken away too.

She shook her head. She could never have given up the twins
– but she'd never had to consider it. She had all the Normal
Things, like a husband, and money, and a roof that didn't leak
and windows that closed and opened like they were supposed to.
She took a deep breath. *Be grateful your life isn't hers,* she thought.

Mara checked the box again: it was empty. She put the books back in the box and stood up, hefting it into her arms.

Abby's diaries didn't belong here. The beach house was a different place now than when she had lived here. It wasn't the place of horror and humiliation her mother would have remembered.

This was a good house now: it had been rebuilt and repainted, John and Franny had played in it, filling it with laughter. Mara and Brian had made love in the bedroom. This was a good place now. These memories couldn't stay here. This house was for someone else now.

Finally, the beach house could start again.

Chapter Twenty-Seven

Mara wrapped a tartan fleece blanket around the twins as they sat on the beach, drinking soup from a flask. The day's viewings had gone well. It was late afternoon and Mara had promised them a beach picnic and, if they promised not to mess anything up, a sleepover in the beach house. Plus, a special surprise. They'd been trying to guess all day: a dog? New bikes? Cookies?

'Hey,' Paul called out as he walked down to where they sat, waving.

'Hi.' Mara waved back. She pointed to Paul.

'That's your surprise,' she told them.

Franny looked nonplussed. 'Is it a delivery man? With a new dog?' she ventured.

'Nice try. No.' Mara laughed. 'Who did I tell you about? Do you remember?'

She stood up as Paul approached. 'Welcome to Magpie Cove. Properly, this time.' She hugged him and turned to the kids. 'So?'

John was quiet, watching Paul, but Franny jumped up, spilling her soup on the sand. 'Is this our uncle? Is it? Uncle Paul?'

'I am. Hello.' Paul smiled awkwardly. Mara had told the twins about Paul a few weeks ago, now that they'd cautiously become friends. She'd helped him throw out lots of old, broken furniture and buy some new stuff as well as redecorate the lounge so that now it was clean and new. They planned to do the hallway next, after she sold the beach house.

'I'm Frances. This is John. We're fraternal twins, which means that Mum made us by releasing two eggs at once, both of which became fertilised by different sperms, which made two zygotes: one was John and one was me.'

'Oh. I see.' Paul nodded seriously.

'We share fifty per cent of our DNA,' Franny added.

'Right.'

'If we were monozygotic twins, we would share up to one hundred per cent of our DNA. Monozygotic means identical twins—'

'And this is John,' Mara interrupted.

'Hi.' John scuffed his toe on the sand, looking away shyly.

'You and Mum probably have fifty per cent of the same DNA too, even though you're half-siblings,' Franny continued.

'Well, that's why I thought we should all get to know each other,' winked Mara. 'Because of the DNA. Have a seat, Paul.'

'Thanks. You didn't say what to bring, so I brought crisps and beer.' He looked blankly at the beer bottles, and then at the twins. 'Sorry, I didn't think…'

'That's OK. We'll have the crisps.' Franny took them from him, opened the large sharing bag expertly and started eating.

'I find it's best to let her get on with it.' Mara laughed at Paul's discomfited expression.

'I can see that. So how did the viewings go?' Paul sat down cross-legged on the picnic blanket and opened a beer.

'Good, I think. The estate agent seemed pleased. I think there were maybe six viewings today, so we'll see. I've promised the kids we can stay here tonight and have a sleepover. It might be sold by Monday.'

'It looks like you've done an amazing job.' Paul stared at the house. 'So strange to think…' he shook his head. 'I still can't get my head around it. This is where she lived.'

'For some of her life.' Mara looked at the house, pensively. 'I can show you where she and I lived. If you want to, some day.'

'I'd like that.' Paul hugged his arms around himself. 'She grew up here, then? Can't have been bad, living on the beach.'

'Um, I guess it was fun when she was younger. But she left when she was seventeen. I never knew about the place at all until she died.'

'Why not? It would have been an amazing thing for you to come here as a kid.'

'I know.' Mara took a deep breath. 'Kids, why don't you go and play for a while? I need to have a talk with Uncle Paul, okay?'

John stood up, picking up his Frisbee.

'Wanna play? After?' he asked Paul, shy again.

'Oh. I'm not very good…' It was obvious Paul hadn't been around kids much, Mara thought; he didn't know how to talk to them.

'John'll teach you, won't you, sweetheart?' She smiled up at her son. 'Ten minutes, okay?'

'Sure. I'm not that good either, but it's just for fun.' John had that way about him of making people feel at ease, even though he was only a kid. She watched as Paul visibly relaxed. Franny scowled at being excluded from the conversation, and took the crisps with her.

'She's a character,' Paul observed, smiling.

'I don't worry about Franny. Well, not until the next time she falls out of a tree or jumps into a pit of quicksand. Freakish injuries aside, she'll be all right in life.' Mara watched as Franny stuffed fistfuls of crisps into her mouth whilst running to catch the Frisbee.

'Won't she choke?' Paul watched his new niece with concern.

'Probably. It's not like I haven't told her a million times. *Franny! Swallow!* Mara shouted at her daughter, who ignored her completely. She shrugged.

'Anyway. I wanted to show you something I found at the house.' She reached into her handbag and passed Paul two of Abby's diaries. 'There are more, which I'll show you, but these are the ones that maybe you need to see first.' She was nervous about this, somehow. She still didn't know Paul that well, and even though Abby's diaries were also about him, it felt like she was telling her mother's secrets.

'What are they?' Paul took them, frowning.

'Two of Abby's diaries. I found them when I was doing my last clean-up of the place. They… they explain why she gave you up.' Mara bit her lip and looked away. 'You should read them.'

Paul looked at the diaries in his hands without saying anything.

'You don't want to read them?' Mara asked, after a pause.

'No, it's just that… I don't know. This is kind of out of the blue.' He frowned. 'I mean, I went all this time not knowing anything about her. All I knew was that I hated her for leaving me. Then you turn up, and then this. It's kind of a lot.'

'I know.'

'What does it say?'

'In the diary?

'Yes. I feel like if I'm prepared, before I read it, it'll be better. Is it bad? Was she…' He avoided Mara's eyes. 'You know. Was she… forced?'

'When she got pregnant with you? No.' Mara watched the twins playing Frisbee for a few moments. 'She was in a relationship with your dad. He was called Dave, but that's all I could find. They were seeing each other – I dimly remember him, actually – but it turned out he was married and he hadn't told her. He went back to his wife when he found out.'

'Oh. Wow. But, what does that mean? That when she was pregnant with you…?'

Mara nodded, unable to say the word.

'It's why she left home. It's strange – it's not what the house means to me at all. For me, it's a new start, you know? It's beautiful in there now. To her, though, it was the place where the worst thing in the world happened.'

'Oh, no.' Paul closed his eyes.

'She was seventeen. She ran away. Cut all ties. Our grandparents must have left her the house, though, when they died. That must mean that she had some contact with them over the years – maybe just before they died, I don't know. She never talked about them to me, anyway. Apparently, she'd started coming down here to stay in the house in the year before she passed.'

'You didn't know?'

'No. She was secretive.' Mara traced the outline of her nails with one finger. 'Right to the end.'

'Uncle Paul, come and play!' Franny ran up to them and held out her hand for Paul's. 'You've been ages. It's getting dark! Then we'll go inside and have hot chocolate. With marshmallows. Mum promised.'

'Okay, I'm coming.' Paul stood up and handed the diaries back to Mara. 'Look, I can't read them. It feels wrong. You can tell me what they say.' He handed them back to Mara. 'I mean, I might be ready to read them one day, but… it's too weird, right now.'

He followed Franny, who beckoned him into their game. John threw the Frisbee; Paul missed the catch. *Life goes on*, Mara thought, watching them. She understood: for Paul, it was a lot to take on board, and she didn't blame him for not wanting to read the diaries. He was like John, she realised. You had to wait for John to come to you – you couldn't force him to do anything he didn't want to. He'd do it in his own time, when he was ready.

It was terrible that Paul had never known Abby. Mara thought about all the ways both of their lives would have been different if they had. He hadn't known Abby, and he hadn't been allowed to say goodbye, either. It was something she would never wish on anyone.

Mara looked up to the darkening sky as something soft and cold settled on her wrist: one, then another. It was snowing.

Chapter Twenty-Eight

'They're asleep, or at least, pretending to be.' Mara sank into the large white sofa she'd chosen for the beach house viewings; it was rented, and she'd draped a red-and-white striped throw over it for the kids to sit on so they didn't get it dirty. 'You can open one of those for me now.' She held out her hand for one of the beer bottles Paul had brought for the picnic.

Paul opened the bottle and handed it to her. Immediately, she was reminded of drinking beer with Brian here, weeks ago, before anything had happened between them. She pushed the thought to the back of her mind.

'I was reading this while you were up there. It's good! Did you write it?' Paul was wearing thick black-rimmed reading glasses, which made him look even geekier than usual. He pointed to her typed manuscript which she'd left on the table earlier, intending to give it a read-through later.

'Yes. It's not much. You know. Just a children's story.'

'It's really good. Have you written anything before?' he asked, picking it up again and leafing through the A4 pages Mara had bound with four heavy duty metal fasteners at the edge.

'Oh, no. Never. I've been writing it on and off at work. At night sometimes. You really liked it?' Mara felt a glow of pride in her heart. No one else had read it, though she had been working up to reading it to the kids.

'I do.' He flicked the pages thoughtfully. 'You know, I know a couple of book industry people. An agent and an editor or two. If you want, I could show it to them?'

'Oh! I don't know. Maybe?' Mara blushed and took a sip of beer. 'I honestly haven't even thought about that. I was doing it for fun, really. And… I don't know. Catharsis? Is that the word? It was a way I could process Mum's death a bit.'

'Lots of writers do that. Probably more people should write their feelings down. Not even in a story or anything, in a notebook somewhere, a poem, whatever. It helps.'

'You've done that?'

Paul looked a little uncomfortable, but nodded. 'My therapist recommended it. It does help.'

'I guess that's another thing we've got in common.' Mara shrugged. 'Well, if you think it's good enough, then yes. Show it to your friends.'

'Great. Can you email me a copy?'

'Errr… okay.' She didn't know what to say. No one had ever taken an interest in anything she'd done for such a long time. There was a companionable silence for a moment.

'Do you think it's going to settle out there?' Paul pointed out of the window where the snow was still coming down.

'Maybe. I hope it doesn't snow too heavily though – there are more viewings next week.' She frowned. 'It's a shame I'm not selling in the summer. It would look really great then.'

'It looks amazing now.' Paul looked around, admiringly. 'Don't you want to keep it? You could live here. The twins obviously love it.'

'I'd love to, but I can't.' Briefly, Mara sketched out the details of her arrangement with Brian.

'Who is this guy again?' Paul gave her an odd look.

'He's the local handyman, kind of. He runs a surf school too.' Mara tried to make her tone light. 'He's been very good, actually. I say handyman, but really he's a carpenter and craftsman. I mean, he made those units over there.'

'Why are you blushing?'

'I'm not.' Mara glared at him.

'You are. Why are you…? Oh, I see.' He raised an eyebrow. 'You like him.'

'I do not!' Mara cried.

'Methinks the lady doth protest too much.' Paul grinned. 'You're separated. If you like him, then you can do something about it.'

'I'm not separated,' Mara mumbled, tipping the beer bottle into her mouth.

'You're what? Not separated? I thought you said your husband slept with his assistant.'

'He did.' Mara smiled too brightly and put the bottle back down on the table.

'And…?' Paul looked confused. 'Sorry, am I missing something?'

'It's complicated, Paul. You wouldn't understand.'

'Try me.' He sat back and fixed her with a quizzical look. 'I've seen my share of weird human behaviour.'

'It's not weird at all. We're doing the responsible thing and staying together. For the twins.' Mara tried to make it sound as though she was happy about what she was saying, but when she thought about having to go back to her old house tomorrow, after the sleepover, she realised she was dreading it.

'The responsible thing…' Paul repeated. 'Wow.'

'What do you mean, wow? I mean, I know it might not be the most exciting thing in the world, but when you have kids, you have to put them first.'

'I see you putting the kids first every minute you're with them, Mara. But making them happy and you being with their father isn't necessarily the same thing. John and Franny love it here, and they love you. Do you really want to stay with him that much? It doesn't seem like it.'

'How do you know?' Mara said, defensively. She wanted to believe that Paul was right, but she was too scared of making the wrong choice.

'It's obvious, in the way you talk about him. I don't need to have met the guy to know you don't love him. And, that you do really like Handyman Guy. Your face lit up like the Millennium Falcon just then when you mentioned him.'

Mara blushed and frowned at Paul. 'Shut up.'

'They were talking about him earlier, when you came in and we were on the beach,' Paul added. Mara had come inside to make the hot chocolate. Franny had insisted that she, John and Paul catch snowflakes on their tongues.

'Were they? What did they say?'

'Something about Gideon always being on his phone. Taking calls and walking away, talking in whispers to mystery people.' Paul looked at her questioningly. 'That's what John said. Franny was running on, you know, talking a mile a minute, then she took a breath and John said, *He never says who's on the phone, he says it's work, but once a lady called him when he was reading to us at bedtime and it was on speakerphone and she called him "darling".*'

'John said that?' Mara felt her heart lurch. If it had been Franny, she would have been less inclined to take it seriously. She always listened to both children, but Franny would quite often make dramatic statements that she absolutely didn't mean, as if she was trying them out for maximum shock value. Sometimes Mara would recognise a line from something Franny had seen on TV (on one memorable occasion, Franny had shouted, *The truth? You can't handle the truth!* at Mara when she'd asked Franny to tell the truth about how permanent marker had got on two of her white cushions). But John, if John had said it, then it was true.

'Yup.' Paul put his beer on the coffee table and reached for her hand. 'Look, Mara. You seem like a good person, and I know you love the twins, so please hear me when I say this. You are not a bad mother if you choose happiness for yourself and them, away from someone who doesn't love you. I know you grew up without a dad, okay? I know that's what's going on here. You think them having Gideon around will make their life better than yours was, just for him being there. But it won't. Abby loved you. You love John and Franny. Your love is more than enough. And he can still see them, anyway.'

'It's not that easy,' Mara argued. 'You don't have kids. You don't understand.'

'No, I don't. But come on, Mara. You're dreading going back home tomorrow. I can see it in your eyes.'

'It's early days, I…' Mara trailed off. 'Fine. You're right. I'm not looking forward to it. But I have to. I have to try.'

Paul shrugged.

'You'll do what you have to do, at the end of the day. If going back to that idiot – and he is an idiot, Mara – if that's what you need to do to get closure, then that's what it is. But let me tell you that my mum – my *adoptive* mum – she stayed with my dad far longer than she should have, and it ruined my childhood. She had her issues, and she wasn't a great parent either. But most of it was because of him.' Paul's voice cracked. 'I wished he'd die. I used to sit up in bed at night, listening to them arguing, and I wished him dead. Is that what you want for John and Franny?'

Mara stared at her hands. She was still mortified about what John had said.

'No, of course not,' she whispered. 'But Gideon's not like your dad was.'

'No. But you don't have to go back to Gideon to make the twins happy. They're happy here. Now.' Paul finished his beer and reached for his coat at the end of the sofa. 'I've said my piece, anyway. Think about it. If you get half of whatever this sells for, it can still give you a good start on a new life.'

'Paul, don't go.' Mara got up, feeling as though the evening had been spoilt. 'I'm sorry.'

'Don't apologise. You haven't done anything wrong.' Paul hugged her, unexpectedly – it was the first time he had showed her any kind of affectionate gesture. 'Just value yourself and your feelings, Mara. Have confidence in yourself. Okay? If therapy has taught me anything, it's that *my feelings are valid.*' He intoned the last four words in a faux-American therapist voice.

'All right,' she conceded. 'I will *value my feelings*. Right now, as soon as you leave. I'll be valuing my feelings for at least the next hour.'

'Good. Don't forget to email me the book, too. This could be the start of something great.'

They hugged again and Paul crunched out onto the snow-covered porch. The whole beach was blanketed in white and lit by the moon. Mara stood there for several minutes, hugging the red-and-white striped throw around her shoulders, watching the snow drift down.

She waved as he got into his car and drove away. Snow made everything look clean and new, but it was always the same as it had been before, underneath. She had the distinct feeling that was exactly what Gideon was offering her: a snowed-over version of the life she'd left – the life that, she realised, she didn't miss one bit.

Mara closed the door, picked up her manuscript and sat down at the wooden dining table. She opened it to the first page and began to read.

Birds Fly Me Home by Mara Hughes, she read, and then the dedication. *For Abby: though once your heart was heavy, now you are made of light.* A tear rolled down Mara's cheek. She sat back in her chair and stared at the ceiling. *Oh, Abby,* she thought. *What would you do if you were me?*

Chapter Twenty-Nine

'But we already had a funeral for Grandma.' Franny tugged at the formal dress Mara had made her wear. 'At the church.'

'I know, but Uncle Paul didn't get to come to that. And we still have Grandma's ashes.'

When she'd brought the kids home from the beach house, she'd suddenly realised that she still had Abby's ashes, and it would be something at least for Paul to be able to scatter them with her. A gesture; a way to make him included somewhere in Abby's story.

Mara held Franny's head still so that she could finish the plait she was halfway through. 'Hold still. It's like trying to dress an octopus.'

'Did you know that octopi are very intelligent creatures? The mimic octopus can change its shape and colour to resemble at least four other creatures. A sea snake, a—'

'Then the octopus is definitely your spirit animal.' Mara frowned as she plaited. 'There. Done.'

'So are we going to put Grandma's ashes in the sea?' Franny asked. 'What do ashes look like? Do they look like ash? Or are there bits of bone in there? Do you think Grandma will know when we've scattered her ashes? Do—'

Mara shushed her daughter. 'Franny, what have we said about asking questions? If you ask a question, wait for the answer.' She walked into the long hallway and knocked timidly on Gideon's office door.

'Gideon? We need to leave in ten minutes!' she called out and opened the door warily. It was the Saturday after they had stayed at the beach house, and Gideon had promised to come to the scattering of Abby's ashes. But when Mara peered around the door, he was on the phone and staring at his laptop. He smiled tightly at her and beckoned her in.

'Tom, can I stop you there for a minute? The missus is haranguing me about something,' he joked. 'Hang on. Yes. One sec.'

Gideon pressed mute on the phone, and his bonhomie disappeared at exactly the same moment. *The missus,* Mara thought in disbelief. And *haranguing? Yes, I'm haranguing you to come to my mother's ash scattering, you bastard.*

'What?' He frowned.

'Mum's ashes. We're going to scatter them at the beach today?' Mara explained patiently.

'Ah. Thing is, Tom's going to need me for quite a while, it turns out.' He made a not-very-apologetic face. 'The case is all over the place. Sorry.'

'But you promised…' Mara stammered. Gideon was still being Good Husband, Gideon 2.0, but she'd noticed the mask slip a few times. A few snarky comments here and there.

'Sorry. I'll see you when you get back.' He returned to the call.

Mara watched him re-animate his face for Tom, his colleague on the other end of the call. It wasn't even a video call, but there was Work Gideon and Home Gideon, and Work Gideon was constructed with fervent attention to detail. Work Gideon was jolly, a team player, generous, a work hard/play hard kind of guy. Home Gideon was fun for the kids – last night, they'd ordered in a Chinese takeaway and eaten it whilst watching a family game show the kids loved, and after that, he'd helped them build a fort out of sheets and pillows in Franny's room. But when it was just the two of them, it was a different story. Mara found herself missing the hotel: its brown curtains and aged furniture had become homely.

Fine. Not like I really wanted you to come, she thought as she shut the door. It was better if it was just her and the kids; then, they could enjoy the day with Paul, Serafina and Simona. Gideon didn't know any of her new friends, and she suspected they wouldn't have much to say to him, knowing what he'd done.

She's considered inviting Brian – he'd got to know Abby a little, after all, in the last months of her life – but it had felt wrong if Gideon was going to be there, and anyway, she wasn't sure what she would say if she saw him. It was all too raw. He'd stopped texting her completely, and though she knew that was probably for the best, she still looked at her phone all the time, wanting a message from him. They were in touch about the house sale, but that was mostly through the agent, Rebecca, who had kindly agreed to update them both separately.

'Okay, kids, let's go.' She ushered the twins downstairs and picked up her bag, and the silver urn that contained Abby's ashes.

'Is Dad coming?' John asked. Something softened in Mara's heart, and she enveloped them both in a hug.

'No,' she murmured, resting her hand on his head for a moment. 'It's just us.'

When they got to the beach at Magpie Cove, Paul was already there, talking to Simona outside the beach house. Mara remembered that Simona had been with her on the day she first met Paul. If you'd asked her then whether she would have invited him to help her scatter her mother's ashes, she would have said definitely not. Life was unpredictable like that.

'Hey.' She gave Simona a hug. Paul shook John's hand a little formally, and then Franny's. 'Hi, Paul. You remember Simona, don't you?'

'Sure. We just said hi.' He smiled at Simona.

'You okay?' Mara asked.

'Yeah. This is weird, but I think, nice too?' He shivered. 'I should have put a warmer coat on, though. Any offers on the house yet?'

'Not yet. Still waiting. Lots of people saw it this week, so, fingers crossed.' She rubbed her hands together. 'It's only a week and a half until Christmas. I hope it sells before. Just so we can go into the holidays with it done, you know?'

'Sure.' Paul rubbed his hands together and put on some gloves.

'What are you doing for Christmas?' Mara wriggled her foot in the sand. 'I mean, if you were available, it might be nice to spend some time together.'

'Did I hear you mention Christmas?' Simona leaned in. 'I was going to ask if you and the twins wanted to come to us, Mara. Paul, you'd be very welcome to come too.'

'Oh, that's really generous, but I don't know. I'd feel a bit strange about it. I mean, we've really only just met…' He frowned.

'Oh, please come, Paul.' Mara squeezed his arm. 'It would be so nice to be together. We'd love to come, Simona. I bet the farm looks amazing at Christmas.' She realised that she hadn't even thought about preparing her usual Christmas at home; Gideon would expect it, now she was back. But the thought of a Christmas at home really didn't compare to a Christmas at the Gordons' farm with her friends and the twins. *I'll cross that bridge when I come to it,* she thought: one of Abby's sayings again.

'It's not bad. I've already had the boys hard at work with the decorations.' Simona grinned. 'You're all welcome, anyway. I've got a table that seats twenty. Will you be bringing hubby, then?' she gave Mara a penetrating gaze.

'I guess so.' Mara shrugged.

Simona raised her eyebrow. 'You sound so enthusiastic.'

'Think about it, at least?' Mara gave Paul a hopeful look; she didn't want to talk about Gideon right now.

'Okay. I'll think about it. Listen, I finished reading your book.' Paul looked at her shyly. 'It's really good. I gave it to my literary agent friend to read. I think she'll really like it.'

'Oh. I don't know how I feel about that.' Mara made a face.

'You didn't want me to? You said it was okay…' Paul looked discomfited.

'No, no, it's fine. I just feel… exposed, that's all. Thanks for being kind about it, anyway.' Mara hugged her arms around her body.

'I'm not being kind. It's genuinely good!' he argued. 'You have a real gift.'

'Oh, well…' Mara was embarrassed. 'I don't know about that.'

Simona leaned in.

'What don't you know?'

'Oh. I… wrote something, but I don't think it's probably that good,' Mara explained.

'What kind of something?' Simona crinkled her eyes as she smiled. 'And you've got to stop talking yourself down, love. I bet it's a lot better than half the rubbish that gets produced nowadays.'

'It's a children's book,' Paul interjected. 'It's brilliant.'

'Anyone seen Serafina?' Mara changed the subject. She wasn't comfortable talking about the book, if she was being honest. It was so personal.

'She's on her way. Said she was bringing champagne,' Simona commented. 'I've invited her for Christmas too, by the way.'

'Great. I guess today is kind of a mini-wake.' It felt wrong to be happy when their task was to scatter ashes. But her friends were here, the kids were happy, and champagne was on the way.

'No Brian?' Simona looked up and down the beach. 'He would have liked to pay his respects, I think.'

'Ah. Well, I thought about it, but…' Mara trailed off. 'Complicated.'

'I bet.' Simona gave her a knowing look. 'Oh, come on, as if I don't know. Serafina told me you two had got close. But you've gone back to your husband? He's not here either. I'm confused.'

'He had to work.' Mara explained. Simona raised a perfectly drawn eyebrow.

'It's a Saturday, love. We're scattering your mother's ashes. Wasn't that more important?'

'You'd think so.'

'So how's that going? Being back with the hubby who isn't here today and you don't really want to bring to my house at Christmas?'

'Ah. It's early days…' Mara began her spiel, then realised she didn't even believe it herself. 'D'you know what? It's going terribly,' she confessed. 'You're right. What kind of man wouldn't be here today? What a mess.'

'Brian would have come. He's split up with Petra, you know.' Simona gave her a look.

'Yeah. I know.' Mara's heart skipped at the mention of Brian.

'The handyman? Oh, he had a girlfriend? When did they split up then?' Paul raised his eyebrow at Mara, who gave him a frowny look.

'Oh, a few weeks back. Petra told Serafina all about it. Brian said he'd found someone else, had fallen in love with someone else and he wanted to give it a real try. That it was the real thing.' Simona nudged Mara with her elbow. 'Then you went and broke his heart and decided to give your crappy husband the benefit of the doubt. Poor fella. He's had a face like a wet Wednesday ever since. Didn't think I'd ever see the day Brian Oakley got his heart broken.'

Serafina appeared at Mara's side, holding a bottle of champagne and some plastic cups.

'Sorry I'm late, I couldn't find the cups.' She kissed Mara on the cheek, then stepped back and frowned. 'Hey. What's up? You look as though you just lost a pound and found a penny.'

'We were just wondering, as Brian Oakley's now single, why he and Mara aren't an item already?' Simona said archly.

'Riiiight.' Serafina pursed her lips. 'Free as a bird, that one. And crazy about you, Mara Hughes.'

'He. Loves. You,' Simona repeated loudly, as if to a deaf person.

'What? No, he doesn't!' Mara dismissed the comment, though the thought made her feel dizzy.

'Oh, come on, babes. You must have known how he felt. It was obvious that you pushed him away, not the other way around.' Simona shook her head. 'I saw how he looked when he talked about you. I saw him in the café at the Halloween party, staring at you like a lovesick calf. Come on, Mara, don't pretend like you would have married him by now if not for Petra. It was never about Petra.'

Mara's phone rang.

'Damn. I forgot to turn it off!' she muttered, hugging her coat around her, happy to have a reason not to reply. She was about to put the phone on silent when she realised it was the estate agent, Rebecca, calling.

It was true. She had pushed Brian away, even though she had known he had ended things with Petra. *But I didn't know that was because he loved me*, she thought, knowing that she was lying to herself. He hadn't said it, but she had known. She had known from the way he touched her, the way he looked at her after they made love.

Nerves jumbled, she answered the call.

'Hi, Mara. Sorry to bother you on a weekend, but I thought you'd want to know as soon as possible. You got an offer for the beach house!'

Mara's heart started to pound again. She turned away from Serafina and Simona and started walking up the beach, careful not to slip on the ice that covered some of the stones.

'Okay...' Mara replied, thinking, *please, please let there be a reasonable offer.* Something decent. Even if she was going to stay with Gideon, it would be good to have something in the bank if he ever pulled a stunt again. She realised that the fact she was even thinking that wasn't a great sign. *Money in the bank. A waterfall-ready barrel in the cupboard, just in case.*

'Well, as you know, we had lots of viewings,' Rebecca continued.

'Uh-huh.' Mara chewed her fingernail, watching the sea churn. Why wasn't Gideon here? He should be here. But the truth was she didn't want him there. She knew who she missed, and it wasn't her husband.

Brian. *Brian loved her?*

'We had three initial offers,' Rebecca continued. 'The lowest bid didn't want to raise their offer, so we went to a bidding war between the other two offers.'

'Okay.' Mara stared at the house. *Brian loved her.* He wanted to be with her, and she'd thrown that away to be with Gideon. *No,* she thought. *That's not what I want. It's not who I want.*

'So I've got the final bids here.'

Rebecca's voice didn't change when she read out the final offer that had been made on the beach house; Mara guessed that in her job, large sums didn't have much meaning.

'Say that again?' Mara coughed, not believing what she'd heard.

Rebecca repeated the exceptionally high number. There was a pause from her end as Mara stared at the sea in disbelief. Never in her wildest dreams would she have expected anyone to offer so much for the beach house, but Brian had done an amazing job. It was a beauty, and now, someone else was going to own it. Her heart ached.

'Er... right.' Mara didn't know what to say. 'Have you spoken to Brian?'

'I wanted to speak to you first, but I can call him now,' Rebecca said. 'Do I have your agreement in accepting the offer, though?'

'Yes,' Mara whispered. This was unbelievable.

'Okay. I'll call him now.' Rebecca's voice twinkled. 'Good job, Mara. I have to say it was a great call getting Brian involved in the refurb. His work really sold the place: so much so, I'm going to talk to him about some other development projects he might be interested in.'

'That's great,' Mara answered woodenly. She felt slightly untethered from her body.

'Speak soon! Congratulations again!' Rebecca hung up.

Mara walked slowly back to her huddle of friends and accepted a cup of champagne from Serafina.

'What is it, Mara? You look terrible.' Her friend looked concerned. 'You okay?'

'We sold the house.' She drank the entire cup of champagne.

'How much?' Paul asked. Mara repeated the offer. He started laughing and picked her up, twirling her around the beach. She started laughing too, still shocked.

'You're free!' he said, setting her back on her feet and giving her a hug. 'That's what that money means, Mara. Freedom.'

Chapter Thirty

Mara spent the whole drive back from Abby's small wake on the beach practising the words she was going to say to Gideon in her mind. *It's over, Gideon. I'm sorry, I tried, but I'm in love with someone else.*

I'm sorry, Gideon, I'm in love with Brian Oakley.

I sold the beach house for a fricking huge amount of money, so I don't even need your money anymore. See ya!

She couldn't imagine saying any of it, but she knew she had to say *something*.

Yet when they got home – the twins were almost feral with hunger, even though they'd eaten a ridiculous number of Serafina's sausage rolls and mini Cornish pasties when they were in Magpie Cove – Gideon was sitting in the lounge with his work colleague Tom, watching football and drinking beer.

'There's my superstars!' Gideon called out as the twins thronged into the lounge, finding new reserves of energy when in the car they'd claimed they were too hungry to move.

'Daddy!' Franny jumped on Gideon's legs, and John sat on the armrest next to him. 'Why didn't you come with us? We scattered Grandma's ashes in the sea and we had sausage rolls.'

'That sounds awesome! Well, sort of, in a respectful-to-Grandma way.' Gideon kissed the top of Franny's head and gave John's arm an affectionate squeeze. 'I had to work. I'm so sorry. Say hi to Tom.'

'Hi, Tom,' the twins chorused obediently.

'Hi, Mara. Tom came round to go over the files here, and we finished up about an hour ago.' Gideon tilted his head around and gave her a polite smile. 'I said he should stay for dinner. Okay with you?'

Great, Mara thought. She could hardly have the conversation she needed to have with Gideon with Tom around. It would have to be later tonight, when the kids were in bed and hopefully Tom had gone.

'Sure,' she answered instead, and walked into her gleaming kitchen. She started pulling out ingredients to make fajitas, which she had promised the kids in the car.

'Hey…' Gideon walked into the kitchen, carrying two empty beer bottles, and added them to the recycling bin. 'How was today? Sorry I couldn't make it.'

'That's okay. It was good, thanks. Paul came.'

Gideon came to stand behind her and touched her waist lightly. 'Want some help with dinner?'

'No, I'm fine.' Instinctively, she pulled away from him. It was wrong, sleeping in the same bed as Gideon. They hadn't had sex since she'd come back, and it was a huge bed, so they didn't even touch when they slept. And they were still married. But her heart belonged to Brian.

'So weird, this long-lost brother stuff. You'll have to fill me in on the details.'

'Yes, well… we got an offer on the beach house when I was there. Scattering the ashes?' she said, pointedly.

'Yeah, I'm sorry about that… work, and everything.' Gideon scuffed the tip of his slipper on the slate tile floor of the kitchen. It had taken Mara a month to find exactly the right ones he approved of.

'Definitely more important than my mother.' She peeled three large avocados and started to mash them for the guacamole, not looking up. No, she hadn't wanted him there, but that wasn't the point. 'You know what? You're supposed to show up to those things, Gideon. You're supposed to support me. Since you care *so much* about our marriage.'

Mara crushed some garlic into the avocado mix and added lime juice and olive oil. She wondered what he was going to say about the beach house – the offer was so much more than she'd expected. And, of course, it might affect what Gideon was prepared to give in a divorce settlement.

'You should have said you wanted me to come. I'd have come if I knew it meant that much to you,' he protested, weakly.

'You didn't know that scattering my mother's ashes meant anything to me? Wow, Gideon. Top marks for perceptiveness,' she snapped.

He licked his lip, looking like he wanted to respond, but shook his head as if he was choosing not to.

'You're right. I guess I felt uncomfortable at turning up to hang out with your new friends, and them all thinking about me as the cheater husband. There. That's honesty. Happy?'

'Not exactly, but I appreciate the truth.' Mara cut open a package of raw chicken and put it in a glass bowl, rubbing it with spices.

'So, how much was the offer?' he asked, watching her as she moved around the kitchen. Her heart lurched – it felt like a secret she didn't want to tell. Maybe Gideon would refuse to settle with her at all when he heard it, but there was no point in lying about it and pretending the offer was lower. He could easily check – and, knowing Gideon, he probably would.

Suddenly, Mara realised she didn't care. She didn't care if this meant a month more of wrangling between the solicitors. It was over between her and Gideon, and she had to tell him and then move on with her life. She told him the number. His eyebrows shot up in surprise, like a cartoon dog.

'That's way more than you expected!' He gave her a long stare. 'This contractor guy you did it with must be pretty good.'

'He is…' she replied, levelly. Did Gideon suspect something had happened between her and Brian, or was it a throwaway comment?

'So, cause to celebrate?' Gideon frowned. 'Is something wrong? I can tell Tom to go home, if you want.' He stepped backwards, his tone guarded. 'I'm sorry again about not coming with you today, Mara. I should have.' Mara knew he was making an effort with her, but it wasn't for her benefit. She knew he didn't love her. Not in that way.

She sighed, and bowed her head.

'This isn't right. It's not working,' she said in a low voice. 'I'm sorry. I shouldn't have come back.'

'What? What d'you mean? You just sold the beach house. Stuff is moving on.'

'I know. I'm happy about that. But you and I aren't moving on. It's over, Gideon.'

'I thought we were going to give it another go?' He lowered his voice to match hers.

'It's not right between us. I know you love the twins. I do too. But we don't love each other.' She turned around to face him. He looked as if he was going to argue, but she cut him off. 'Don't. I know you're perfectly capable of spinning some kind of scenario where you love me and I'm the one who broke your heart, but we both know that's not true. If you loved me, you would never have gone off with Charlotte. She left you and you realised how much you missed John and Franny, and you wanted them back. I don't have to come with that package,' she replied, staying grounded, breathing steadily. 'I'm making a life for myself, and I like it. The twins can still see you every week. You can take them on all the holidays you want, do all the fun stuff. But I am still leaving you, and I want the divorce to go ahead,' she continued.

He looked at her suspiciously. 'It's like you rehearsed this.'

'Of course I rehearsed it! What difference does that make? I mean what I say.' She stood with her hands on her hips. 'And I want the settlement terms as advised by my solicitor.'

Gideon turned away and walked to the sliding doors that led to the garden from the large kitchen.

'They're quite ambitious terms,' he remarked, his voice returning to the usual cold tone he used with her. 'Especially given that you just got a lot more than you expected for the beach house.'

'They're fair,' she shot back, calmly. 'Anyway, that's for the lawyers to fight about.'

'I don't want a divorce, Mara,' he stated, coldly.

'Because you don't want to pay me what I'm asking for?' She looked at his back, wondering why she hadn't thought of this before. 'Was that why you wanted me back, all of a sudden? You thought I'd roll over to an easy settlement? And when I didn't you… what? Thought it would be cheaper to stay married?'

'No, of course not,' he replied, but didn't turn around.

'You're lying.' She walked over and spun him around by the shoulder. 'I'm right, aren't I? I know you don't love me. That's why you're always so… cold with me. You can't bring yourself to be anything else. But you love the kids. So you'd rather stay married to someone you don't even like, and save money.'

'That's not true.' Gideon refused to meet her eyes.

'It is! Did you ever love me?'

Gideon sighed.

'I don't know,' he muttered.

'You don't know?' Mara shouted.

'Shhh! Tom's going to wonder what's going on.'

'I don't care what Tom thinks!' Mara yelled.

'Fine. I… it was a long time ago, Mara. We were younger then. I didn't know what I wanted. Maybe it wasn't right, the two of us. But we both love the kids. We would never have had them without each other.'

'I know.' Mara lowered her voice. 'But I think we should follow through with the divorce. The twins and I have a new life. With the beach house sale—'

'That's it, isn't it? Now you're much richer than you expected, you don't need me anymore.'

'That's not it and you know it, Gideon! You left us! Don't turn this back on me. Yes, selling the beach house gives me more financial freedom than I expected. But I had a job in Magpie Cove. I had – I *have* – a life of my own. I'm happy.' She took a deep breath. 'I'm happier than I've been in years, and I don't want to move backwards. I won't.'

He stood with his hands in his pockets, head bowed.

'There's nothing else I can say to persuade you?' he asked, after a long silence.

'No.' Mara felt as if she was weightless: as if she was sailing over Niagara Falls, but not in a barrel. She was free. It was more like flying. 'I'm going back to Magpie Cove.'

Chapter Thirty-One

As Mara walked over the snowy beach to the beach house, a flock of magpies flew over her head, coming from the house and heading towards the village on the shore. She turned her head to watch them: there were seven. She racked her brain for the saying. What was it again? *Seven for a secret never to be told.* She watched them go thoughtfully.

Every time Mara had come to the beach house, she'd watched magpies circle it. She'd never been able to shake the idea that they were connected to Abby, that somehow, her spirit was caught in Magpie Cove.

Yet, now, for the first time, she felt different. Something had changed: perhaps it was Mara herself, but the nagging feeling that her mother was somehow still present at the beach was suddenly gone. If Abby had once had unfinished business with the beach house, then it was over. Mara knew her mother's secrets, and had found Paul. Was that what Abby had been waiting for? And had Mara's story for children been her own method of processing her mother's death? The story was written, and the secrets were told. Perhaps that was why the magpies could now fly away freely.

She approached the beach house, opened the door and stepped inside. This was a home again. Whatever once happened here, it had been left behind. New stories could be written here: happier stories, with no need for secrets.

'I guess we did it.'

Mara turned around at the sound of Brian's voice. He stood uncertainly in the doorway, as if he wasn't sure whether he could come in any further. Mara felt a flush of happiness, seeing him, just like the one she'd felt earlier this morning when he'd texted and asked to meet her at the house. They'd mainly been in touch through the estate agent for the past few weeks, but Brian had still sent her a message now and again. She was glad he'd kept in touch, even if she hadn't been ready to talk before.

'I guess we did. Come in, don't stand with the door open.' She smiled. She still wasn't a hundred per cent sure she had the courage to tell him how she felt, but she was so glad to see him. She was addicted to the light-hearted way he made her feel. Like a teenager. *Utter cliché,* she berated herself. *You are pathetic.*

'Tea?' Mara held out her flask.

'Thanks. I should have brought champagne.' He grinned. 'Can you believe it?' He was wearing a dark blue insulated parka. As he pulled it off, Mara tried not to watch his white T-shirt ride up and reveal his stomach, but it was almost impossible not to. She cleared her throat and focused on pouring tea into the flask lid.

'It's insane. I thought we'd get the asking price, but not so much more…' She handed him the cup.

'The power of a bidding war.' Brian raised his eyebrow, grinning. 'I love whoever it was that drove the price up so high.'

'Agreed. Here's to us.' She held his gaze for longer than she meant to.

'Mara…' He stepped towards her, an earnest look on his face.

'Please. Can I say something first?' She took a deep breath.

'Of course.'

'I'm sorry.' She let out a long breath. 'I didn't think… when I went back to Gideon, I didn't really know how much it would hurt you. I'm sorry. It was wrong of me.' She looked down. 'I told myself you were just having fun. You always have girls around you. I convinced myself I was just another one of them.'

She searched his face for a response. Perhaps it had only been about sex between them after all? Serafina and Simona could easily be wrong…

Brian placed the flask lid carefully on the pine table and turned away from her.

'You were never just some fling, Mara.'

Her heart leaped, but she couldn't be sure of what he was saying.

'Working on the house together put us in a difficult position. On one hand, I got to spend all this time with you. And you have to know, I loved every minute of working on this house.'

'It's been a great project,' Mara agreed, looking around. 'I'm so happy that we did it. For Abby, too.' She felt a lump form in her throat as she said her mother's name.

'Sure. It's a great house, Mara, but that's not why I loved it. It was you. I loved being with you.' Brian turned around. His gaze was serious and unflinching. 'I fell in love with you.'

Mara swallowed hard.

'I…' She wanted to say it back, but he took her hands in his.

'Please. Please let me say it. And if you still want to go back to your old life, you can. I'll never bother you again. I understand if you stay with Gideon, Mara, but this is eating me alive. I have to say it.'

She wanted to tell him that it was over with Gideon, that she had walked out, but he was pacing around; he clearly wanted to get something out.

'Since Lucy, I've never been in love. You're right. I've been with a lot of women. I didn't treat them all very well, either, and I'm ashamed of that. But I was terrified after I lost Lucy. I know it's not an excuse, but I was terrified of falling for anyone again because I couldn't lose anyone again. It was too hard. And then you came along. Maybe it was because I knew you'd lost Abby, and Gideon had left as well, I dunno. I felt… protective of you, at first. As if I was looking at myself.'

'I don't need protecting,' Mara warned. She'd had to toughen up in the past months; she was proud of being able to look after herself and the twins. 'If you think that's what I want, then you can forget it. I don't need some… big, strong man to look after me.'

'Oh, don't I know it. I found that out at the supermarket that day. You're lethal with a shopping basket.'

'Don't you forget it!' She laughed, despite herself.

'I won't, don't worry. I don't think my thigh will, either.'

'Before I ran into you, I'd been crying in front of a chocolate spread display. Then I was mortified because all I had in my basket was cake and wine. Damn, Brian. Every time I saw you, you seemed to have some girl or other hanging around you, and you were so nice to everyone, I didn't think you thought anything different about me. Other than to pity me, perhaps.'

Brian looked blank.

'Oh, right. Yeah, I remember the box of wine now. I mean, I didn't think anything of it. You were just so… so beautiful. Every time I saw you, I realised how beautiful you were and I'd get tongue-tied, I didn't know what to say to you… um, this is embarrassing.' He moved towards her on the sofa and held her face in his hands tenderly – 'And you just have no idea about it. You're like this… queen among women. You don't notice how people respond to you. Not just men. You make everyone feel welcome at the café. You just give them a quiet smile and you listen to them even when they're talking rubbish… like I am now. Yes, I'm a friendly person. I like women. What can I say? They like me too, for some reason. Maybe because unlike a lot of men I talk to them like they're human beings. But you…'

He gently drew his hands away from her cheeks. She wanted to grab them and put them back.

'But I thought you'd think I was such a loser – that day in the supermarket. I had half my make-up running down my face. How could you not have noticed that?'

He shook his head.

'Don't know. Just didn't. Look, I'm saying my piece here. Let me get to the end.' He gave her a boyish, anxious smile. 'This is hard, okay? Believe it or not.'

Mara's heart glowed with happiness. *He loved her. Brian Oakley loved her.* That was all she needed to hear.

'When we…. When we made love for the first time, upstairs? That was…' He shook his head, disbelievingly. 'That was… I still don't have the words. It was a totally different experience. Even than it had been with Lucy. There were times it felt like we were… I don't know, like these two beings on some kind of other plane. Wow, I can't believe these words are actually coming out of my mouth.'

'Neither can I. Brian, you don't have to do this. I…'

'Please, I'm almost there. I have to say it all. I owe you this. I owe us this. I understand if you want to stay with Gideon. If you love him, or even just because you think it's best for John and Franny, then I get it. I totally get it. But I love you. And I want to be with you. And if I didn't give this everything I had, then I'd regret it for the rest of my life.'

Brian leaned forward, his elbows folded on his knees, and lowered his head into his hands. 'OK. I'm done,' he muttered.

'Brian? Look at me.'

Mara moved up the sofa next to him. She stroked his hair.

'I love you too. And I'm sorry about leaving you. I was wrong. I'm not going back to Gideon. I mean, I did, but I left last night.'

He sat up, hope in his eyes. 'Really?'

'I was stupid to think it was ever a good idea. He can be very persuasive. He's always bullied me into getting his way. But I saw through it this time. Thanks to you, in part.'

'Are you serious? You're not going back?'

'No. Rebecca seems to think the sale of this place will go through pretty quickly, so I guess when we get that, we can find somewhere. I think it'll be enough.' She reached out for him. 'I loved you then. When we were together, upstairs. But before then too. I was just… too afraid, as well I guess.'

'Oh, Mara. Didn't you notice how awkward I was around you? Sure, I'm nice to girls. Maybe I flirt with them. But I don't sleep around. And I certainly don't have the kind of… once-in-a-lifetime sex like I did with you.'

When they'd kissed before, Mara had felt the electricity between them, but when Brian's lips met hers, this time, she shivered.

'What is it? Are you okay?' He pulled away, but she leaned in, returning his kiss passionately. There was a new delight in kissing Brian – a silk thread underlying what there had been before. Mara wondered at the feeling until she realised what it was: she knew, finally, that he loved her and she loved him. The silk thread was certainty – it was the absence of doubt, self-doubt or insecurity.

Brian's kisses became more urgent; Mara pulled him on top of her on the sofa. She couldn't get enough of him; she peeled off his T-shirt and kissed his muscled chest.

'I want you. Now,' she breathed in his ear. Brian kissed her again.

'One last time in the beach house,' he murmured, and, helping her up, he picked her up in his arms and carried her up the stairs.

Afterwards, they lay together on the white bedsheets, catching their breath.

'That was…' Brian kissed her.

'Interstellar?'

He chuckled.

'Yep. Agh, I'm too blissed out to even think of a sexy space pun.' He rolled onto his back and pulled Mara into his arms. 'I love you. Have I told you that?'

'Once or twice. I love you too.' She laid her head on his chest. 'I'm so sad this is the last time we'll make love in this house, though. I wish I could keep it. The house, I mean. I love it.'

'I love it too,' he breathed, playing distractedly with her hair. 'Hmmm.'

'What do you mean, hmmm?' She looked up at him. 'Won't you miss it?'

'Yeah. Of course I will. No, not that. I just had a thought…'

'Dangerous.' She laid her head back on his chest, listening to his heartbeat. 'I could stay here forever.'

'Hmmm,' he said again. 'What about if you did… stay?'

'What do you mean?' Mara frowned, sitting up. 'In the house? I meant I could stay in bed with you forever. Like John Lennon and Yoko Ono.'

'Yeah. Me too. But what if we didn't sell the house?' He raised his eyebrows and sat up in the bed, next to her. 'We don't have to.'

'Of course we have to. That's what we agreed. Otherwise I can't pay you for all the work you've done.'

'Mara. I… I love you. And I want us to give it a try, being together.'

'Me too.' She nuzzled into his neck. 'We should go on some actual dates though, maybe.'

'That would be wonderful. But listen. You don't have to sell the house. You and the kids love it here. So, stay.'

'But…' She didn't know what to say. 'How would I… I mean, you paid for a lot of the materials. And all your labour. The plan was that we were always going to do the house up and sell it.

Just because you love me and I love you doesn't mean I'm going to take advantage of you like that.'

'Well, for one thing, please know that I'm always up for you taking advantage of me.' Brian grinned. 'Seriously, though. Rebecca talked to me yesterday about some other development projects she wants me to do for some clients of hers. Seems that she really likes what we did with this place. I'm going to get a lot of work based on this. I mean, enough so that I could probably sell the surf school. We talked in quite a lot of detail. There's no hurry about paying me back. Call it a loan, if you want.'

Mara traced a line of dark blond hair on Brian's chest with her fingertip.

'Maybe. I mean, I spoke to my solicitor this morning. She thinks we can get a pretty good settlement from the divorce…'

'So you should. Your ex isn't short of money, Mara, right? It's his responsibility to look after you and the kids.' Brian raised his eyebrow.

'So, I could pay you back from the settlement.' Excitement unfurled in her stomach. *What if she and the kids could stay here? They would be overjoyed.* 'But why would you sell the surf school?'

'It's time. I never really wanted to teach. I'd prefer to just surf for fun. And, yeah, I admit it. The surf school was a great way to meet women, but I don't really feel the need to do that right now.' He hugged her to him. 'Anyway, carpentry and renovation's been what I've been concentrating on for a while now. And I think you and the kids should live here. They love it. You love it. This is your family house. Abby lived here. It's right that you should have it.'

'I would love it. I'd be lying if I said I wouldn't…' Mara admitted. 'But Abby had a difficult time here as a teen.' Mara didn't want to explain it in great detail right now, but the pain her mother must have experienced still troubled her.

'Does it have a bad feeling for you?' he asked. 'I didn't know Abby that well, but I could see she was carrying some stuff. She had a sadness in her. You don't have to tell me what it was.'

Mara sighed. 'She was… attacked here. It was a friend of the family. Her diary didn't say who. That's how she got pregnant with me.'

'Oh, I'm sorry.' Brian shook his head. 'I just don't know how anyone could do that. It's unthinkable.' He looked away, and then back at her, his eyes widening. 'Hey. You don't think… whoever it was… he might still live here? In Magpie Cove?'

'That hadn't even occurred to me.'

Mara thought for a minute. 'He could still be here. There's no way of knowing. And I don't think I can really entertain that thought at the moment, you know?'

'Of course. Sorry. I shouldn't have mentioned it.'

'No, but that's the thing with things like this, in the past. Old secrets. Bad things simmer under the surface of these little towns, and you never know who people really are. I found out the hard way that you can think you know people, and you never really do. But no, I don't have a bad feeling about the house. I don't think it happened inside. I think it was somewhere on the beach, maybe. And… since we've renovated it all, it feels like a new place, anyway. It feels safe and clean. Abby was here before she died. I think maybe it was more about her parents and the fact that they didn't support her when it happened, rather than an echo inside the house itself. I think she made peace with the house. And I think she'd be really happy to see it restored so lovingly.'

'So? What do you think?'

'About living here?'

'Yeah.'

'I think it would be a lot of money to say no to,' she said, thoughtfully. 'But money isn't the most important thing, is it?'

Mara snuggled up against Brian Oakley and kissed him. This time it was a long kiss. Mara took her time to make sure he felt the sweet tenderness he inspired in her; a heady mix of that and a heady passion she could feel around them both, like incense smoke.

'I think I'd love to live here. And I'd kind of like to put Paul's name on the deeds too, if that was all right with you? We'd live here, but I think it would be a nice gesture. He lost Abby and he never even knew her. Legally, he doesn't have any right to anything of hers, but… it would be nice, you know?'

'Of course. I'm looking forward to meeting your brother.'

'You'll like him. He's kind of a cool geek guy. He's sort of similar to John in temperament.'

'I love you for thinking of your new brother like that. Adding him to the deeds. He's lucky to have you.' Brian kissed her shoulder.

'We're lucky to have found new family,' she said, and closed her eyes. Finally, her life could start again. A new beginning, where she could be free and happy with the ones she loved most in the world.

A sudden thought popped into her mind, and she started laughing.

'What is it?' Brian nudged her, grinning. 'Mara?'

'The chocolate-spread family,' Mara giggled, remembering the day she'd cried in the supermarket. 'I'm part of the chocolate-spread family again. I'm the chocolate-spread mum! I'm back!'

'What are you talking about?!' Brian started laughing too, though he had no idea what she was talking about. 'Who's the chocolate-spread mum?'

'I am!' Mara laughed. 'No. Wait. I'm not. They were models. Actors. It wasn't real. Pretend smiles. That's not who I am.'

'I have absolutely no idea what this is about, but for the sake of clarity, who are you, then?'

Mara paused, thinking. She thought of her old life with Gideon – she thought of John and Franny and how happy they'd be when she told them they were going to come and live in the beach house.

'I don't know. Annie Edson Taylor. The woman who went over Niagara Falls in a barrel, maybe. I survived something as bad.'

'Your costume at the Halloween party?' He laughed. 'That was the moment I really knew I loved you. You looked over and we saw each other, and you just gave me this really cross, honest look, like we'd known each other all our lives and you weren't going to let me laugh at what you were wearing. That you knew you looked ridiculous and you didn't care at all. Plus, you liked my shark outfit. That's very important to a man.' He grinned at her.

'That's when you knew?' Mara propped herself up on her elbow and stared at him, amazed. 'When I wore a cardboard barrel to a party? Are you serious?'

'Yup.'

'It was such an unsexy outfit.'

'Depends if you're into barrels or not.'

Mara nudged Brian's arm.

'Idiot. You were so mean to Petra that night. I really did think you were an idiot then, by the way.'

'I know,' he lamented. 'She did, too. I was. I knew I liked you and she could tell I wasn't comfortable being there with both of you. I know. It was stupid. But you always made me feel like a teenager whenever I was around you.

'So, who are you now that you don't need the barrel anymore?' Brian snuggled up to her and traced his fingertips across her collarbone; she shivered in delight. 'Apart from a resident of the best beach house in Magpie Cove? A beautiful queen who enchants the sweet woodcutter to build her a house where she can spend the rest of her days being cherished and cared for. Possibly with some chocolate spread on toast in bed if Her Ladyship would like it now and again.'

'Her Ladyship would find it acceptable.' Mara grinned. 'No. No fairy tales. Women never do well in fairy tales, even if you think they will at first. No fake advert families either. How about I love you, and you *adore* me, and that's more than enough for now?'

'Sounds good to me,' Brian said. 'How long do you think we can stay up here? I don't want to get up.'

'Nor me.' Mara snuggled down under the sheets, next to him. 'Let's try and stay here forever.'

'All right.' He smiled and closed his eyes.

A Letter from Kennedy

Hi! I hope you enjoyed *The House at Magpie Cove*. If you did enjoy it and want to keep up-to-date with all my latest releases, just sign up at the following link. Your email address will never be shared and you can unsubscribe at any time.

www.bookouture.com/kennedy-kerr

In every family, there are secrets, and, sometimes, those secrets simmer under the surface in little villages like Magpie Cove. I enjoy writing about small towns and villages, perhaps because I grew up in one, the only child of a single mother, like Mara and Abby. Smaller communities can be loving and warm, and they can also be cruel and vengeful: there are definitely pros and cons to everyone thinking that they know your business. Families live in seaside villages like Magpie Cove for generations, and they don't forget.

I wanted to write about a woman, Mara, who was rebuilding her life after the kind of year we all hope we'll never have. The things is, that perfect storm of everything going wrong at once does happen more often than you might think, but it can also lead to unexpectedly wonderful things.

For Mara, her mother's death and a divorce on top force her to re-evaluate what she wants for her own children, and what her own experience of childhood with a single parent has taught her about motherhood, strength and independence. But while Abby leaves Mara her emotional legacy, she has also left Mara a way to mend her broken heart with the beach house, and with Paul, the brother she didn't know she had.

Our parents, and particularly our mothers, may break our hearts even when they aren't trying to, but all we can do is accept that they are fallible humans, just like us. I wanted Mara to go on a journey to better understand Abby, and herself, and understand that in imperfect situations we all make the best choices we can.

There is a freedom and a power in making a choice, whatever that choice is. Never let the fear of making the wrong decision stop you making it; trust that life has a way of leading you in the way you need to go.

With all my good thoughts,
Kennedy

If you'd like to hear more about my books, you can find me on Facebook and Twitter:

kennedykerrauthor

@kennedykerr5

Printed in Great Britain
by Amazon